TRADING DREAMS

J.L. Morin

New York

Harvard Square Editions

2012

Published in the United States by Harvard Square Editions

ISBN 978-0-9833216-2-0

Harvard Square Editions web address:
www.harvardsquareeditions.org

Printed in the United States of America

Trading Dreams by J.L. Morin,
nominated for the Pushcart Prize in 2011,
author of the award-winning novel *Sazzae*

"An ideal read for suspense lovers interested in the current financial crisis."

— *Booklist*

"...juxtaposes vivid scenes at a kinky sex club on the outskirts of Greenwich Village with references to the bursting economic bubble and the federal government's bank bailout."

— *Publishers Weekly*

"Morin's wit can be delicious."

— *Canberra Times*

"...exposing enough greed, hypocrisy, and blatant illegality to make even the least informed reader deliciously angry."

—*Harvard Independent*

"Set in the world of sleazy banks that cost people their homes, *Trading Dreams* is a mystery as well as a call to action! An intriguing blend of one woman's awakening to her own power, an unsolved killing, and the inner workings of the Occupy Wall Street movement, this book will keep you up reading 'til the last page."

— SUSAN RUBIN, *Ms Magazine* Blogger, Feminist Majority Documentary Filmmaker, Playwright

"J.L. Morin's voice sparkles. Once again I revert to fandom, with praise and blame gratis. Jerry terrifies me. I miss my youth."

— D. E. TINGLE
Author, *Imperishable Bliss*

"Superb fiction with a side of harsh reality and a heaping of humor!"

— Yuko Nakanishi,
Harvard Writers and Publishers

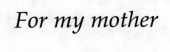

For my mother

Be careful what you wish for . . .

CHAPTER 1
FABLE

When I posted the job, I had in mind an aggressive young bull, bright on the future with no past. There were over three hundred résumés on my desk, and the last two guys I'd interviewed were qualified. One was a tall, fiery Duke graduate who had played hockey, and another was a Latino black belt who crunched up a numerical *tempestuoso*.

But they gave me that cold stare when I brought up doo wop. Hummed a few bars of 'Give Me the Taco' like back in the good old days. Neither one cracked a smile. I couldn't see myself making conversation with them for two years.

•

Next.

After the bloodletting of 2008, the market had to be flooded with candidates. There couldn't be only one hope left. A broad. Where was my young bull? Instead, they sent me this vessel with the management potential of clay. At least we were hiring again.

She didn't see me peeking at her in the waiting room, so I went back to my desk and sat down.

"Your four o'clock is here," my secretary said, blocking the door with her pregnant belly.

"She's early," I said.

"You know my leave starts tomorrow, right? You asked me to speed up the interviews. She was the only one who—"

"Never mind." I had forgotten to ask for a replacement secretary from the temp pool! Her maternity leave would be over by the time they gave me a new secretary.

"You might have to hire a girl trader so she can do both jobs. You only give three months maternity leave anyway."

"Send her in."

Jerry slunk into my office, her stockings rasping as her legs rubbed together.

"You can call me Dick."

". . . and that's short for Richard?" Jerry's shoulders slumped forward, giving her tweed suit the appearance of a coat pile. She could have been pretty if she'd learned how to carry herself. Pale skin, translucent under dark hair, fragile as an eggshell. She nodded at everything I said. I couldn't get a word out of her sad lips that knew

2

only compromise.

If freedom's nothing left to lose, Jerry was already 'free', expectations deflated. Dark curls mopped a doubtful expression under watery eyes. Skimming her résumé, I could see the job was a long shot.

I told her that Global American Bank was a second-tier institution grown out of early settler trade in coffee and gunpowder on the southern tip of the island. "The bank's trained its share of bean counters who might have been lacking in the social graces, but who were true to the search for the golden egg. We grew on their faith, upward with each generation, through the clouds."

A tilt of her head affirmed that she already knew all that. Blue veins throbbed at her temples.

"And here we are on the 53rd floor of One Liberty Plaza, which is what they called that square down there before it was Zuccotti Park." We'd made our share of human resources errors, and I was keen on avoiding another one. "We have a strong reputation for giving a man a chance."

Things had changed from the days of suspenders, although I was still wearing mine. Now, in 2010, you had risk managers, quality control seminars and master agreements. I was expecting to hire a guy with the raw potential of an Armani suit. "What's our mission?" It was a rhetorical question, and I answered it myself: "To be the top tier-two bank on Wall Street."

I looked at the girl in the chair across from me, with her sunken shoulders, and cursed New York Head Hunters. She wore flat loafers and was trying to hide a tattered briefcase behind her left thigh. She looked like she was about to pitch it at me. A southpaw. If I called the headhunter now, I might be able to schedule another round of interviews for next week.

"Let's take a walk. I'll show you around." Computer screens blipped across the floor. Phones murmured. I grabbed my Greek wild card trader as he glided by in his summer wool, and introduced him to the girl. "Sasha runs the proprietary trading desk."

Their faces lit up. Her body took on a catlike aspect that made me stare for a moment. "Where are you from?" she asked, standing a tad too close to Sasha and gazing up into his black eyes. Hmm, competition. Sasha gladly took her off my hands. I hesitated, watching Sasha's curly head above the others as he chatted up the boys on the oil desk. He showed Jerry off like an antique coin.

I was on hold with the headhunter when my cell phone rang. It was a friend who had done me a favor with the admissions committee at my daughter's university. Now she was in her first semester coping with midterms. I was afraid she might not pass. Good ol' Bernie. I owed him one, and he was calling to collect.

My back tightened. "Hi Bernie." My eyes followed Jerry's long legs proceeding across the trading floor. She was wearing sheer black stockings. Her hips wagged.

"You see a little robin redbreast hopping around up there on the trading floor?" Bernie's sense of humor was off, but I laughed loudly, holding the cell phone to my mouth, and asked him, "How did you know I was watching a chick? That's uncanny, Bernie. What do you need?"

"Since you ask, I would greatly appreciate it if you

could help the lady out. How far did you get with her?"

So the chick was connected to Bernie, and he was on my case. A wave of fear descended to my shoes. I might not be able to get rid of her. "Not that far, if you must know. I'm interviewing her now, showing her around the shop. She's right here. Want to say 'hi'?"

CHAPTER 2

VOYEUR

i t had only been a month since I'd hired her, but from day one I knew something was not right. It still bothers me that I didn't check her references. If only I *had* put her on with Bernie. That would have been the end of it right there. I wish I could forget that day!

Each moment with Jerry piqued my suspicions further. Finally, my curiosity became unbearable. Desperate, I took her laptop over to the yellow couch Sasha had hijacked from the elevator on its way to the CFO's office. Sasha had a way of coming up with the gift horses.

I opened the laptop, punched in her user name and proceeded to tackle her password. There had been a scrap of paper on her desk with 2Vc214@ written on it, but that didn't work. I tried 3Vc214@: no go. I tried everything I could think of to pop her cherry:

    4Vc214@
    5Vc214@
    6Vc214@
    7Vc214@
    8Vc214@

I laid back on the yellow couch. I let the blood run to my head. Usually that helps me think.

The problem with spying on someone is you get obsessed. Not that I'd let a dame get the better of me. But I'm losing my train of thought. I didn't need to start a competition with Jerry. I needed to relive that first day with her . . . coming back from the elevators, finding her sitting with the municipal bond traders. How did I let it happen? The memory is so delicious, who cares!

I remember I was about to hand her the phone when she said, "Excuse me. Where's the bathroom?"

Decisive. That's what she was. I paused at the glint in her eye. Now it was what *she* wanted. To pee. That was her master plan! To mark her territory. The bitch had done it. Now she had me working for her! As soon as I moved to execute her order, I felt myself falling. I rationalized away her untraditional approach, since she was a friend of Bernie's, and told him, "Call ya back."

We only had men working on the trading floor, so I had to look for the women's bathroom key. I went over to the security guard by the mirrored elevators. Ten of me appeared in the tunnel of mirrors, singing an a cappella tune from 1961 like the good old days before the hippies took over at Pace University. I made up the lyrics myself, *To pee or not to pee . . .*

Jerry had guessed my sign right off the bat. She could sense that I'm two different people, something I only discovered recently. In college in the sixties, I was so mixed up that I went around with a varsity sweater and hair down to my shoulders, trying to fit in with both the jocks and the hippies. She'd said, "That's normal for a Gemini." I grew a moustache, which I keep because I have thin lips, and felt disoriented for two years trying to reconcile my Russian background with the American mold. For a while, I succeeded in becoming more American than most Americans. That's not to say I don't understand Europeans and their inability to break with the past. There's a certain wholesomeness to the Old World, still married after all these years to America in the 1950's. So my savior was doo wop music. Doo wop gave me the strength to hold a steady course as I went through the changes of the seventies, eighties, nineties, and the new millennium.

I came back, key in hand, to find that my geeks had surrounded her with their swivel chairs and were asking, "What's the square root of point one?"

Women weren't expected to have opinions: she leaned her head back, shaking her dark mane as if someone had told her a joke, and took the bathroom key from my hand.

The position is filled.

At the time, I knew I was giving up control, but figured she wasn't going to do half of what I was going to do to her. Now, a month later, I was stuck. I sat up on the yellow couch and grabbed her laptop again. I tried 9Vc214@. Nothing, locked out.

10Vc214@

I stretched out on the couch. The blood ran into my head and made me feel lighter. People only had those higher case and special character passwords when they had to. On our laptops, you didn't have to. You could choose any password you wanted. A simple name would do. Somebody's name or a favorite thing. Like that song Jerry sang to Sasha, 'You Are My Sunshine'. I went over to the laptop and typed in 'sunshine'. No.

I mistakenly punched 's' into the user name field, and a menu of suggestions came up. Jerry had punched her password into the user name field, and the computer remembered it!

's un shine'.

The machine spun and paused. Unusual. My heart leapt into my mouth. Something was happening. Where was the error message? Something different was definitely happening this time. Now would I find out the truth? The screen came to life with icons and a background of Mount Fuji. My heart raced.

I was in!

Her emails started her first day on the job, and there was a large file, her diary. I began reading from the beginning.

CHAPTER 3

NATURE'S CONFESSION

i move for men. Acquiescing to whatever conditions. Throwing my clothes into a box. I moved to Australia for one and to Paris for another one. Red stilettos, in the box. Moving domestically seemed like progress.

Ever since Mom was murdered, the warmth of a familiar being over breakfast outweighed any risk, even with a break-up rate of one hundred percent. I used to zap around the planet taking the best of each relationship as it came along one right after the other. No more. Now I wondered wherefore I bought the yin when they kept selling me the yang.

I suppressed the memory of Mom and looked to the future. My thirtieth birthday was creeping up on me with no prospect of a husband or children. For the past year my body had been screaming that it was time to have children as if a siren had gone off. I dreaded turning thirty. Where was my guardian angel now?

I'd felt my guardian angel once, the day before my mom was murdered. I'd been driving my jalopy down a dirt road in the August heat. It was as if someone were behind me. I suddenly had a great feeling of well-being. I looked in the rear-view mirror and saw the road stretched out in back of me and the sunlight through the leaves. I understood. It was as if someone had said, *Everything is going to be all right.* I was glad that everything was going to be all right. "OK," I thought. "But then that means I get my First Love back. Right?"

Yes. All right, you get him.

I dared to hope and pray that my first love would love me again. I had the idea that I had to go backward to go forward. Now I know better than to wish for that kind of thing. This is a base kind of negotiation. You don't want it once you get it. It comes to you in a twisted way, and you don't know what you're giving in exchange. But I didn't know that at the time.

Wait a minute, you said I got First Love back. Where is he? Manhattan! Years later I learned that First Love was in Manhattan where my brother was, and I knew it was time to hope again. On my own again, I called Information. Nietzsche says doing the same thing over and expecting a different result is the definition of insanity.

A rickety voice came on and asked for the name and number. I found First Love. "I can't believe it's you," he said. "How long has it been? Fourteen years?" He said he

11

had just broken up with his girlfriend. That's New Yorkese for, I'll dump her when you get here.

I did not question the astuteness of moving in with F.L., *oh mistake of mistakes.* I only know one person who can see through optimism untamed by the rod of experience, Saphora. She must be laughing at me now. She never lets anyone sway her, an advantage of having an IQ of 180. *Summa cum laude* from Harvard but not smart enough to show *me* the way out. We knew I was going to do it. I was on automatic: move to New York to be with F.L. Go back to where it all started going wrong. That'll solve everything. After all, he had taken my virginity.

He'd climbed in through my bedroom window when we were in high school. He descended into my bed, surprising me with his size. We rubbed against each other all night, and he left in the morning before my mother came to wake me up. A month later, in a tent in the Smokey Mountains, he penetrated me and made my legs shake. There was blood and pain, but it was beautiful in high school. We didn't try to *live* with each other back then.

But that was then. This time, I'd have to play for keeps. I arrived in New York under the cover of night with one small suitcase. The boxes were being shipped. We were so happy to see each other that first night, we kissed all over his neighborhood. It was going great. I looked over his shoulder in case anyone was following me.

He had to go to work the next morning. I disguised myself and went to the most incognito grocery store I could find. Out in the street with my grocery bags, my heart stopped when I heard footsteps behind me. I casually glanced over my shoulder as I crossed the street. A man behind me crossed the street, too, just as a taxi passed. "Taxi!" I called. I jumped in the taxi and drove around before getting out almost where we'd started.

I cooked meat for First Love, which repulses me as a vegan. When he came home, I was in a G-string. I handed him a beer as he walked in the door. He sat down on the couch, took a sip and said, "I want a professional woman," to see how much he could get me to bend. "You went to Harvard. Go out and be a professional."

I embarked on the folly of trying to be exactly what First Love wanted. I'd failed a load of interviews by the time I got to the dingy office at Global American Bank.

Now Richard sat facing me in my two-sizes-too-large $1,200 Chanel suit I'd put on my credit card at Sax Fifth Avenue. I returned the suit afterward. My legs were crossed, loafers dangling.

"You know this is a male-dominated field." Richard was wearing a mushroom suit jacket and a vomity tie.

"You gotta lotta nerve telling *me* about domination," I said. He seemed to like that. The guy had no idea. He was looking at my big diamond ring.

"Are you married?"

I was, in fact, married, technically, to a man in France who refused to divorce me because it would look bad in his village. The limbo marriage gave me a sense of security, free airline tickets (he was a pilot) and another passport. I just looked out the window and said, "There are plenty of women in finance." I feared that he would discover the truth.

Richard studied my ring and repeated, "You're not

married, are you?"

There was that illegal question for the fourteenth time. If somebody asks you an illegal question, you're not obliged to tell the truth, are you? Another lie I had to tell to live. I didn't want to cause any confrontation. The easiest thing to do was to be agreeable. I knew what was coming.

"I said, YOU'RE NOT MARRIED ARE YOU?"

I *had* to get married. I needed someone to take care of me after my mother was murdered. The thought sent me to the bottom of my consciousness. I struggled not to blow the interview. Hell, it was against federal law for employers to ask if you were married in an interview. It was my *duty* to my rebel mother and the suffragettes before her who fought for the few rights I was supposed to have . . .

"No," I whispered, real nonchalant. My head felt light. It's more convincing if you whisper lies. I looked at the big diamond ring sparkling on my finger and added a truth: "It's my grandmother's ring." Always stick close to the truth, a technique I learned only after rampant truth-telling at fourteen failed interviews.

My grandmother's ice was more impressive than the tiny scrap I had bought myself for *my* wedding. Look what's happening to us women with each generation. And now you have to be single to get a job. What a load of crap. Like your husband was going to take care of you these days if you were married. And they called themselves men. It wasn't about taking care of anyone. It was about *not* taking care of kids. Neglecting boys. Raping girls. How were you supposed to found a family? I was sure Saphora would have lied, too.

CHAPTER 4
DIVINE FORCES

i hummed a bar of doo wop, daydreaming about that first day with Jerry. I still don't know what drove me to help her, but having her in my life gave me hope. The divine forces set me up to go to bat for Jerry.

I remember I took a deep breath before wading into the stale air of our new CFO's office. I could see Mort's shriveled figure through the haze on the dais of his oversized black swivel chair. He had just smoked his morning cigar. His face was tombstone gray, his hair combed over his bald spot. He ignored me for a minute and a half, and then stood up all at once as if he had just switched me on.

He came around the desk toward me. I overcame the urge to take a step backward. I stood face-to-face with Mort and hit hard. I said we had a new Ivy League candidate who had out-crunched all the others and explained how well other Ivy League employees had done in their careers at the bank.

"A woman?" Mort said.

It was time to use my trump card. I had a feeling about her. A feeling I hadn't had in a long time, not since 1997. I swung as hard as I could. "Not since our record year, before your time, Mort, but trust me on this one. We made a fortune in interest rate swaps. I can still taste the money." Mort licked his lips. I heard the bat connect with the ball.

"I'm telling you, Mort, I got an itch in my nose. I only get this itch when there's a hunger that hasn't been satisfied in a long time. Don't laugh. This is strictly about our bottom line."

"Speaking of your ass, you might need someone in Mortgages." His skin was ashen.

I was struck with a sudden fear of losing her. "Mortgages, Mort, come on. We'd be better off just holding onto our mortgages until maturity."

"Maturity! Securitization helps banks sell mortgage portfolios freeing up funds to finance more mortgage loans."

"Sure, Mort, strip off predictable payment streams from securitization-candidate-trust-pools before the fakeaway loans start misbehaving due to unexpected delinquencies and defaults and dump 'em on insurance companies still anxious to buy toxic subprime paper."

"Exactly. What about all those mortgage bundles we bought from Nantucket? We don't have the titles to show they're ours."

"Don't worry, Mort. I got Sasha signing notes for all of 'em."

"Sasha! His uncle's the president of the board. How's Sasha going to appease the stakeholders? We need a scapegoat we can fire. You're underestimating Jerry's value. A good scapegoat is hard to find. You want to hire the girl? Have her sign those bogus notes." Cigar smoke camouflaged his skin.

We brought Jerry in. She skulked to the empty chair. Mort appraised her like a butcher considering how to chop up a side of beef. Jerry's bulky tweed seemed to baffle him. Suddenly, he shrugged and went into his Global American Bank spiel. Jerry nodded and chimed in on the ends of the key phrases I'd fed her earlier. He asked if she had any questions. She surprised me with, "What's GAB's mission?"

"To be the top tier-two bank on Wall Street," Mort wheezed. "You got family in New York?"

She seemed not to hear. I thought I was imagining her unwillingness to be forthcoming, but when I brought up the family for the second time, she just looked out the window, hunched forward on her seat, watery eyes skimming the jagged building tops.

Mort's phone rang. This second phone call was unnerving. Could she be *that* connected? He watched her as he spoke. The lines in his forehead meant that he was on the verge of acquiescence. He licked his cracked lips again, took out the Mont Blanc pen I'd impressed him with at Christmas, and scribbled on his pad, all without taking his eyes off Jerry. "Uh huh," Mort repeated. I tried to quell my reservations, while she pretended to read a company brochure.

Who else did she know? My curiosity got the better of me. "Don't you have any brothers or sisters?"

Her eyes clouded over and she turned her head to the window. She looked like my daughter watching TV, only the movie was in Jerry's head.

I pressed her for more family details, thinking about my own girl waving from the step of the dormitory porch as I turned away.

She stared back.

I tried to get Jerry to tell me how she knew Bernie. Not his type. Bernie liked redheads as a rule, and he was not a leg man. With her nomadic legs, Jerry might be related, although I'd met most of Bernie Blankenfein's family over the years. Maybe one of the new in-laws after Bernie's son's second marriage down in Boca Raton. I hadn't noticed an accent, but there was something of a Southern belle about her lingering manner. A woman from the Deep South. It fit, probably some distant relative come up to the big city.

Jerry was still staring out the window, pupils open wide on her inner space. An embarrassing silence ensued. At last she came back to us.

"I have a brother. Don't imagine that we're close, darlin'. He provided me with the tools to keep men at arm's length. He's temping part-time somewhere." She pointed out the window. "Maybe over there." Sitting next to her, I couldn't dispel a peculiar feeling. She didn't seem to feel the need to elaborate.

Now that the favor was almost done, I was looking forward to seeing Bernie again. The whole plan was making me hungry. French or sushi? I would call Bernie back as soon as we hired her and tell him where I wanted to go. He could pick me up in the Town Car, maybe call his cousin at my daughter's university on the way, now that midterms were coming up.

Jerry was muddling through OK for someone with no idea of politics. I think what finally sold Mort was her stubbornness. It made him overlook the obvious, that she didn't fit the 'aggressive' cast. And when Mort changed the subject to numbers, she was easygoing under pressure. I knew he was thinking that she'd be good for overhead: we'd only have to pay her seventy percent of what we were paying the boys. If only I had known about the harassment suit. I wouldn't have let him get carried away with her. A few reference checks would have stopped the whole snowball. "How do you feel about mortgages?"

"They're a necessary evil," she said.

"I'm impressed," Mort said. The deal was done.

And then, my favorite moment, when I offered her the job. Now I play it over and over in my head. A thick cloud enveloped the view out the bay window up on the 53rd. She looked relieved. Things were falling into place. She mustered a little speech and accepted my offer. I shook her trembling hand. Her chest heaved under her lumpy suit as if I had saved her. It made me feel like a hero.

She had me going. One minute she's some damsel in distress, and then I run the credit report and find out she's suing her former employer! How that escaped me, I do not know. That is just the kind of thing I like to find out about right away in a phone call after the first job interview. I thought I had a malleable clump, ha! Little did I know that

I had hired a hottie with a bullwhip. But let me get back to my *favorite* moment.

She turned to me. "Richard, why did Mort ask me how I felt about mortgages?"

The Hudson was gleaming below. I pretended I didn't hear her and quietly noted in the back of my head that she'd put a spell on me. Screamin' Jay Hawkins, 1956. I followed her into the mirrored hallway. Our reflections splintered into six more of us in the tunnel of mirrors. My boys followed the reflection girls to the elevators. Her girls all knew we were watching their asses. Me and the boys were whistling, *"I Put a Spell on You."* The girls turned around and shook our hands. I watched the real Jerry open her mouth.

No words came out.

Was anyone watching us? Only the horizon. My gaze crossed the bond desk and traveled out to the blue horizon. That solemn line recalibrated my sense of proportion. Her hand trembled in mine and did not let go. I felt my temperature rise as I stood there holding her small hand for I don't know how long until she turned away. All six of her reflections turned away. The reflection girls walked through the mirrored hallway to the elevators without touching the ground, like a long line of ancestors accompanying her. Then they were gone.

What a day that was. Now she was ours for better or worse. I knew to cover myself I'd have to find out what made her tick.

It was dark outside. Everyone had gone home except a few clerks. I snagged her laptop and plunged back into her diary on the yellow couch.

CHAPTER 5

TWO TRUTHS AND A LIE

I only had to lie once to get a job.

He glanced at my résumé. "Nobody from Harvard interviews here."

"Your bank hasn't been around that long," I said, looking at my watch. "You know what, sugar? I've got another interview now." I stood up: *the discussion is over.* "Nice meeting you." OK, I lied twice. I had to say that to survive. I pumped his wobbly arm. He stood up, stunned.

"Wait a minute," he said with a return-on-investment smile. "I want you to meet our CFO."

Ha! I got the job.

Outside the mirrored building, I jumped when I saw that familiar person in the window. I looked at the crowd around me for a killer and then realized there was nothing to be afraid of. It was just my reflection with all the family traits. Dark hair, a little thin. *Why couldn't I be blonde like my mother?*

The building's mirror walls framed the pedestrians. Within the silent mob, my slender form rippled along the building. Then I had an idea. I threw back my shoulders, as if I were a new person. Surely I wasn't continuously myself, but rather a distant relative of my past selves. My hopeful reflection struggled along behind the other trench coats. I watched my old self move through the tinted mural like a forbearer parading across a Grecian urn. The people around me rippled and shouted in tongues unheard. My feet pounded to the rhythm of the masses. I daydreamt that I was a vessel, manifest, on course, uncut. At the street corner, the mural came to an end. The ancestors disappeared, and I sputtered out onto the pavement.

I had been re-hired even though I had sued my last boss at a stock exchange. The metropolis was never civilized enough to protect me with its laws. The –polis was only civilized enough to divide my consciousness against my wilder self. The rest was up to me. A shocking realization, a low point in my life. "Oh Muse, lift me."

I broke from the crowd on the street and walked past the sculpture of the Charging Bull, Wall Street's mascot. We should bronze some greedy bankers and put them up there instead, I thought. Steam rose from the manholes, and the taxis allowed pedestrians to pass through the traffic. The stairs leading underneath the streets were crumbling. Time to get back into the work force, burrow underneath New York opportunities and enjoy the privilege of working days into nights. I descended further into the dilapidated subway, hoping I wouldn't see another rat. It was an uncomfortable commute on old trains. I thought of all the time one could save if one were to give up on relationships, in bloom at thirty. Getting some goals, acquaintances aside. No one to interrupt, curl up with, or dissolve into. No forgetfulness, no roots, no moss.

CHAPTER 6
REINS OF POWER

*A*s soon as she disappeared behind those elevator doors, I started to ache for her. My hands let slip the reins of power. They burned.

I had been on Wall Street for twenty-one years, and here I was, still paying my dues. I was thinkin', I'll just let Bernie thank me and then go home. Maybe just one *crème caramel* with him, and then drink a quart of water and get a good night's sleep, get up early in the morning. It was over-ambitious of me to expect to hire anyone normal, what with New York being so full of nutcases.

A tune from the Belmonts came on, and I started getting into my doo wop groove. Or we could go to that new bar on the Upper West Side with the open-air terrace and Brazilian waitresses. I'd seen it in *New York* magazine.

My secretary was away from her desk. I opened my office door and poked my head out into the waiting room. An empty coffee cup rested on the edge of the coffee table next to the pile of *New York* magazines. Today's newspaper was refolded on the seat. There was a new woman in the waiting room. I tried not to stare as she uncrossed a pair of elephant ankles. My interviews were over, so what was this disproportionate monstrosity doing here?

Old Bernie Blankenfein had been scarce over the past few months. I was looking forward to hearing Bernie's perspective on the repo market, especially after the heavy turnover in our relationships with some of the major banks.

Breathing in the leather scent of the little redhead's perfume, I leaned over an empty chair and snagged three *New York* magazines. A Hermès scarf with silken chains on ermine print hung on the back of her chair. It looked like something Bernie would buy.

Maybe me and Bernie should go back to that Japanese restaurant on 51st with the *sake* and the kidney-shaped bar, where you could scoop up raw fish from locomotive cars. I flipped through the magazines, but couldn't find what I was looking for.

Long fingernails flipped lazily through the magazine I wanted. Her foot tapped, her milk white chin pointed down. Maybe one of these other magazines listed a restaurant where we could talk over a decanter of red wine. I tilted my head to read the back of her magazine. Her red suit jacket opened onto the cleavage of an enormous bosom. The golden zipper caught the light as it swung back and forth. Great blue eyes peeped out from frizzy red bangs. "Excuse me for staring." She glared back at me. Her gaze stunned me, and my eyes slid down to her red breast.

Robin redbreast.

My heart stopped.

I ducked out and leaned my back against the door. The heavy metal latched under my dead weight. CLICK.

Bernie was not going to understand.

There was no uprooting the seed I had sown in the new CFO's mind. My legs felt like jelly. I wandered over to the spot desk and sank into a chair. I called my secretary. "I know she's been waiting! Just cancel everything. You go home, too. You're welcome. You deserve it. Good luck with the baby."

I feared the worst. If Bernie didn't recommend Jerry, who was she? A nobody?

An hour later, I got a return phone call from the credit agency telling me that Jerry Gold's name was Geraldine Goldman, no credit history. I hung up.

The report was coming in on the fax, one piece of paper with a lot of white on it. There were no stains. Nobody had a credit report that clean. I had a feeling something must be very wrong. I had hired a nobody. She seemed to appear out of nowhere a year ago and since then had changed addresses every six months. I read over her application again and noticed that her home phone was a 1-800 number. Of course she lied about not being married! The good women are already taken. *Putz.*

All this should have been done before I recommended

her to the CFO. Fudging for Bernie, but not for Bernie. Fudging for who? Now it was up to me to smooth over the red flags. What if my wife found out? I kicked myself, calling my daughter at school to tell her to study hard. Fudging for God.

CHAPTER 7

HELL

My first day in Equities they gave me a bagel and a calculator. I waited with anticipation as Richard made his way over wearing that vomity tie. He stopped to talk to my immediate supervisor, a guy they called FatSo because of his girth.

I couldn't hear what they were saying above the noise of two traders bidding up March Endco put options. It was hard enough to wrap my mind around that, the noise was so nerve-wracking. FatSo left Richard and got in the middle of it. He bought the lot and shoved the trade blotter into his clerk's hands. The blotter fell on the floor, and the clerk scrambled to pick it up.

FatSo grabbed the clerk's collar. Pieces of FatSo's Egg McMuffin flew at the clerk's face. "When you win the lottery, you come back here and take shit right in the middle of the floor. Right here, and then never come back. Got it?" The clerk nodded. The way he nodded made me sad. Coming all the way to New York to have some fat guy hold onto your collar. It made me so depressed seeing that clerk shrink into his heels with FatSo holding onto his collar, laughing at him. I lowered my expectations when I saw the ghoulish look on FatSo's face. What if he did that to me? The bank was mired in a cult of mediocrity. How could I get out of this hell?

"And you." FatSo turned on me. "Understand one thing: there's no such thing as sexual harassment here. We're pullin' down the average."

I looked at the men around me. It figured. It hadn't been that long since slaves had cleared this land. This was where they established the city's first market, trading 'Negros and injuns' only three hundred years ago at the end of Wall Street. Did they really think a culture of enslavement would go away just by changing a few laws? Evil couldn't be legislated away.

The ugliest feature of the equity desk mob was their disrespect for everything except evil. Even Richard despised honor and feared evil men like Mort. Utility was their only morality. If questioned about trading, their faces would become serious. I would try to listen above the din to understand the rules. There seemed to be two sorts of game, the intelligent game and the game of the plebs. The first belonged to proprietary traders and involved weighted probabilities of a desired outcome. The second was based on how much the margin traders could scam executing trades for big customers. Companies were not disposed to letting traders take risk. Almost every woeful peon trader was scamming margin because it was less risky. I was the lowest peon. It took fifty years for FatSo to allow me to even make markets.

First I had to understand the slave mentality. I watched traders moving slowly — a freed slave remembers being forced to hurry up, and goes slow. It was hard reading the herd. You'd get some poser staking twenty-five thousand to put some bait out there just to observe the reaction. A seemingly small trade could be a prelude to an even bigger game about to surface. Once everyone jumped on a morsel, the real money would come in, usually going in the other direction — Slap!

Their acts spring from weakness and unfathomable cowardice. They will forsake anything to survive. Saphora was right.

I learned not to feel guilty when I lost and tried not to arouse too much jealousy when I won. I had come to the floor to breathe it, count it, shuffle it and lose it. Still, I tried to hold myself above the basest money-grubbers. I followed the biggest bettors stampeding to whichever robbery was going on. I watched the most cunning of slaves. They were instruments, the nuts and bolts of the financial machine.

The best way to make money off other peons was to look casual. You had to exude this recreational indifference. Then they would expose their hands. If they smelled a loser, you were dead meat. The herd would flock to exploit any weakness. Any mood could be assigned a percentage and modeled into a probability. I'm sure you could prove this mathematically if you wanted to. My mask projected an innocent view of mankind, but underneath, as I became aware of the realities of human nature, a staunch cynicism set in.

CHAPTER 8
YELLOW COUCH

*D*amned to re-live the day I met her over and over for the rest of my life! I stopped wearing my oatmeal tie and had to fight with myself to keep from helping the bitch! It was the sensitive Gemini twin in me.

I remember I did a double-take when my new hire stepped off the elevator her first day on the job. A myriad of reflection girls mimicked Jerry's curt half-turn with a thousand bouncy hairdos — dyed blonde! Her high heels made each step end with a bounce. Gone was the bulky tweed, and in its place, a tight olive-green turtleneck sweater-dress that hugged a generous bosom and voluptuous curves even *I* hadn't guessed at. But the clincher was the short skirt. I am a leg man.

I didn't know how to react to this blonde bombshell. I watched Sasha fall over himself leading Jerry to her desk and pulling out her chair for her. The rest of the boys received her bleached blonde hair with fascination. They surveyed her from the corners of their eyes. I know dames have the right to change their minds, but Jerry had changed everything *except* her mind. I was considering whether there had been a breach of trust, but for all my years at the bank, the only woman employee I had any experience with was my secretary.

It was dizzying. I just hired the bitch from hell. I had to lie down. I kicked off my Guccis. My shoulders sank into the soft leather cushion, and I welcomed the delicious guilt of being horizontal at the office. Maybe the answer was in the yellow couch. I had a feeling things were lurking in Jerry's past, but nothing that Sasha couldn't charm out of her on this very yellow couch. He could take candy from a babe. The room continued spinning. Her brilliant blonde curls burnt into my eyelids reminded me that I had to call Bernie. I decided to let everything go for now.

That's how Jerry took her place on the desk back in the day. We were rolling. Despite the financial crisis, some of the traders were making serious profits for the bank. The first two months we had her sit there watching the boys. When we did give her a bit of work to do, she jinxed it. Everything she touched went south. Customers got deleted, trades were put on backwards. She lost more money than she could count. I was ready to axe her, but the CFO was waiting for my *feeling* to bear fruit.

Mort came up and patted me on the shoulder. "We

have our first dame on the floor."

The boys acted gentlemanly around her, if that was a good thing on a trading floor. I mustered a smile. There we were, joined in a vast global network up in the clouds, trading for peace with Jerry.

CHAPTER 9
FAMILIARITY

*H*ow First Love astonished me when I came home at the end of the day! His bronze muscles made up for most of their trading floor baloney. He was the most endowed lover I had ever had. He called me his butterfly. I was glad to have re-found The One. After all, he had taken my virginity in high school.

F.L.'s railroad apartment in New York was one room wide with the bedroom window on 4th Street and another window all the way in the back of the apartment. The living room connecting them was nothing more than a hallway. We would make love in the bathtub the first two weeks. He knew my body like it was his own. *I* could have kept going like that forever with a capital F.

Why does familiarity have to set in? I tried not to accept my deepest fear: he was only interested in what he didn't have yet, and he'd had enough of me. It only took three weeks for him to get tired of seeing me every day. He only saw light from the shadows it cast. I would be putting on my bra, and he wouldn't even look.

I realized that he was more than ignoring me when he insulted my outfit on Valentine's Day. Forget about flowers or chocolate. He had started to *hate* me. He passed his cruelty off as absentmindedness and left the getting angry to me. Passive aggressive. Who wants that? I should have been jumping for joy when our relationship fell apart, but instead I was thinking, *what could have been, what could have been, what could have been.*

The final blow came when I got my first paycheck and bought myself a faux mink coat. I was resentful that *he* didn't buy it, and he was resentful that I was 'such a materialist'. He accused me of consumerism. "Vegans don't wear mink." He reminded me that my mother was a civil rights activist, and called me 'inconsistent'.

Ha! Look where consistency got Mom. Living in a ghetto she couldn't save, enmeshed in social problems too heavy to overcome. We might as well have been living in a Third World country. Some America.

"It's not real mink, lamb," I said.

"It looks real," he said.

Maybe I had to find someone whose clothes weren't threadbare. It's hard to live with someone if all your stuff is better than theirs. *I* started to hate him for being so poor.

One night when the sun was setting behind the brownstones, I found a letter F.L. had written in his jacket pocket, to a man. I screamed.

He screwed up his mouth and put down the paper in order not to crumple it up. "So what?" he said. His muscular legs were crossed in front of him, calves of youth, not of a damaged animal, better left untouched after all, after all these years. "Thirty percent of men are gay."

"You mean 'thirty percent have feminine tendencies'."

"If you count them, it's sixty percent. At least I have political convictions. All you think about is making money and buying things."

"That's not true." F.L. was gay! "I'm . . ." How could I compete with that? "I'm a vegan. For your information, there's a food revolution going on. It's a whole movement to eat locally-grown vegetables for the health of the planet. Hey, at least I don't treat people like ideas."

"You're a petty bourgeois," he said. "The only thing you ever rebelled against is your mother."

Ahh! That was below the belt. "Why are you with me then?"

"I'm not. I'm sleeping in the living room. Could you please move your books out so I can go to sleep there?" That is exactly what F.L.'s father had said to his mother twenty years earlier. Forced back into F.L.'s childhood, I watched him re-enact his parents' divorce. He carried pile after pile of books out of the bedroom, despite the fact that there was no other more qualified lover than me, his first love who had gone through every contortion to keep him interested.

And I thought that he had become a New York boy, leeching off women for a few months and then tossing them aside like Kleenexes — after all, we let men do it to us with all our modern promiscuity. That F.L.'s sufferings were the cumulative outrage of a boy who'd grown up without a father at home to take care of him, and everyone was to blame, including women. That one woman couldn't stop the philandering alone as long as men could always go find another willing female, and he didn't love much.

But women weren't even in the equation. "My lawyer will be in touch with you," F.L. said, just as his father had said.

"For Christ's sake, we're not even married." Middle-class poser, rebel revolutionary, my ass.

He pulled the covers up to his chin like an old man on a stretcher in the hallway.

I turned out the light. "OK, I'll be right over here in the bedroom."

"Don't think that you can keep the car."

"Why not? It's my car."

"My name is on the title, too."

I felt a pit open up in my stomach. "It's very important that we don't fight."

Our childhood romance resided in the realm of dreams. Was there such a thing as repetition? F.L. left for the other man.

He'd been gone for two days. I was lying in bed thinking, It's not the man I miss. God knows he had enough annoying habits. It was the closeness. It was the bond, like a mother and child bond. Probably the very thing that annoyed him. The man could only love from afar.

I rolled over. I was so tired. I missed my mother.

That's what hurt me. Not having family to back me up. I was relieved we weren't going to have a baby. What if the baby grew into an evil person? What if the baby became another murderer . . ? I heard banging on the door. I tried to get up but couldn't move. I tried to yell that I was coming, but no words came out. I had to go and answer it because it must be my child who wanted to come in, but my fear of the child had me rooted to the bed. The baby had grown into a murderer.

I woke in a cold sweat. I could feel my mother's presence in the room. I smelled her blood. I got up and turned on the light. I felt the horror all over again. It was my blood. My period. Any sign of blood sent me back to the day my mother was murdered. Dripping red splotches onto the parquet, I ran to the door and checked all the locks. I pushed the desk against the door. *He won't kill you for a reason except that it must be done.* Saphora was always right.

F.L. came home to pick up some stuff. I moved all the furniture and unbolted the lock. He laughed and disappeared again. He must have found another squeeze, and I must be crazy hunting for The One all this time. I had to get some goals.

The second night on my own in his apartment was the night of the Harvard Club dinner. I wouldn't have gone if I hadn't forgotten about it until the last minute. With a sense of urgency, I pulled the furniture away from the door and grabbed a taxi.

It was like stepping onto another planet: the 'Haves' planet. The solid wood paneling and women on burgundy leather sofas. It filled me with hope. They made the world seem sane and fair. You worked hard, got paid, had a loving family. They had every advantage and never had to deal with things like sexual discrimination. I supposed that when I got up the nerve to ask them about it, they'd say, Harassment doesn't exist anymore, we got rid of it in the sixties. Especially in Law. Law was supposed to be open to women now. I asked one of the women lawyers if there was equality in her law office.

"Hell no," she said. "Every so often, one of the partners chases his secretary around her desk."

Ah, they suffered, too.

Another alumna said, "I don't identify with my job at all. It's something I do every day, but that's it."

Maybe that was the key: not to identify with your job. Not to identify with anything they could take away.

CHAPTER 10

WEED

I wondered what to do with Jerry as I walked across Zuccotti Park. The park looked nice again all cleaned up after the heavy damage on September 11. They were setting it up for another event commemorating the anniversary of the attacks.

Jerry's only responsibility to date was watching the Equity boys and reading anything she could find. I knew Mort wanted her as fodder for his shadow banking operation. The thought of losing her to corporate distressed me. In an effort to wrench her from his talons, I ignored his recommendation about shoving her into Mortgages and shoved her into Equities instead. In Equities the boys could show her the ropes.

She was allowed to come over to the proprietary desk to use my Bloomberg on the coffee table next to the yellow couch. That privilege raised a few eyebrows, so I made it known that the Equities desk was also invited to use my yellow couch any time they felt like it. Everyone jumped all over the invitation, and there was no room for Jerry on the couch. Even when there was only one hairy lunk reading my newspaper on it, Jerry stayed away. She didn't seem to be thriving in Equities.

I was thinking about how to get her into something she could understand. I figured, as a consumer, she would be able to relate to asset bundles that included auto loans, student loans, credit cards securitizations, and to keep Mort happy, residential mortgage-backed securities, or Structured Investment Vehicles. SIVs were a helluva lot sexier than Equities. The SIV market had assets under management in excess of $400 billion. They had an evergreen structure — new debt entered as old debt matured. She could work with the SIV manager, Sasha.

I was commuting back up the elevators headed for a nice siesta. I was already dreaming of teaching Jerry about SIVs. Whoever was on my couch was about to get kicked off. I was sure Jerry would like SIVs. I threw open the door ready to bark at the whole bunch of oversized teenagers. Sasha was sipping a *latte* and laughing and crying at the same time. Jerry jumped up from the yellow couch with a startled look.

"Oh. It's you," I said. "I didn't know you were funny. I'll have to try you out in Sales."

Sasha started. "Uh, I wouldn't put her in Sales, Dick." He stood up and waxed into one of his emotional effusions ending with, ". . . and besides, Jerry's too honest to sell clients the toxic stocks you're trying to dump."

"Sasha, a closed mouth gathers no foot." I walked by their couch and inhaled the aroma of *lattes. Lattes*, huh? I pretended to ignore the two of them but bought five September coffee futures.

The atmosphere lightened up with Jerry as our pet. We fed her chocolate and let her go at four o'clock. I lay down on the couch waiting for Sasha to come and sit down. I heard his feet pad over. "Shoot," I said.

"She's too attractive for us," Sasha confessed.

"Beauty is only skin deep."

"Ugliness is through and through."

"You're not ugly, Sasha."

"I wasn't talking about me, Dick."

"Any news?" I asked.

"She grew up in a slum in New Orleans."

"N'awlins!" I *had* detected any southern accent. "Have you ever been down there?"

"No. I didn't know we had Jews in Gatorland."

"You have Jews everywhere, *malaka*. N'awlins is like another country. A culture of its own. It's a violent town, a black and white town, and to think, our little Jerry squelched out of a swamp."

"She's running from someone," Sasha said.

"Running? From who? There's no one to run from here."

"Not here, out there. She thinks someone's chasing her."

"Are you saying she's nuts?" I asked.

"I don't know. Her baggage is pretty heavy."

"Like what?" I asked.

"Like she came into the trading room and sat in her swivel chair looking past me with that dilated stare."

"The equity boys have been giving her a hard time," I said. "I'm sure she was vulnerable."

"That could have contributed, Dick, but then I said, 'You better lie down on the couch. Go ahead, talk to me. Tell me your dreams. I know how to interpret them. I was in therapy.' "

"You were in therapy! Give me a break."

"I was," Sasha said, "after the divorce."

"Come on, she didn't lie down because you were in therapy."

"I told her, 'Dreams directly express unconscious psychic activity.' "

"And then?"

"And then I said, 'Throwing light on the causes makes you conscious of the source of your troubles. Tell me about your pain. Pain is cleansing. Pain is beautiful.' "

"*That* worked?"

CHAPTER 11
BARBIE SACRIFICE

i was standing with my mommy in the tall backyard grass in New Orleans. We had just come off the swings. The grass was deep green and full of wild flowers, daffodils, mulberries and morning glory that climbed up the wall. I was praying for a Barbie doll and came out of my hiding place to try to get Mommy to buy me one.

Mommy said, "We can't afford it."

"What's 'afford'?"

Mommy was saving up for college. That was better than toys.

"What's college?" I asked.

"It's a school you go to when you're eighteen. You'll be seventeen, though."

"What's the best one?"

"I guess it's Harvard."

"I'm going to Harvard." I looked down at the grass around my feet. Mommy was saving up for college. That was better than toys.

I remember lying on my mother's stomach, and my mother putting her arms around me and saying, "Mommy loves you." I felt close and floated off to sleep. Or Mommy would say, "You love your Mommy, don't you, little sweetie . . . "

Yes.

In the beginning, I was growing like a weed. I was five. Mom's uncle in Florida got Paw a job at a 'multinational', and the family was transferred to Leningrad, Russia. In less than a month, we were back in New Orleans with Paw out of work and hanging around the house.

My beautiful Mommy came and sat with me on their green carpet at the foot of the staircase and said, "Your Paw isn't going to live with us anymore."

I looked at my mother's white arms as they reached down to hug me. Mommy was sweet and wonderful, and all I wanted as a little girl.

"Doesn't that make you sad?" Mommy said.

I thought about it. If I could have Mommy, what more would I ever want? "No," I answered. I was too young to think about how my little brother would feel growing up with no dad. I always protected Raif, but I was just a child. He was still a bottomless pit of neglect.

Paw was usually in a bad mood, and never had time for us. He left. He came back. Mommy threw him out like so much trash. So what?

So Raif cried and cried. I rocked him in my arms. I had no idea Paw was so important to Raif.

CHAPTER 12

SURROGATE FATHER

I stood up from the yellow couch. "Sasha, I'm not by any means the nicest guy to be around, and I'm not even particularly monogamous, but my kids have a father. I disagree with divorce. I'm against it. Call me old fashioned, but I don't want my son to grow up gay, or my daughter to get raped before she has her period."

"Dick, plenty of single mothers do just fine—"

"Who says they do just fine? I bet I can tell you what happened next with Jerry. Mommy became Mom, and was never at home from then on. She had to go back to school. She had to go to work. I bet Jerry spent her childhood alone with drugs and alcohol as friends. When you take the father away, it's the kids who are divorced. The only thing they understand is neglect, and everyone wonders why they need more space, choose flaky friends and can't have relationships."

"OK, Dick. Relax. There's nothing to be afraid of. Your wife's not divorcing you."

"I'm just sayin'. The mother hires a therapist who costs more than the father and faces the bills alone. I don't care if a divorced father holds a degree in law or medicine. Divorced fathers keep the money. They don't provide financial support. A quarter of them cut off their children at the age of eighteen." But now she had me. I would finish her education.

I kept her résumé on my desk as if it wasn't too late. It helped me daydream about that first day in the job interview when I skimmed her résumé and then her knees and her ankles in those black stockings. A chill rippled down my spine, all the icier remembering how she looked when Sasha asked her what the square root of point one was. I was in a hurry when I hired her. I had a vacation to get to. I'm usually not so sloppy. I am, however, a leg man.

"Zero point three," she had said, taking the bathroom key from my hand.

We picked her up and brushed her off. Now Jerry had us bringing her coffee and competing to finish up for her at the end of the day. She gathered her gym bag and swept toward the door. "See y'all tomorrow."

A chorus of *goodbye's* from the boys.

At the end of the day, I sat back down next to Sasha on the yellow couch. "What else?" He didn't answer. "Come on. I know you've got something."

A strange expression crept across Sasha's face. *"Re,*

49

she has a younger brother. I think their mother was murdered."

I drew in my breath. "Murdered! That really is too bad." Was that what it was about her? Some of the guys argued that she wasn't beautiful in the strictest sense, but I thought she was. She had a tragic beauty about her. And she was kind of bowlegged, like she just got off her horse. That kind of thing fascinated me, but I couldn't pinpoint what made me *need* to find out more. Which man could have destroyed her family and caused her such grief? Or maybe it was a woman. You could hardly tell the difference these days. I would find out if I had to *piece* her together.

I'm not the most sensitive guy, but I could see from reading her diary that she had changed more than her hair these last few months. "You're like clay, Jerry," I told her the next day. I was serious.

She smiled that Cheshire cat smile.

The creature that crawled out of her old skin was cynical, doubtful, a lump of human material trying to live. She had struggled through college, marriage and separation with the buoyancy of a statistic, grew *fascinated* with statistics. Teaching her to track the momentum of prices, I could see she identified with anything that went up and down. I would follow her up and down like a damn wheel of fortune.

CHAPTER 13

STATISTIC

My white male colleagues were doing the same job I was and getting paid $27,000 more. Head traders were yelling and screaming and firing us clerks, a maneuver to increase their own bonuses. I had to fill in, and they finally let me trade.

Mort came onto the floor regularly to check on me. He didn't seem convinced that I was a good 'fit'. I showed him my trades to prove that I'd made over $1,000 per day. He glanced at the handful of papers and said, "I doubt that. I don't think you're getting the hang of trading." Every time I came up for air, he pushed me back down. "You'd probably do better in an office job. They're short of people downstairs in the mortgage department."

"Yeah." Mort rubbed his eyes. "I've got to deal with

this do-good lawyer who's convincing homeless people to move into our abandoned properties in the Bronx."

"That's illegal!" I said.

"The City of New York housing agency says it's 'legal homesteading'. They develop the abandoned properties."

"Well, that's more than we were doing with them."

Mort glared at me.

I shrank in my shoes. "But without bank loans, they'll never make it."

"This lawyer is a pain in the butt. Since 1994, he's secured over $10 billion in commitments. They're using the Community Reinvestment Act to force us to give them loans and capital. It turns out we were required to loan within the community all these years since we have several branches and plenty of deposits coming into the Bronx. They want us to open a South Bronx branch and lend to the community."

"Sounds interesting." Mortgage department! I disappeared as soon as Mort turned away. I was about to sneak into Richard's lounge area. Richard didn't have any use for me at all, even though it was me that he was talking about to the rest of the traders. I heard him say, "I wonder if she takes off that jacket when she bends down to say hello to the head."

The proprietary trading desk saw me and broke out laughing.

My ears rang until I felt dizzy. It was already too much that all their screen savers were throbbing with Playboy bunnies. I stumbled back out of the lounge.

A week later, one of the traders missed his hedge. Mort was furious and blamed it on me. His nostrils flared and he started yelling, "You're not a team player. You shouldn't add up the profit and losses from your trades and show them to Richard. Separating your profits and losses from the firm's is not a team-player thing to do."

I didn't notice any team players watching *my* back. To him, a team player was someone he could yell at when the bank lost money. "I made over $3,000 today. You're nicer to me when I lose money."

"Three thousand is peanuts. I'm losing real money!" Mort yelled. "Listen to me, you're a smart girl, you went to Harvard, and you're not helping us one bit. Wipe that smirk off your face." He rested his head on his desk and said, "I'm unreasonable. I'm losing my mind." When he calmed down, he said he was sorry. "The mistake was everyone's fault. I didn't mean the things I said. Sorry if I ruined your day."

When I showed my trades to Richard at the end of the day, I had to show losses due to sales that Mort had told me to make. "These are all losers. I didn't want to sell this stuff, but he insisted. Now's the time to be buying options."

Whoever trained that philistine to manage other people . . . The next day, Mort on the equity desk again accusing me of things I didn't do. "You should have sold more than fifty contracts! You just admitted that you didn't sell more because you were nervous."

"Nervous!" I was shocked.

"Shut the _@#* up. I want you out of my sight. Go get a cup of coffee." He pushed me away.

"I don't want a cup of coffee."

"Leave the trading floor right now."

I stood there, paralyzed. "Do you want me to go home?"

"Yes. Go!"

I went to get my stuff. Sasha was there. I nudged him out of the way. "I'm in a fight with the CFO."

"What happened?"

"What happened was that we've been making a lot of money over the past three weeks, and he wants to keep it all for himself." I realized as I said this that I wasn't going to get any support. Cutting me out could only be good for Sasha's bonus, too.

Sasha did a double-take when I told him Mort sent me home but only said, "I admit that he is too hard on newbies, but he's nice to me."

As I ran my hand along Sasha's desk, my ring caught on something jagged. There were several notches carved into the side of his desk. I knew he wouldn't answer me if I asked what they were for.

There was no way out. At least my best friend from high school was coming to visit. I wandered over to the lounge area to text her. Regina texted me back. She was on the way.

Sasha followed me to the lounge and said, "OK, OK, Jerry. Relax!" He was so cute with his muckle mouth going in every direction. He told me to stretch out on the couch.

I was so stressed, I complied. Then I saw Richard out of the corner of my eye.

He was talking to Mort. Richard came over to the couch.

I bolted upright and put both feet on the floor. I was sure he was going to fire me.

Instead, Richard handed me an iPhone. "It has a Mortgage-Backed Securities Alert. Now you can watch the markets twenty-four hours." The prices on the screen flashed red or green depending on the direction of the market.

I held the iPhone in the palm of my hand. "This is cute," I said, relieved.

"I got one for my daughter, so I thought I'd get one for you, too," Richard said. "iTunes, iPad, iPhone, iPay."

"Does it vibrate?" Sasha said.

"Yeah," Richard said.

"Jerry, put it in your front pocket, and I'll text you," Sasha said.

"This is for mortgage-backed securities, though. I'm in Equities."

"Not anymore. You're fresh as new clay. Now you're with us on the prop desk."

On the proprietary trading desk! The best place in the bank to be. I won the lottery! I threw my arms around Richard's neck and almost kissed him.

Sasha turned gloomy.

I just glared at him and lifted my foot behind me. Heaven.

CHAPTER 14
BANK JOB

*i*f you ever wonder what it would be like to be inside your love object's head, don't. It's shocking to hear someone else's thoughts. There are things you're better off not knowing.

By now I had her passwords for everything web-based. I was constantly inside her head, waiting for her to say something about me, and when it came, it hit me like a bag of bricks. After I read what she really thought about me, I had to start taking my ulcer medicine again.

My new boss is goofy. I feel sorry for him. He thinks that nothing should be done for the first time. Nobody really likes him.

Ha! I knew it! And,

He makes you sit there nodding as he describes what he ate for lunch for fifty years and how he cheats on his wife. These aren't leadership qualities. People just wait for Mr. Structured-Reality to go into his office so they can get on with their lives.

And I moved her to the prop desk so I could *protect* her! Boy, did she do a job on me. She was outta my league. And what she said about Sasha!

Sasha makes up for it, though. He's tall, dark and handsome enough.

If I had another chance, I'd fire them both then and there. Anxiety set in when I realized my most trusted colleague was my nemesis. My wife I'd stopped trusting a long time ago. But my colleagues. We were a team. Goodbye peace of mind, hello sleepless nights. I tried to rationalize that I was after all her superior: it wasn't that she didn't like me; she just couldn't stand the *idea* of me. Too late. I should never have looked in her diary. She got me. I was hers.

I knew for sure I wasn't the only one. Men were her playthings. She adroitly used them to protect herself. From what? I was wary of her, even back then. I knew not to trust her like one of the boys. We didn't let her mix in our business until we had to. There was a rally in tech stocks, and all the other desks started to get busy. There was just too much work *not* to use her. Somebody would have to train her. Me and Sasha started showing her how to clean up residuals, how to execute client orders, how to be aggressive.

"Like Achillia, the woman gladiator!" Sasha said.

With her there, the boys relaxed a little.

"See 'dat? All we need is a little more love," she told us. The hours slipped by. Pretty soon she was keeping track of all of her boys. Phones rang, orders flew, Sasha's dark skin flared up to his curly top. He yelled at her, and she yelled at the clerk on the phone, and got the order filled.

"Done!" She was on the team.

She didn't necessarily do what we were telling her to do, but she came up with some things that no one expected. It seemed like she knew what everyone had to do at what time. With her rolling our positions and checking the orders, business took care of itself. She started to come up to speed and think like a trader, read between the lines, see commonplace happenings as indicators of market sentiment, connect news to prices, visualize graphs. Sasha lighting a cigarette prompted bar charts of the mind.

After two months in the clouds, I began to fear that I would never have the pleasure of firing the bitch. I shouldn't keep her 'diary' on this old laptop. It's no example of the discipline I demand of my staff, and definitely not the kind of thing I would want my wife to find, although when she did find some evidence against me on a scrap of paper, it served as a decoy so I could pursue some real mischief. But that's my own affair, and nothing to do with the issue at hand, because I never had anything, not even platonically, and regrettably so, with Jerry. She was one of the boys.

How Jerry had the time to keep up her correspondence, I do not know. What I wonder is, when did she have time to trade? But the trader in me says that her mailing list might have served as a necessary distraction. Maybe it kept her from churning the account and helped her stick with the position beyond the normal threshold. Most people would have taken profit too early going up, or been too weak to cut their losses in time on the way down. *She* would have said, Women have a higher pain threshold than men. Women can multitask.

Sasha and I watched her open the real estate section and draw circles around ads. Life would start going like clockwork again. She was moving to an apartment in Greenwich Village with its townhouses and loonies, and she was too impressionable. Jerry was already a little nutty.

I congratulated my own originality for scraping her up off the street and educating her with my collection of golden oldies. How could I know she would take it so personally? My doo wop filled some need. To her, a broken record suggested itself as the structure of life. A loop that would close with the end of time. She was so impressionable I guess because we were the only family she had in the city, not including the part-time brother. I studied the picture of the brother, thin body filling up an ornate picture frame on the crowded trading desk. His pale image was as polished as a vampire's in black suit and tie. I imagined it suffering the loss of its mother alone in the silver frame.

She was lucky, that's all. To be young, free and alone in the big city in its heyday, gliding down the street clad in Armani, blonde curls wagging behind, among some of the most eminently qualified bachelors in the country, stopping in a shop to buy perfume, maybe trying on a dress, or meeting a girlfriend for a tête-à-tête. All that freedom must have been something. At least it looked like pie in the sky to me.

She was with me on the job. It was hot outside. I told her, "Get outta here. It's four o'clock." She looked fine with her knockout legs. I had no idea how much pain she was in over the dead mother. No one guessed she was reliving the horror with each breath. Life's funny that way. She might look better than ever, but on the inside, with each screech of the subway train slowing on the tracks, she was the one screaming.

I keep the diary because it's a good one. She made the American dream look good. Who'da guessed she wasn't happy? She had us going. One look at her made you fantasize about winning the lottery, when deep down you knew you were as replaceable as a soldier. We said goodbye to her at four o'clock.

Sasha scowled at me as I followed her out of the building. "Dick, come back here! Have you lost your mind? We have to check our profit and loss."

She watched herself walk alongside the building outside. Looking at her cascading reflection in the side of the building, she seemed startled by her own face under the curls, with a train of followers behind her, their faces concentrating on going faster, putting in longer hours. What did she do at night? She seemed like she could change into anything, a fragment, a torso, a ripple, reflection. Freefall in Manhattan, where anything was probable. Surely others were not as good at being her. Someone would have to do it. Might as well be Jerry dissolving into the throng. She tried to pull herself together, would have to find her own way.

A bitch on a mission. Who knows what women really think, functioning in a man-made world? To hear everything, yet come to no point. No doubt she was trying to grasp at some male construct: the foundation of an indecipherable, alien labyrinth. What was the question? If it was given, it was wrong. I feared I would never be able to piece her together. No one would ever know Jerry graphed out over time.

She heard sirens and felt the darkness afoot. That I didn't get. What darkness? It was daytime. I remembered what one of her friends had said about Jerry wandering the streets of New York. Jerry watched her own reflection with suspicion, following the march downtown, proceeding along the building walls, blurring into a cloaked painting on pottery. Why would she be suspicious and afraid of her own reflection? I've heard of low self-esteem, but fear of oneself?

And what about all the crazy mythical delusions her confidants were feeding her? *The daughter of Zeus would not be silent plodding to the rhythm of the street.* It was a friend named Saphora, convinced that we're re-living the fall of the Grecian empire: *You there, like Athena shedding the soft, embroidered robe made with her own hands. You assume the appearance of a warrior reflected on a building wall, marching off to do your lamentable work.* Saphora sounded crazy enough. I would be on the lookout for her.

I surprise myself sometimes, drawing conclusions from the fluff in Jerry's laptop, but after all that's happened at the bank, I need her company here.

Where is she? Sirens wail, time's up. This is a book in search of a mistress. She was here a minute ago. Long legs, curly hair, color: Ash Blonde #6A. Have you seen her? Black eyes glare and light up her face. She was either in a hurry, or about to forget what she had to say. Couldn't follow a simple recipe, taking up too much space in a *man's* man's world. People didn't necessarily think of her as an outsider, but she was far away, with her own screwy logic for every crisis, as if clay could talk.

(HAPTER 15
MR. MAYBE

*T*he crowd on the building wall rippled past my blonde reflection as I circled the building. I was relieved they didn't invite me out after work for any of their grotesque crony rituals. I was thinking about my last words to my mother: "Don't worry," today and every day. Broken piece, twisted, lonely, never alone. I'd tried to make Mom proud of me, but every outward success was tainted by personal failure at men and their gods. I didn't want to miss F.L. so much. I tried to dissolve my loneliness in the closest relationships possible in the big city — not with my brother — with my diary.

This is the hand I was dealt:

- Abandoned
- Afraid of Intimacy
- All I Need is Space
- Do You Want to Fight?
- Every Victim Needs Two Therapists and a Lawyer
- Move on NY
- "Hi, I'm Jerry"

How to function in solitary refinement? I shouldn't have let slip what happened to my mother when I was talking to Sasha at the bank. It was becoming impossible to hold it in. The second month on the job, I decided the best solution would be to get some Prozac. As if they can't tell when someone's on that stuff. It makes your eyes bulge. I'd heard it was supposed to have some useful side effects, like making you stop needing sex. On Prozac I would be able to grow by myself, alone, never mind all that bonding we did in college. I knew pills were unhealthy — the fit thing to do would have been something long-term: meditation or painting. But I looked at my problem as a passing cloud. I didn't think there was anything particularly wrong with me. I just wanted something that was not available in modern man.

Trustworthiness, consistency, a sense of commitment. I believed that if I had a whole man, I would stop hunting for more in the goddamn relationship and achieve some goals. Unfortunately, I had not met a whole man. I had conducted in-depth searches of many half-men, their dance moves, their ponytails, summer houses, mole on the chin, and what was not there was really not there. Soul mate was always unable to recognize that (forget about *what*) I was trying to achieve. How could I obliterate my own obstacles when I was too busy fighting to exist? To dwell on it would be idiocy.

Faced with my own irrelevance in their eyes, I was forced to admit it. Men had become irrelevant. I had to mine my own soul to find what the world had ignored. If only I had the strength.

Hell, in New York you could get anything, couldn't you? And if we're all interchangeable, so were they. I had to ignore the sense of loss that the memory of closeness brought. Looking backward would be my undoing. Rather than dwell on the memory of my last failed romance, I would repeat it with naïveté from the beginning, with someone else. I wondered who I would become next, and felt an inkling of potential. If only I had the strength to bear it out. Wasn't I always able to find another fix for my loneliness? My lack of necessity, as a beauty, was crippling me.

I listened to my footsteps resound on the brick buildings. I had passed a police officer earlier, no consolation, but I was anxious now that he was nowhere in sight. The Village was always so crowded, I usually didn't mind walking alone in the wee hours of the morning, but tonight the streets were as empty as . . . murder.

I looked over my shoulder. Someone was following me. My legs began to feel numb. I wondered if I would be able to run if I needed to. I quickened my pace. Now that I thought about it, it wouldn't have been hard for a murderer to find me. A murderer could have heard where I was living or might have seen me coming home from work. Maybe the right opportunity had only just come along.

I had just reached the end of Bleecker Street when fear seized me. I could feel a familiar presence nearby, perhaps behind one of the cars parked along the other side of the street. With each step the thought of being attacked increased until, in my terror, I started to run. My feet clacked down the block and resounded on the brick walls. I heard footsteps running but didn't look back. I ran faster than I knew I could, past the garage and the antique shop window. Suddenly, as I turned the corner, I saw the lights of Anyway Cafe shining just across the street. Another block. I forced myself to run the rest of the way to my doorway. I had made it home. But the door was open! Something was not right.

I scurried inside and quickly closed the door. The lights were out. Could the murderer have followed me here to finish what he had started? Was anyone inside? I tried to remember whether I had locked the door on my way out . . . it hadn't even been yesterday morning. I had stayed out all night the night before, too. Had someone broken in? I was already in the living room, though, and none of the furniture had been upset.

A man sat up in the bed.

I screamed.

"Be quiet!" he yelled and came and put his hand over my mouth, which made me try to scream more. He flicked on the light.

What was happening? He was sleeping in my bed. My eyes adjusted. Everything was in its place, but it was not my place.

He squinted at me through dark eyes and said in a British accent, "You're not Lisa." His eyes widened, as if this was not such a bad thing. He had a sexy nose.

"Who's Lisa?" See dat? When you fold, you get a new hand.

"Women! I don't even know you, and you want to know who bloody Lisa is."

"Your door was open, lamb."

"And so you thought you'd just come in here and start screaming?"

"I'm new around here, and must have—"

"What planet did you come from?" He was putting on his socks and went into the kitchen.

He had a nice butt. "What are you doing?" I asked him.

"Making coffee."

"At this time of night?"

"I don't think I can get back to sleep after that display."

"Sorry."

"Oh now you're sorry." His chest was hairy.

I looked out the window at F.L.'s apartment building across the street. I must have gotten turned around.

"What's your name?"

"Jerry." He put on his glasses, and looked like a big mouse hiding behind them. It was time to go, but I just stood there like an orphan. I'm not kidding, I must have been really desperate to stay there with him. Excellent timing. Should I thank you, Mother?

"Jerry. I'm Ivan. How do you like your coffee?"

"With milk."

"No milk."

"Black, then."

"Quite right as well. It's decaf."

"Never mind. I think I can make it home." I loathe black coffee, and never saw the point of decaf.

"No, stay. It's a zoo out there at this time of night. At least you're safe here. There's your coffee."

Instant. But there was something arresting about a man serving me for a change. "I'm coming."

His eyes fixed on mine.

I must be getting dumber and dumber. By the second sip, I was half way in love with Ivan the medical student. I really don't understand men at all. One minute they look like rodents, and the next minute they've got you talking in double meanings. "Who is Lisa?"

"Not that again. If you must know, she's my ex-girlfriend. She walked out on me and slammed the door. Sometimes it bounces open if it's slammed."

She was gone! There was hope. "I'll keep that in mind." I smiled at him, but he looked like he was crying. At that moment, I felt so sorry. Sensitive guys have it hard. When I thought about some good old fellow just lying there wondering if his door had bounced open or whether his girlfriend was going to come back and close it, it made me sad. I put my arm around his shoulders.

Ivan flinched. He knew how to take himself apart. He said, "I'm afraid of intimacy."

That would become the signal to run.

CHAPTER 16
THE MURDERER

When I walked onto the trading floor with the fifteen oil futures I'd sold short on my mind, Jerry jumped up from the couch.

Sasha stood up. "Dick! Good morning, sir."

"Cut the crap, Sasha." I don't tolerate spoiled rich kids making fun of me. I waited all day watching Brent crude make new lows. Pretty soon I'd be back to zero. I let Jerry go home. "Any news?" I asked Sasha.

That's when he told me.

"What!"

Tears came to Sasha's eyes. He was really serious about Jerry. I felt sorry for both of them. We let the phones ring, and I closed my eyes, saying, "You *are* fast. She really said her mother was murdered?"

"I swear, Dick. She's hiding from someone."

"Who?"

Sasha's gaze swept around the room as he bent forward and whispered, "The murderer."

"The what?" I jumped up and looked around the office. The Hudson gleamed below. The doorway was empty, and the fax machine was printing a report.

"Even her father doesn't know exactly where she lives. All he knows is she's on the East Coast. She calls her brother every couple of months from her home, a borough away, and says, 'I'll come visit soon. Right now I'm still getting settled into my new life.' She is a woman alone. You know what I mean?"

"Give me a clue."

"She's looking for love in building windows."

"And she's hiding from a murderer? Does she know who it is?" I asked.

"She wouldn't say," Sasha said.

We weren't qualified to sort out this kind of a mess. Sasha could suggest a structured financial product at best. His parents had sent him to a Swiss boarding school in the mountains where he looked out the window at the snow while he ate fillet goulash stroganoff with waiters standing behind him. I grew up in the bosom of a New York Russian neighborhood ripe with thieves and pimps. I would have been able to handle Jerry better if she *were* some kind of criminal. Still, I felt relieved that she was running away from somebody else. At least Jerry was clean.

I wanted to protect her, help her find out who did it,

or just be there for her. Maybe I'd been a little hard on her. All traders messed up in the beginning. We were going to see this through together. She really was here for a reason not of human design.

Sasha paced the room with a look of determination. Neither one of us had the slightest clue as to what to do.

"She can stay," I said.

CHAPTER 17
GOING FOR BLOKE

*M*en were irrelevant. They couldn't see me, so why should I see them? My phone rang. All the guys on the desk turned and looked at me, except Sasha. Ivan in his British accent came on the speakerphone. "Would you like to come around for tea?"

Sasha's back stiffened.

I pressed the button for a private conversation. "Yes. I'll come get you at your place." I didn't want Ivan to see F.L. seething. I thought it might turn Ivan off. I was still learning.

Ivan and I lounged around his little apartment with our pot of tea listening to jazz. "It's claustrophobic in here," he said. "Let's go for a walk." It was a relief to be walking past the brownstones with a neurotic man. It made me feel healthy in contrast and less likely to be singled out as the object of social charity. I liked the fact that he was working on himself. It was inspiring. Maybe I would learn to take myself apart.

I discovered Ivan had a black belt and showed him the little kung fu I had learned after my mother's murder. He had kept things on a strict 'just friends' level until now, so I was surprised when he put my hands on his shoulders and showed me some more moves. Ivan was surprisingly muscular. Very sweet and cuddly, would make a great father.

"We have more in common than just being neighbors," I told him. The kung fu excuse offered a way around his intimacy issues, and it was me who was afraid this time. Afraid that he was stronger than me, that he would discover my weaknesses, that he could hear my biological clock ticking. He leaned down and kissed me softly, just once, on the lips. I felt the other half of my heart drop. Nothing to do but fall in love with Ivan.

In bed at the crib, I straddled Ivan under my hips. I stretched my pantyhose and tied his wrists to the bedpost. He acquiesced. Then he looked down at his limp dick and started explaining. "My mother neglected me and left me in England with my stepmother when I was nine."

It was hard to arouse fickle Ivan. All he'd ever wanted was his mother, and now that he could finally have her, he was a man and she was an old hag.

One windy autumn morning, I segued out of F.L.'s railroad apartment and into Ivan's mother's doomed abode. This despite the fact that after twelve years, my First Love from high school, who said things like "supposably", was supposedly my last try at domestic bliss.

I was still aspiring, though haunted by memories. "I've always loved you," F.L. had whispered. My blood boiled remembering that. It was a daydream over a cigarette. Sometimes I thought I was in a movie, and life was organized by Hollywood. Romantic love wasn't circumstantial, and if he couldn't do it, no one could. *And I have always loved you.* My lips brushed his. But now he was Ivan.

Ivan was like a series of hot and cold showers. When I was on fire, he would start telling me how he had been neglected as a child. He'd moved back to America to be closer to his mother. I tried to make up for it by giving myself to him completely. Every time I advanced, his lousy fear of abandonment made him retreat. I confronted him: "Come on. It hurts when you withdraw." Even though I'd promised myself that F.L. would be my last try, "I'm still twenty-nine. We could have a home life. At work, everyone acts like a sexist myrmidon. At least I can argue with you." Why did I have to try so hard? If only my clock weren't ticking. It was nerve-wracking and lonely and I *did* want children.

It would be nice if I could only give the pieces of me that men wanted and keep the rest for myself. But I repressed what was left of my personality to further bend to their whims. I read Freud and Jung in search of answers, and found out that if you are conscious of repressing things, the damage is less than if you don't know you are doing it: when you conceal part of your personality from yourself, it splits off and lives under the protection of the unconscious where it develops its own subterranean fantasy life.

Ivan was in eTherapy. The consolation was that his parents were real lawyers, which gave me some hope of saving my car. I didn't want to lose my life savings to First Love, who was trying to steal the little I had. I walked along eagerly past the delis and newsstands to Ivan's mother's apartment on a summer night, past the sidewalk café, past the convenience store with the same bum sitting outside. I arrived at his doorstep.

Inside the apartment, I took off my jacket and pulled Ivan onto the couch next to me. He was into honesty. He talked until I couldn't hear what he was saying. I looked into his fearful green eyes and decided he was either dumb or just wanted sex, or both. I lunged; he dodged.

When the relationship was at its best, he would have an anxiety attack. He took a step backward. "I can't take this pressure. You're too intense for . . . for most men."

"What men? I'm trying to have a relationship with *you.*"

It was fall. Me and Ivan lay by the radiator, a four-legged animal wrapped in a blanket. "I like the fact that you're working on yourself," I told him. I tried to sound encouraging. "And it can only get more creative. That's the way to heal yourself, by following your inner voice and being creative."

"And what are you doing that's creative?" he asked.

"I have some ideas. I just haven't had time to follow them through."

"Like what?"

He called me out! I lay on my back. "It will be vegan."

"Vegan? That's vague. How is not eating meat because your mother was murdered being creative? "

I struggled to defend myself. It was really Saphora's idea. "It would be something edible that's tangible and practical and shows real conviction. Something healing."

"Like?"

"Like. Like a vegan restaurant. 'Vegan Cure'."

Ivan rolled his eyes.

"Your eTherapist liked the idea."

"Oh, OK." But that evening at the 230 Fifth Avenue roof bar, Ivan said, "I need my own space. I want to see other people."

The eTherapist was right! Ivan couldn't think about anyone else for more than five minutes. He had an intimacy issue. It was easier to push love away than to deal with the pain that might come if the relationship turned out the way he feared.

I tried to get him to talk honestly about us.

Ivan said, "You're needy."

"You were neglected as a child, and now you think *I'm* needy!" I wasn't going to give up on the damn relationship until it worked. 'Fear of intimacy' seemed so silly that he should be able to solve it. Were American men becoming gay? Behind him, the skyscrapers throbbed with colored lights, each building holding the capacity of a town. Amazing that these enormous buildings didn't sink through the ground into the subways.

The weight of the –polis does cause mutation. Man's torn consciousness divides man against himself.

76

I ignored Saphora and took Ivan's hand. "The eTherapist thinks that to be happy in a relationship with a woman, you have to overcome your deference for women and confront the notion of incest with your mother and sister."

"I don't have a sister," Ivan said. He pulled his hand away.

You had to be a real sucker to fall into this racket of telling some lazy schmuck what to do and how to think. It was easier to take Ivan apart than to put him back together again.

At home, Ivan was typing faster to the eTherapist. What a lot of words per minute! They could at least produce something with all this discussion, a poem or a song. "Do you know anyone at a record company?" I asked as Ivan transferred one hundred dollars to the eTherapist's account.

"I'm thinking of trying Autotherapy."

"Is that what your mother did on my car?" I asked.

"I'm serious. I'm canceling my next appointment," he said.

"I'm proud of you," I told him. "Sometimes you have to steal what's yours back from the thieves."

We struggled for closeness on the velour couch. He had to degrade me into a lower type of sexual object, since his respect for me was 'hampering his potency'. "Good girl. Now bend over."

"Like this?"

"That's it, little hussy."

For the same price, travel seemed to be a better remedy. He flitted around. We couldn't plan. Things had to be spontaneous, which left me guessing. The flip side was that adventure awakened the hero in Ivan. He left his fears behind. We went on camping trips, to islands. I put a strain on my job running off to Paris with him at the last minute. We had good times hiking in the mountains on the weekends, avoiding eye contact and skirting around any happiness that might catapult Ivan into anxiety. We wrote a song and barbecued on the roof and looked for a restaurant space for my vegan restaurant. We woke up in each other's arms. The minute we were happy, it stopped working. Nothing is more insurmountable than someone else's cowardice.

It stopped working when I was camping with Ivan on the Appalachian Trail. I wore my new hiking boots and expensive red wool socks. It was so romantic, I got my period and bled all over the sleeping bag. He grilled fish on the open fire while I washed the sleeping bag in the stream. Ivan decided to spend the second half of the vacation on a separate trip to Los Angeles.

I went nuts. "Why aren't you inviting me?"

His eTherapist wrote back to me, "Being with a person with those issues can take a great emotional toll on you since you are constantly exerting effort to fix things by trying to create intimacy or an open environment only to be rejected and pushed away."

"I know."

"Believe it or not, fear of intimacy comes from his parents emotionally abandoning him in his childhood. As long as he is still reacting unconsciously from his childhood emotional wounds, he'll keep repeating the same old pattern." I knew about repeating patterns having looked everywhere for The One. The eTherapist was starting to make sense. "He's hiding behind emotional walls and setting himself up to be abandoned all over again. Instead of hiding, he needs to step out and reveal himself to his partner! *Yeah, sure.* Sharing your worries with your partner dispels the negative feelings, and his fear of intimacy will gradually disappear. Unfortunately, you cannot make him do this."

Deep down, I must have known that Ivan was a black hole, but I felt I owed it to mankind to help him. Work had been all-consuming, and I risked losing my vacation if I didn't take it now. So I progressed from disaster to disaster, flying to Los Angeles to get Ivan to allow Ivan to feel vulnerable. If I could just get him to open his heart to me and practice self-disclosure on a regular basis, I was sure I could prove I was worthy of his trust. According to the eTherapist, this was supposed to increase our physical intimacy beyond what he'd ever experienced.

His waning approval of me was his only contribution to the relationship. He slouched forward in resignation.

"I came here to talk about how you really feel," I said.

"I feel like I don't want to be in this relationship."

"Go ahead, then. See other people. I just did," I lied. We were sitting in a grunge café looking out on Mount Rainier. The down-to-earth Seattle clientele was refreshing after New Yorkers who couldn't do much beyond bantering. Ivan's eyes lit up so bright that I had a flashback to our week together. The other patrons looked at us. Ivan watched me intently as I took a bite of my eggs Florentine. He followed my every movement as if we had just met.

"You're lying," Ivan's lips said. His eyes said, *You little slut. Who'd have guessed?* He was looking at my blue eye shadow, which I had worn anyway, even though I knew he didn't like it.

I glared at him. "Why not. You whittled my needs down to nothing." More heads turned. I was going to get my share somewhere, anyhow. "It was good. He was hard for a whole hour. We did it twice, once at a club and once at his place."

"He was hard on the way home?"

The fantasy I built to please him! "Oh yeah, and I gave him a blow job in the taxi, but he didn't come."

The things Ivan would incite me to do. He gave a surprised laugh. "Good. You should be even wilder."

I kept taking the bait and losing more respect. If I could just be the bitch that he wanted, we could be happy together forever as masochist and dominatrix.

CHAPTER 18

"JUST SIGN HERE"

i gave up on taking the subway in high heels and took a taxi along the East River toward our pie-in-the-sky-scraper. It disappeared as the taxi went into the tunnel. We stopped. We were stuck in traffic inside the tunnel again. Reality cuts deep. I had to pay the driver, get out and hobble alongside the cars toward the light at the end of the tunnel. I kept my nose plugged. The light was a lot farther than it looked. I finally had to breathe in the carbon monoxide. I took off my heels and broke into a sprint.

I was late, with a cut on my foot and runs in my stockings. At the doors to the skyscraper, a hundred people were standing around smoking their last cigarettes of the morning, because it was No Smoking inside. I had a blister on my toe from my new high heels, but I hustled across the huge lobby and stopped at security. I dug through my briefcase for my new security badge and filed into the elevator with all the other people in trench coats.

The walls of the elevator were covered with gray padding for moving furniture. Transients were always moving. It might as well have been a freight elevator. I entered the lobby of the 53rd with its tunnel of mirrors, and did what everyone who entered that lobby did: walked over to the window and stared at the magazine view of the Hudson Bay sparkling below. Toy ships, Statue of Liberty, islands quietly resting in the blue water.

I crossed Mort's shadow getting out of the elevator. He ignored my greeting. The snob only talks to you if you're a big shot. He was too busy laughing all the way to the bank, so to speak. *I* have to laugh at nitwits who don't say hello back. They sap my energy if I don't take a moment to laugh out loud at how ridiculous they are. He pretended he didn't hear me. The trading floor was 20,000 square feet of office space, a football field. The smell of Mort's cigar smoke was lingering at my desk.

But there was Sasha, sitting next to me. When I had first laid eyes on his back, I thought I was standing behind a younger version of my stepfather. He was tall with my stepfather's dark curly hair. Not that I was close to my stepfather, but he was still there in the back of my head. An archetype. Despite Sasha's sense of humor, there was a look of sadness on his face.

"Mort left some busy work for you to do. It's an easy job, Jerry. When we get through it, we'll be able to get back to sitting here every day developing trading strategies and talking about your fashionable American murder."

Sasha hadn't said anything about the murder since I'd told him, and I was relieved that he could make light of it. He was funny and smart. A little silly. He was technically one of my bosses, but the hierarchy was never enforced. His temperament suited me fine for this potentially high-stress job. There was nothing worse than a trader who'd lost his sense of humor. That's what gets you through the hard times.

"Speak *Geek* to me," I said. I chuckled at my own joke, a little worried about my future at the bank. He looked suddenly older, and I sensed the beginnings of a rivalry between us. We both let it go. I was already applying my strict no-office-romance code of conduct. Richard was going on vacation on Thursday, and had to have everything running like clockwork before he left.

"Jerry," Sasha said, "I'm gonna need your help with these SIVs. Do you know what an SIV is?"

"Yeah, a sieve is that mesh thing for sifting flower—"

"OK, forget about Structured Investment Vehicles. Pull your chair over here, baby." He said it with such ease, I couldn't help imagining him over me. "That's good. Now there's something else that Mort needs right away. Your signature. Here, let's simulate. I like simulating, don't you? Imagine Mort lends you 100 dollars. Now you owe him 100 dollars, and then a few weeks later, I come to you to collect his 100 bucks. You'd say, 'I didn't borrow 100 dollars from you. I borrowed it from Mort.' I say, 'Well, Mort gave me that note. Here, I'll prove it.' And I write out a note saying, 'You now owe me 100 bucks,' and I sign it."

"That doesn't seem like proof to me, but OK." Sasha was dangerous all right.

"Exactly! To avoid any real questions our debtors might have about whether or not they should actually be paying us their mortgage payments or paying the original bank, we need to provide notes to these clients.

"Don't we have a department for that?"

"We should, but in fact they're too busy selling and buying mortgages from other banks to leave a clear paper trail that proves that we're the bank they really owe the money to."

"How do we know we are?"

"We wouldn't be fabricating documents and pretending they owed us if another bank had the notes."

"I see. Nobody has the notes."

"Exactly. No one has the notes. These mortgages were bundled more than three years ago by the millions, and the originating banks have gone through mergers since then."

"Right."

"We wouldn't put ourselves in a position to be sued by another bank holding the actual notes, right?"

"I hope not."

"Correct. You're really quick, Jerry. See, here's my signature on all these notes. They don't profess to be the original notes. They simply say, you owe us now. These are just a few documents we have to clean up before we get to trading."

My head was swimming. I skimmed the documents in Sasha's bronze paw and reminded myself not to stand too near to my male colleague. Hell, what did I know? "So, you want me to sign these?" I didn't like the idea, but I wanted to get it out of the way so I could trade.

"Yes, if you could. I was going to do it myself, but I don't have time. After you go through this pile, I'll let you trade."

I couldn't believe this was still going on in 2010. I thought we were past the mortgage crisis. As I signed the notes, I liked myself less and less. It wasn't that it was busy work. I wasn't sure it was right. Maybe Sasha was going to throw away all the ones with his signature on them and only keep mine.

I watched him put on a trade for two million SIVs, which became a winner. He didn't take profit, but left his winnings out there. They earned more, and he still didn't realize the gain. But by the end of the morning, the trade was losing one-third of what he'd made. I watched him close it out. "It's virtually impossible to get over the shock of a small loss before you can appreciate the gain from a trade. Almost no one closes a winning trade out at the peak. The key is to appreciate what you *can* get."

I couldn't believe they stuck me with signing mortgage notes. I had lots of ideas about shorting credit default swaps, but they just wanted me to stay out of the way. The bonds Sasha had sold were big losers. "We should have let you do your credit default swap," he said, "even if we didn't understand it. Look at the price now!"

Richard came in to check on the mortgage notes. "Thank you, Jerry." He flashed me his user-friendly smile. "I know it seems mundane, but we all had to pay our dues before we started to put on our own trades."

"Her swap idea was a good one," Sasha said.

"Listen, Sasha, she doesn't trade any real money until *after* I get back. I don't want any risk on vacation." Richard closed down Sasha's positions at a $35,000 loss. "Now it's time to sleep on the beach."

"You know, Dick, she could have covered your back side with that swap," Sasha said.

"With that swap, she could have covered my back side and my front side." Richard gave me a lecture on not doing anything. I wasn't sure he was happy with me. The guys on the desk were all into their own games, and I was getting bored.

"You're fine," Richard told me, "and I'm only sayin' it once. Just keep doin' what you're doin'. You know you've bumped up a level when somebody gets jealous." He nodded his head in Sasha's direction. "Don't expect any thanks from fallen Greeks."

She turned to me and gave me her full attention.

"The only thanks you'll get is a kick in the butt. Just use the time while I'm away to get organized on a personal level. Go apartment hunting, sign up for courses, whatever you have to do, now that you have a new job. And don't worry. I'll be back soon, rosy cheeks. You look nervous, and cute."

"Right. I'll go look for a place somewhere Queensish." I glanced out of the corners of my eyes at the expressions on the faces of the currency traders as they executed a yard of Indonesian rupiah. I counted the zeros in a 'yard' and tried to remember back to the days when this white-collar scene made me feel humiliated in the pursuit of money. Now it was routine, and I knew that there wasn't that much money lying around after all.

The newspapers presented the splendor of Wall Street bonuses with heaps of money in the form of stock options dished out to corporate executives annually. But that was because journalists had no interest in writing about the daily humdrum of small losses and inglorious exploitation. They complied with editorial exigencies and perpetuated the capitalist myth of the big winner, the stray lottery ticket holder who despite all odds, was able to retire at the age of twenty-six. This was the food of the newspapers that kept the masses commuting in freight elevators up to the top of the world with hope ticking in their hearts.

There was little splendid about Global American Bank, beyond the view of the Hudson; there were no heaps of gold to be seen cluttering the aisles. Very little cash lay out in the open. When a big number like unemployment came out, some crazy man or sheik might make an appearance and win or lose a virtual pile of money, but as for the rest of the players, we scuffled over petty cash.

Richard took a deep breath and left for vacation.

The next day, Sasha and I were much happier with the desk to ourselves. Sasha went out twice as often to smoke cigarettes. We talked on the speakerphone to our people in Dallas and Chicago. Our broker in Chicago called to say he would come up to New York to take us out in two weeks.

Sasha rolled his eyes. "Don't worry," he said into the phone. "I explained to Jerry that you're married and have twelve kids."

"You ruined everything," I muttered under my breath without looking up from my screen. "What day of the week is the broker coming?"

"It's a Thursday."

"The day that's most inconvenient for you. Richard will be on vacation, and you take your daughter out on Thursdays. That's the day you arranged for the broker to come to New York?"

"You know, you learn fast, Jerry. You'll have to go instead of me." The phone rang. Sasha picked it up and started laughing. "Is she hot?"

"Somehow, I don't think you're talking about his wife," I said.

Sasha was about to introduce me to some Global American Bank people in Paris. He called them up and said into the speaker, "I'm going to introduce you to the lady that has come to work with us. She's nice, she's charming, very elegant and stylish, subtle, not like you, so don't be a slob when you talk to her. Eh? Try not to be disgusting. All right, this is Jerry."

I picked up the phone. *"Bonjour. Vous-allez bien?"*

"Bonjour!"

What's going on with mortgages in the U.S., Jerry? We're hearing that 'robo-signers' have approved thousands of documents. You're not one of those 'Burger King kids' people are talking about who walked in from the street and barely knew what a mortgage was?"

"Give me that phone!" Sasha said. "Knucklehead. When are you going to learn how to talk to a lady? She's getting her MBA, for God's sake. Have some respect." He slammed down the phone. We ate our bagels in silence.

Sasha was in a bad mood for the rest of the day. He said he hated to work. He would be much better relaxing on a beach in Greece. "My girlfriend's moving out tonight."

I don't know what prompted that revelation, but I thought that maybe now his spirits would improve. He'd wanted her to move out for a long time, but he didn't have the strength to live alone, even if it meant "rescuing a whore".

I went back to watching prices. "You should have let me buy the 30-year at 11:30."

"I should have let you buy it at 10:30. On Monday, you will trade for real."

"Yesss." Three more days to go, I thought as I got back into the freight elevator and passed swiftly down the tube with the other trench coats.

CHAPTER 19
SUSPECTS

i was crawling out of my skin with curiosity. I won't say she ruined my vacation, but I had to start investigating the murder. Under a palm tree in the Imperial Palace lobby, I mined Jerry's web-based email for clues. It was clear that she thought the murderer was still around. I began with the hypothesis that it might have been someone Jerry knew.

There were a few people in Jerry's life from her past who I considered suspect, starting with First Love, a Southern man. His Mexican heritage put me on guard for the unexpected. I had a mental picture of him as muscular, about her height, physically able to commit a murder. Her descriptions of his brooding character fit the profile. The fact that she was living with him had been a source of constant worry for me, and I was relieved at their breakup.

The second doubtful person in her life was a friend from high school, Regina. She had always been in enough trouble to put her at odds with Jerry's mother. She seemed so crazy she hardly needed a motive.

And the third was this Saphora, the friend from Harvard with the Greek fetish. It sounded like she spent her vacations during college with Jerry's family, a strike against her. She knew the mother. She seemed to have been a big influence on Jerry's thinking, though mired in passive intellectualism. I suspended judgment on her involvement but decided that she was capable of plotting a murder. She was in New York, so it would just be a matter of time before she materialized.

There was one more shady suspect, a man named Angel. Jerry seemed to know him by reputation only. He was a party person who appeared all over the New York Club scene.

I couldn't crack the case with this information. I'd have to see what new material Jerry would produce.

This speculation reminded me how proud I was of the crew I'd put together back at the office. There were no major personality conflicts. If anything, harmony caused the most trouble. I couldn't say that Jerry was a 'good fit', but we all waited with anticipation for her to join us up in the skyscraper each morning. At least that's how *I* remembered it looking up at that palm tree . . .

CHAPTER 20
SOUL MINING

"*I* might have found a new object," I told Saphora.

"Ooo. Do tell."

"Sasha."

"Sasha! Not Sasha of the dying empire? — You said yourself that he was a player."

"He is. But I'll win."

"Do the math. You only want him because you can't have him."

"You never see the point if it's not to found a family. Here's someone who can understand tragedy."

"Understanding and avoiding are two different things."

"I can't believe you even think Sasha the Greek is not

good enough for me."

"Honey, no man is good enough for you. You just pick whichever one you want."

"He has a sweet side. Underneath there is a classical manliness beyond description."

"I'll bet there is. Sasha, huh? That sounds like a fine dude. That's a feather in your cap, I'd say."

"This is not a collection. I'm trying to have some real reciprocation. Something lasting. Maybe he's too fine."

"What about Ivan?" she asked.

"You can say that again."

I really couldn't understand men. They made you want to give them everything when they couldn't appreciate ten percent. And then for the ending to drag on like this with Ivan already as much of a basket case as F.L. and threatening to leave me with two breakups on my hands.

I was stumped. I knew they wouldn't make good fathers or even lovers, so why did I care so much about losing them? They didn't meet my hero specifications. Why was I trying to figure them out? There must be something missing in me, in my soul. Who had time for relationships? It was time for soul mining. I had things to do, like open my vegan restaurant.

But a woman's mind doesn't let her stop believing in man until she sees proof as solid as a brick wall. What could have been a painless exit turned into trench warfare. I stayed at work late with Sasha so that when I arrived home, Ivan was almost happy to see me. I made Ivan wait as I showered, but he still seemed relieved when I went to sleep without demanding physical gratification.

I held onto my stomach and managed the situation with endless compromise on the one hand, and watering Ivan's unquenchable thirst for drama on the other: his sexual perversion required that I parade men in front of him. That's what got him off. Seeing me with another man. Unavailability.

I invited acquaintances over before he came home from work and introduced them to him when he got home. One guy did me hard against the bathroom door.

"How did the bathroom door get broken?" Ivan asked. Then he saw the condom in the garbage can. Ivan thrived on humiliation. We both knew this was part of some grander bargain. That evening, he listened to my stories with newfound fascination.

Someone up there must have decided to give me trouble before allowing my children to be born. I didn't know which god was responsible for this turn of fate, but I was aware that things were happening on another level, a re-enactment of an archetype on the Grecian urn. We were the etched figures:

Aphrodite used her powers once more. She whisked Ivan off and put him down in his own fragrant bed.

I felt the gravitational pull toward the man who had provided a home for me for the past months.

"Come!" said the goddess. "There he is in his room."

I was exasperated, and looked at the man with his beautiful neck and full chest. His eyes sparkled when he saw me, and I smiled even though he was no better than a wall. What was the object of this game? Why had Fate plotted again to carry me off to a distant city for this favorite of hers?

Unable to share the coward's bed again, I turned away from Ivan, possibly invoking the same rebuke dealt unto Helen, and accidentally knocked *The Iliad* off the bedside table. It was Saphora's book.

"Do not provoke me, or I might desert you in my anger."

Saphora? I was cowed. I wrapped myself up in my white and glossy robe, and went directly back to the dim bedroom. There she was, the goddess herself, laughter-loving Aphrodite. She picked up a chair, carried it across the room and put it down for me in front of Ivan. I sat on the chair, turned my eyes aside, as Saphora would have done, and began scolding my lover. "I wasn't interested when you introduced yourself to me," I said. "We struck a bargain. I thought, maybe in the short term. Then, OK, 'til the end of summer. You offered me a scientific explanation of this male fear of intimacy. Is it enough to be wonderful to be with? To charm everyone?"

"For now, yes."

There, you see? It was just for a brief thrill, as if love were only a drug.

He took my hand, leading me. I followed him, and we lay down together on the bed. He took off his tie. Then he had an anxiety attack. He pushed me away. Rolled onto the floor. "I can't handle the pressure. I need my own space. I don't want to feel obligated to call you every day at work. I want to see other people." We had a fight, and he gave up on the whole relationship again.

"I don't like the position you put me in," I said, hurt. Why was it always about him? I had to settle for less and less. "OK, if that's the way you want it."

Don't give in! Too late.

"You're just too bloody needy for me," Ivan said.

"You're spoiled," I said. It was such a silly dilemma. I fought to overcome it.

"Our vacation in Paris was one of the best times of my life," he said, lying on the bedroom floor crying.

I was happy he thought so, but it wasn't for me. He broke up with me three times. Ivan was only twenty-eight, and he couldn't get it up in Paris, for God's sake. We curled up on the floor. "It was wonderful," I lied. There, now we were close, with my lie snarling between us. It really was there between us. I saw it: a slimy lizard.

Suddenly he pulled away. I *saw* the lizard's demon face scrutinizing me accusingly in the dark. "What?" I said.

"Nothing," he said.

"What?" I knew we had all seen it.

"Well, I was thinking something, if you must know."

"Tell me," I said.

"I was just thinking that I have to be really sure you love me as much as you say you do, and that you're not going to stop loving me."

"I could *feel* your suspicion," I replied. "I love you so much. I can't tell you how much I love you. Don't you worry." *Ach.* Now he was going to say he wanted to see other people. We were on a psychological merry-go-round with impotence surmountable only by degrading women enough to separate them in his mind from his mother. Who had time for this stuff?

Me. I stretched and admired my long legs. He didn't look. I crossed them Indian-style on the couch and told him point-blank that he had to accept his incestuous feelings for his mother first before he could love a whole woman for being herself and not some degradable object.

"Don't pull that Freud bunk on me." He ran to his anti-intellectual eTherapist who ushered him down the tangent of least resistance. I had started to disappear into his thicket of incongruity. The masochist deliberately provoked rejecting responses from me to stay on familiar territory: humiliated and hurt. The only woman in Ivan's mother's apartment was Ivan's mother. Meat eaters.

"I need you inside me." I looked up at him imploringly.

He lurched backwards, terrified. A nervous laugh escaped his lips.

"And you don't mind my having sex with other men?"

I had his full attention now. He looked helpless. "I want you to have a full life," he said.

"If we have to be abusive to get each other's attention, the love is gone." I went out for a walk, and when I came back, *Ivan* was gone. Haw! I was free to use the apartment as I liked. I took a bath, made us some dinner and called the school. He hadn't been there all day. I felt a chill run through my spine as I hung up the phone. I searched the apartment for a note or a clue, but nothing seemed out of place. His jacket and favorite shoes were gone. He'd taken his gloves but not his hat. I called his mother at work. It was just before Hanukah, and she was on vacation. She hadn't left a phone number. I put his dinner in the fridge.

Around midnight, I started looking around the dim apartment, rummaging through his desk for clues as to the whereabouts of his heart. There was a message on the answering machine, a female voice, "I'm sorry it's so late. I had some phone calls to make. But I'll be coming over around 11:00." What phone calls to make? What kind of work was this mystery girlfriend doing at eleven p.m.? Prostitution? This had gone too far. But exactly how far was too far?

The next thing I knew I was emptying his bedroom trashcan out onto the floor. No condoms. He was still in the terrified-of-revealing-his-limp-dick stage. I wondered if he was going to lay that line on her about how "I can only get it up with girls I don't like, and I really like you." I checked around the bed. No condoms. I opened his bedside drawers and looked under his guns and rifles. Four condoms. Those condoms didn't come in packages of four. Just a bottle of Nivea and a bottle of baby oil. Masturbating. I guessed he had to build up to it. There were directions to her place scribbled by a strange female hand on a scrap of paper on the coffee table. He saved garbage like that.

Now that Ivan was gone, his apartment stopped smelling like a ham sandwich. Two days went by. It didn't feel like Ivan was dead, but it might have been my wishful thinking. You couldn't force somebody to grow, so you couldn't force them to be alive.

I paced the apartment. The trick was in the selection. You had to pick the right people in the first place. It was so obvious to the French. I was worried sick and could hardly eat. Finally there was a phone call. "This is Bellevue Hospital. Are you the next of kin for Ivan Stanovich"

"Oh my God! Yes! What is it?"

"He's in stable condition. You can come and visit him."

"Can't he come home?"

Ivan was recovering from an operation and was going to be moved to the mental ward. They had found him bleeding in the goddamn street. He had severe internal bleeding from a broken light bulb up his butt.

I went to visit Ivan. They opened his door for me and said I had fifteen minutes. Ivan was propped up in bed in one of those blue gowns, hands hidden under the blankets, an absent look on his face. Conversation was impossible. He kept mumbling to himself, "I shouldn't have . . . shouldn't have . . ."

The apartment was lonelier than ever. I'd have to get an alarm clock that didn't tick. There it was as plain as day: it didn't make sense to have a baby. Modern man was going to flake out. I'd have to raise it alone and might end up a murder victim myself.

Ivan's mother called, "I'm going to be staying there to take care of my son. You can call my moving company if you need help moving out."

Why wasn't I in shock? "I just have a few things." This was a new one on me, being replaced by his predatory mother.

I was about to go downstairs to the deli to get some boxes to pack my books in. My 1-800 number rang. Raif! I felt a rush of guilt as I let the phone ring. I should have taken care of my younger brother better in the first place, especially now that he'd blown his relationship with Saphora. When it rang again, I did the responsible thing and ran up the last flight with the boxes and got it on time.

But it wasn't Raif. He must have given my number to my dad. "We don't want to be a part of a relationship if—" my own father who never bothered about me was calling now to break up with me. " —if we don't know where you are."

"Fine. That'll be easier for both of us." I hung up. Family was a liability. I was safer alone.

I sat down on Ivan's mother's white chair. My eyes kept wandering back to the cute photo of Ivan and myself in a checked lumberjack shirt and those big boots with the red wool socks. Hiking with Ivan. How could they turn me out? I could die of something like this. Being that close to a man could kill me — what if we'd had kids! Maybe next time we would, or the next time. I sank further into Ivan's mother's chair. *This is just the kind of thing that could kill me.*

I wasn't leaving him my copy of Freud on impotence after all, and chucked 'Degradation' in the box with my shoes. Then I did something different. Instead of calling another guy with an apartment, I looked through the *New York Times* classifieds and found an attic sublet on Jane Street. Location, location, location. Even if it was tiny, it was gonna be *my* postage stamp.

I carried my books up the fifth flight of that antiquated stairwell, thinking modern man was undergoing some kind of mutation. How much distance could man want? Nobody there to watch him being inconsistent. My last monstrosity wouldn't have known what to do with a woman if she came with a manual. It was the perfect relationship for his insoluble ass. I didn't love him as much as he didn't do me. At the bottom of his personality, he didn't love himself. How could he love me if he couldn't

100

love himself? That was the first thing to find out, whether he loved himself.

I still hadn't met a whole man. My investigations of half-men provided strong evidence that what was not there was really not there. Mutants only wanted half a relationship. They did just fine. There was a glut of low-maintenance to be had. They could find women who watched a lot of TV and had no ideas. If men needed space, it wasn't hard to find women who simply didn't understand. They were all around, never encroaching, never knowing your whereabouts: nowhere. Never mind. *I* was going to find myself. I put down the box and faced the exposed brick wall.

I wasn't looking forward to leaving work that Friday afternoon. I couldn't bear the thought of crawling back into the dilapidated subway and holing up alone in my microscopic attic on Jane. I stayed at the bank late.

"Weren't you going to let me trade for real?" I asked Sasha.

He took it as a rhetorical question and went out fifty times to smoke a cigarette. I noticed a red mark on his forearm and three scars next to it. "What's that?" I asked.

"Cigarette burns," Sasha said.

A bolt of foreboding ran through me. "How did it happen?" I asked.

"I wanted to see how much it hurt."

"You did that yourself? How much did it hurt?"

"A lot."

"You'd think you'd get the hang of smoking by now."

"Tomorrow's another day," he said.

"That's a jazz song. Do you know that song, Sasha?" I

played it for him on YouTube, and he helped me on with my coat.

I stopped over at Ivan's to pick up my mail. Ivan's mother cracked the door and stuffed the pile of letters through.

CHAPTER 21

HACKER

*E*very time I hacked into her goddamn computer, my heart leapt. I knew it would hurt to be inside her, but if she didn't care about me, neither did I. She could play me like a deck of cards for all I cared.

Then again, legs or no legs, I'd have fired her on day one if she'd come to work on Prozac.

There was a black ace crisscrossing the country. This Regina. I was eager to meet her, with long black hair and chiseled Indian nose. She had a motive for every crime. I can't begin to imagine what it would have cost to straighten her out. This more-than-a-woman threw my probabilities into doubt. She had known Jerry longer than First Love and Saphora, and that put her on the suspect list. I delved into Jerry's diary for information on Regina and found this section where they traded dreams as teens.

CHAPTER 22
ON PROZAC

i tried to run in my high heels. There she was crossing the park. "Regina!" Heads turned, but not hers. I called her name again. It was somebody else, just another figure painted on the pottery. Oh God, what I wouldn't give for another warm body to curl up with.

I wished we were back in high school standing by the radiator in Mrs. Elda's microbiology class. I told Regina my dream standing huddled against the radiator. "I want to be a scientist. I want to do research and discover things."

"Not me, girl," Regina said. "They don't make enough money. I wanna glamorous job in New York that lets me travel the world."

One look at her determined, fifteen-year-old face was all it took to convince me to abandon my dream for something 'cooler'. Her dream. And here I am still trading the indecipherable, derivatives that even bankers don't understand. Maybe I could undo it all, my years of useless travel with only a hypothetical Prozac addiction to show for it, everything. That catalytic moment by the radiator resulted in an exchange that merited further investigation. If only I could go back to that radiator, maybe I could undo that moment when we first traded dreams. Maybe I could straighten out our paths, prevent her from following my science dream to that hellish lab job killing rats with a miniature guillotine — I wonder if she knows I'm to blame for that.

Regina's husband had thought transplanting her on new soil would make her grow and change her unfaithful ways, so they'd moved to Los Angeles. But the whole catastrophe started over again within a few months, boyfriends, drugs, lies. Now Regina was headed east thinking to relax in my palace of success and fulfillment. I wanted to impress her with the solution to all our problems. What was taking her so long? She was not here yet; she was still coming, passing through New Orleans, our hometown. Driving across America, coming forever, can make a Sing Sing inmate seem like the Wizard of Oz.

On Jane, the TV rattled off a sales pitch for some dating site. The TV was trying to program me. How could I listen to my inner voice when the TV bombarded me with junk and repressed all my thoughts? I was trying to remember something. It was floating just beneath my consciousness. Yogis think consciousness is what creates our bodies. A cell was a memory housed in fluid and tissue. Repression must be destroying me, then. I looked in the mirror to see if I was translucent. I was opaque, but the only thing I could remember was that commercial from my childhood. A black kid saying, "Why you think they call it 'dope'?" The first suggestion of drugs.

I fantasized about what we'd do when Regina got here. I would show her all the cool places, and when we ran out of things to do and Regina started clicking her heels together, the blind would lead the blind, and I would hit her with the Prozac.

On Prozac, you wouldn't want sex. With your needs pared away, you probably wouldn't even care if your special someone was out there with other lovers; you'd be there in your money-green suit increasing productivity. You could bet your bottom dollar that it was not a woman who invented Prozac. A man invented this new seedless woman who didn't matter. On Prozac, there would be no soul mate not to recognize what I was trying to achieve. It wouldn't be on the menu, but no one would be hungry anyway. Basic human rights? Pah. You'd have no requirements, step on no one's toes, encroach on no one's space. You'd be in your box where you belonged: on Prozac.

The sky had been crying for three days. These things always happen on a Sunday when doctors' offices are closed. In search of Prozac, I burst out of my apartment and rushed over to the Bellevue Hospital Emergency Room in the rain. It was crowded. They asked me if I was suicidal. I didn't know what the right answer was. I hedged, searching for clues. "Well, the thought has crossed my mind."

The nurse's paper-bag expression folded inward.

"But I don't think I would ever carry it out."

The nurse looked at me, her wrinkled hands in her

lap. Nurse said. "What's the matter? You look like a professional. You got the whole world laid out at your feet."

I hung my head.

"Look, the thought crosses everyone's mind. But are you suicidal?" the nurse said.

Tears welled in my eyes.

"It's like this," Nurse said, "If you say 'Yes', we send you one place, and if you say 'No', we send you another place."

"Where?"

"Well, if you say 'Yes', you are not allowed to leave the hospital."

Rutt roh. "No, I'm certainly not suicidal." Whew, I thought. I must be way out there if I am trying to get in here. What would they say back home?

Pft, they would say. *Now, Regina we can respect, because she really is crazy.*

I was trying not to WANT to get laid. I just wanted to talk to a psychiatrist for FIVE minutes. I was going to tell him, Yeah sure, I was already on the medication, but I lost my prescription when I moved to Manhattan.

Nurse wanted blood.

A year earlier, I had gone to an emergency room. They gave me a pap smear, stuck their fingers in my rectum, and sent me a bill for four hundred dollars.

"Here it only costs three," the Bellevue Nurse said.

"It's not fair what they do to women sometimes." But Ponzi scheme healthcare seemed better than no help at all. I hunkered down among the maimed and lonely, my blue hospital gown open in back, and filled out the forms. My roommate started vomiting. I began to doubt my own judgment. An attendant wheeled me half-naked out into the hallway to make room for an emaciated man with a long beard. Someone was singing. New York had an endless supply of crazies falling into cracks like this one. I lay down in my bed across from the pay phone and remembered my family. There was no one to call. Mother, brother, children, failure that multiplied, failure to multiply.

By now, Bellevue had outweighed the Wizard of Oz, and I was stealing back my rights, putting my clothes on, walking back out through the Emergency Room doors. The nurses were busy tackling the bearded man and didn't notice me. He was yelling, "Get your hands off of me!"

They were holding him down in a wheel chair. "My God! Let me out of here!"

I ran, discarding my glass obsession with Prozac on the steps. You can't get there from here, I thought. You cannot get there from here. I looked at my hand and knew which card I had to play:

- Change the subject

It rained that night. A long, calm drizzle. I boiled sticky rice, mixed it with vinegar, and shaped six little rice balls. I put raw salmon fillet on top of each, scooped up slices of ginger with my chopsticks, dipped the sashimi in soy sauce and green mustard, and scarfed them down. The TV newscaster droned on about another sickening murder as if she were reporting the weather. It sent me back to the moment of my mother's death. I changed the station. Same garbage. A pedophile. Mom screamed. I cried. Why should I let them get me? I had *other* thoughts to think. I unplugged the TV and carried it over to the window. There were people walking down below. I turned around and carried the TV through the apartment to the airshaft. Five stories and a crashing TV. No one cared. I shut the window.

I was calmer now writing in my diary in the quiet. It kept on raining, but I had to get out of this tiny apartment. I went for a walk in the rain and eavesdropped on the other patrons at Mojo Coffee. There were others from my hometown in New York. I wondered what they were doing. Pater and Lonnie. I would look them up. I took out my little black book. There were plenty of transients to invest in. This Pater was a gay friend who'd moved to New York from New Orleans.

I walked home through the dark streets alone, along brick walls toward solitude and self-reliance. I trudged through the raindrops. Water seeped through the crack in the sole of my loafer, soaking my wool sock. The harder it was to relinquish my platonic relationship with Prozac, the better. I would win. It was another psychological addiction. Look how I depended on it, never having had it. I felt lighter, as if someone were with me. And came to the point. If only I could remember what it was.

I was still young. I had to remodel myself before it was too late. Jung said you hardened at forty. *After that* it was too late, and the only therapy that helped was painting your fantasies. I had ten years. There was change in the air. I lay in bed, suspecting a god was with me. My arms stretched upward toward the ceiling in the dark, blind human material reaching up from the earth, fingers branching out in the darkness. One hand grasped the other.

CHAPTER 23
PATER FAMILIAS

"*H*ey, Pater. Where y'at?" The trading desk turned and looked at me shouting into the phone. I was going out.

Sasha was outside the bank smoking a cigarette when I came out. I could feel his eyes on my back as I walked down the steps into Zuccotti Park. Instead of hobbling into the subway, I decided to splurge on a ride. "Taxi!"

Sasha was there behind me. He opened the door for me.

I rolled down my window. "Thanks." The cab took all the pain out of commuting. I wound along the East River with the Manhattan skyline gliding by. This day would surely have a happy ending.

Me, Pater and his entourage broke bread at a Mexican restaurant on 5th in the East Village. Pater had a lot of friends, which is how he got his name Pater Familias. His friends were never as bright as he was, though, and they made it hard to get his undivided attention, unless you hadn't seen him since high school.

With his cigarette on autopilot, Pater tipped his egg-shaped body forward on his barstool. His blue hair prickled my cheek as he yelled into my ear. "New York is a machine, churning people. You have to spend all your time looking for new jobs, re-skilling, doing the apartment shuffle. Either it's the owner who sold your pad, or you make it as a homeowner, and it's the banks kicking you out."

"Maybe I should find another warm body," I said.

"A roommate? Don't live with anyone, girl. People are crazy. They're baggage, man."

Crazy? Usually Pater said I was out there. But for once, he said, "You get yourself into these confusing situations where everything is fragmented, and then you pick up all the pieces and make everything work. People think you're vulnerable because you come across as soft on the outside, but underneath, you're a rock." That was one of the nicest things anyone ever said to me, and it came from a punk.

Pater's sidekick, Lonnie, came up to the bar and put her arms around us. Lonnie was a fashion designer, and always had to have something weird on. This time it was pink velvet pants. "Let's go dancing!" she said.

I couldn't remember the last time I'd danced. I guessed I would be OK in my silk slacks and green bodysuit. As I grabbed my raincoat, I looked in the mirror by the exit at my throat under a black pearl necklace and matching earrings. I could hear my husband saying: *Cherie, before you walk out the door, take off one thing.* I removed my necklace and put it in my pocket. I looked over my shoulder into the mirror again. The throaty soft blonde 6a looked back. Elegance.

"Pater, you rescued me from myself tonight," I said, getting into the cab. Pater led the way to Splash. Lonnie split her pants and rode the taxi home, but two of Pater's colleagues from his graphic arts company met up with us in the line outside. They were like the Three Musketeers, all working for the same company and one for all. Pater had hired them, so I wondered how much of their homoerotic shadow boxing was from the heart and how much was to please the boss. Then again, maybe Pater would have hired gay men if he could. But the manchunks were both very friendly toward me, too. "Jerry, come on!" They disappeared into the smoke. I pushed through the crowd to the dance floor. Dancing with the new men, I couldn't help imagining myself in bed with both of them, one in front, one behind. My feet kept the rhythm. I brushed the sweat off my face and held my head in my hands. I knew they were thinking the same thing. Then Pater arrived, and changed their sexuality back to neutral-gay. They'd become a tribe, and danced in a circle. The circle tribe didn't wander far, always a good quality in men.

"It would be nice to settle down and start a family," I was yelling above the din. The conversation trailed off. They only talked to each other now, and a void opened up around me. Lesson learned: If you want guys all over you all night, don't talk about kids.

I watched a fat couple fade off to a couch in an alcove. They'd only just met, but seemed to know each other very well. I wondered if fat people didn't have it easier. Both could be sure the other was overdue to get laid. The Three Musketeers were harder to figure out, though. How often did they go out dancing like this? Did they get laid? By which? Pater led us to another room.

When I wandered off, a homely man came up to me and said, "Filigraine and burlappers," into my ear, and just as I concluded he was speaking a different language, I understood, "Are you going to go home with me?"

"No!"

A skinny queen in a white dress was prancing up and down the aisle. He kicked up his legs in an imaginary chorus line. He was doped up and wearing white barrettes in his hair. It was hard getting back to my friends.

"Do you think that's cocaine or Ecstasy?" I asked Pater.

"Ecstasy. This whole place turns into an X rave after three. There's a guy here from Israel tonight with a million hits."

"That's more than I want to know." I looked around at the yuppie Ecstasy party. I was not into this teen spirit stuff. Weren't people getting into fitness in the new age? In France, we ate three-course dinners at nightclubs. We had crusty bread and a floor show before we danced. They knew how to socialize without drugs. What was I doing here? I wanted to heal myself with vegan cooking.

I followed the boys to the center of the dance floor. The drums pounded through the floorboards. Temptation took the most convenient form here. The drums found out whatever you were trying to resist. *Boom, boom.* I felt my desire, not for sex but for conception. The drums boomed through the floorboards, up my legs and into my heart: *I want my children. Boom, boom. Just like Mom did.* Whatever you were trying not to want, cigarettes, drugs, a loan, that was what came to you here, through the floorboards. The drums said, *boom, I have a RIGHT to my children.* I watched the men's faces as they passed through the spot light. *Give them to me NOW.* I didn't want to die childless at the hands of a murderer.

I pulled myself together and got off the dance floor. Hormones. I would have to find something else not to want. *Maybe success.* I once knew a girl who said she had 'fear of success'. Wouldn't that be convenient now? To be tempted into fame and fortune?

Pater was on the banquette, unconscious. I had to get out of there. I said goodbye to Pater. He waved, and I escaped out into the street alone. I knew Pater was right. I did have more possibilities on my own. So here I was walking home, trying not to *WANT* to get laid. I just wanted to talk to a psychiatrist for FIVE MINUTES. But you couldn't get there from here. You could not get there from here. You had to change the subject.

CHAPTER 24
YOU CAN'T GET UNDER IT

My head lay on the desk. I was beside myself with lust for Jerry. I had sunk so low, I couldn't sleep at night. I was messing up trades daydreaming about her. People were beginning to notice. Bernie's wife had told Bernie that my wife hired a detective to find out if I was having an affair. Ha! If only I were.

I had to keep my ulcer from flaring up, so I minimized my spying. It was clear from Jerry's diary that Saphora had been involved with the brother. And there were hints that the mother didn't get along with her son's first girlfriend. What if the mother didn't think Saphora was good enough for her son? The mother might have talked Raif out of committing to a relationship with Saphora.

There was the motive I was looking for. In fact, Saphora was the only one in Jerry's entourage with a motive.

"What's a matter with you, Richard?"

I started in my sleep. It was Mort. He was losing respect for me.

"You think you've got problems, I had to inaugurate our new South Bronx branch and commit $5 million in loans."

I controlled my smile. "How embarrassing." I would have to get a grip on my other Gemini personality.

"We got off light," Mort said. "Four other banks had to open new branches and commit $15 million each." He stared hard into my eyes. Mort wanted blood.

"Oh, uh, good." I'd have to give Mort free rein on the robo-signing if I wanted to keep Jerry with me on the prop desk.

By the third month, Jerry had become our only robo-signer. She had signed a thousand mortgage notes, never mind that she'd walked in from the street and barely knew what a mortgage was. We called her the Burger King kid behind her back.

Sasha mumbled something about the mortgages being reviewed by outside lawyers. "We don't need to bother with the details. Just get these signed." He shoved them in front of Jerry.

Hell, it seemed harmless enough to me. We were all in on it. The guilt had been transferred from bank to bank. No one could fix it anyway. There was no way to get the information needed to repackage mortgages that had been bought and sold so many times. The whole system was rotten. There was no particular individual who had committed the crime. I didn't think we'd see the day when the shareholders would demand a human sacrifice.

Meanwhile, Mort's inside information paid off. Everything he touched went up. I took profit and was taking the winnings with me back to the casino. "You'll trade when I get back," I told Jerry. "Don't put on any trades while I'm gone. You don't want to get between a dog and a lamp post."

Jerry made sure the names and titles were correct, and stacked the mortgage documents on the desk. I watched her saunter out onto the 53rd floor in those damn black stockings. Then I left again for Vegas.

CHAPTER 25

WHEEL OF FORTUNE

*V*egas? I was glad the high roller had gone off on another tangent. I had no use for Richard's American-nightmare hype. He really didn't get me at all. I was trying to invest, not gamble. With him out of the way I could realize myself professionally, if not personally.

I straightened up, seeing the trading room for the first time. This was it. I resolved to put on a trade. I could feel my heart racing with the pulse of the floor. I suppressed the fact that the other traders intimidated me. If I had been playing for myself, I would have left already. But as long as Raif was in New York, I had to stay in the city in case I needed to protect him. Ironically, to do that, I had to stay away from him, but that was the nature of the beast. It was up to me. I was the only one he had now that Saphora had dumped him. I promised myself that I would never leave Global American Bank until our luck changed. But Fortune, that slut, dropped me cold.

Like all beginning traders, I had expectations of winning, as if I were a mere character in a movie who must win in the end. This is the inescapable folly that marks a wet-behind-the-ears trader. Absurdly hoping for windfalls with one-in-a-million odds.

The big number came out, only 35,000 new jobs added, not enough: it was going to be a busy day. I'd read various books on building wealth, but what I had to learn now was the difference between the bank's trading floor and trading in the stock exchange pit. The rules seemed to be basically the same, but with all the electronic media replacing the open-outcry system, it was more difficult to follow the ebb and flow. I watched the male egos flare as they won and lost the game.

It was my biggest day on the job so far. There were a number of arms deals going through, and we knew this would filter down into other areas of the market, namely oil and insurance. You had to watch where the money went if you wanted to understand news. The more I understood, the more I hated myself for working at a bank supporting the military-industrial complex that runs our country — that which they don't teach you in business school. My mother had fought to stop the War. She protested against the ROTC on campus and against the university making so much money doing research to build weapons that were killing people in Vietnam.

The oil desk was hopping. The Arabs were agitated.

They hadn't gone out for a cigarette since eight o'clock. Sasha was standing next to the head oil trader, looking so much like him that you would have thought they were brothers, until the oil trader clapped one of his boys on the shoulder and broke into Arabic. Sasha's r's rolled from his ancient Aegean tongue.

The proprietary desk, where any kind of trading was allowed, took profit of $100,000 in calls on some weapons manufacturer. The call options were bets that the price of a 100-share block of arms stock would rise by July. Most wars are in July, if you look at the national holidays like 4th of July and Bastille Day on 14 *juillet*. That day, arms calls were bidding over puts — the market was wagering that the weapons manufacturer stocks would go up. Traders with reason to believe a particular company was about to benefit from a windfall of fortune were purchasing calls on weapons. Sasha peeled his eyes away from the screens. "Jerry, look at these arms calls going through!"

"Yeah. What does that mean?"

"Someone's betting arms sales will rise, especially at these two companies. See how these two companies are trading much more than the others? Look at the call volume numbers. People are buying the option to buy arms at today's prices. You know what that means?"

"Uh huh. You're gross." It was hard enough to get interested in mortgages, but arms! "And what's so interesting about oil?" They were wasting my time with this. I had to get some goals.

"Oil!" The head oil trader held out his arms. "That's what they're fighting over. The U.S. is an oil-based economy that shuffles imports around. Our service sector jobs have become poverty-level. Our empire is crumbling."

I hoped the fall of the American empire wouldn't affect my job as I rolled our positions and cleaned up residuals in all the markets we traded, watching the graphs of the arms companies out of the corner of my eye. Everyone was excited. "It does look like arms are going to the moon," I said.

"Yeah. You can do ten million dollars," Sasha said.

Just like a man. He was only there when you didn't need him. I wasn't about to buy arms. "What are those notches carved into your desk, Sasha?"

He stared straight ahead and didn't answer.

CHAPTER 26
BLIP

That must have been when I was sipping a margarita by the pool, looking at my iPhone and thinking that I was missing that arms deal. I had specifically given orders that Jerry was not to do anything until I got back from vacation.

CHAPTER 27
"YOU'RE FILLED!"

$\int$ asha said, "OK, are you with me, Jerry? I said you can buy up to ten million."

"OK, but not arms companies."

He acquiesced. I began to believe in Sasha again. I called the broker.

"Who's this?"

"Jerry."

"Jerry! How's it going?"

The promise of putting on a trade requited, I left an order to buy gold, and Sasha and I watched the graph. The arms stock sat there for five minutes.

"Why don't you move your order up?" Sasha said.

That would be wavering. I didn't say anything:

overruled.

Gold took off! "I missed it."

"Tell us how you really feel," Sasha said. "Get your aggressions out."

I did the calculation. "That's $10,362 I didn't make," I said.

"Congratulations. You have the emotions of an appliance." Sasha resumed his aristocratic slouch in his swivel chair. We sat there staring at the graph for the rest of the afternoon watching it bounce around -.35. "At least you guessed the right direction for the weapons company," he said.

One of Sasha's buddies entered the trading room and made his way across the floor toward us. He was a tall, dark, good-looking Jew.

"It's dead around here," which meant, let's talk. He went into Richard's office and put on a CD. "This is great music." An earthy, Spanish sound crept through me. I tried not to show its effect. I watched the screen and knew I appeared to be ignoring them. What else could I do? I was ready to open a bottle of tequila and start dancing on the desk.

"This is 'Barcelona Tribe'," he said.

"Tribe?" I said.

"Yes, like the Apaches or the Sioux." His teeth flashed.

I looked back at my screen moving as fast as a rollercoaster. I involuntarily reached for my seatbelt and remembered I was at work. The weapons manufacturers were at a new breakout level. I thought they were about to rally. No one was going to stop me now. The price bounced up. I called our broker. "Where is it?"

"32-4, you're filled! Paid 34 for a million."

The weapons blipped up. There were a solid three minutes of victory. Then, in a clip I lost $2,000. We watched weapons crash. I rode the graph downward, losing $4,000, $25,000. The market slid. My hands were shaking as I called the broker back, too late. "Sell them at the market! What did I get?"

"You're done, I'm just waiting for the price."

"WHERE'S THE MARKET?"

The gray area that I was counting on had turned to white, and I was the black speck in the middle of it, eye of the yin, precursor of yang.

The position was flat, and I had lost $78,000. Seventy-eight thousand. A year's salary. It was too ridiculously much money to really care about. I was in physical pain. I think I was counting my lucky stars that it wasn't 1.1 billion, like that French guy in the newspaper who was thrown in jail. I wasn't cut out for this. I just wanted to open my vegan restaurant. No more trading for the day.

The phone rang. "Jerry, pick up," Sasha said.

Ivan said, "Hi!"

"Hi. Are you out of the hospital?"

"Yeah. Look, Jerry, I think I made a mistake about us."

Another weapons manufacturer. I knew he would wake up one day, but now? I was so sure he couldn't change, I said, "I didn't make a mistake, though. Now I'm working on myself. I don't want to be set up as a sadist for the rest of my life."

Sasha stopped typing and cocked his head.

"OK, Jerry," Ivan said. "You sound shaky. What's wrong?"

126

"It's an occupational hazard. Make money, happy; lose money, sad."

"Oh well. You gotta get your feet wet. Listen, I'm not busy next weekend."

I'm damned.

"Jerry!" Sasha was yelling. He couldn't find the blotter with the losing trade. I'd forgotten to fill it out. "Where's your P & L?"

"I'll call you back," I said. I rummaged around for my profit and loss statement, and handed it to Sasha. "Sasha, have you ever lost as much as $78,000 in one day?"

Sasha contemplated the problem. "Once," he said.

Once. That's all you have to say? "What did they do?"

"They held me out the window by my ankles, what do you think? I'm still here, aren't I? I was surprised that Mort had it in him when he defended me to the President. He said, you know, 'It's part of playing the market. Some days you're good and some days you're not so good.' But then he said to me later, 'Just show me on which days you were that good!'"

So it *didn't* matter whether I lost or won.

"At least now you appreciate what you had. Don't freak out on me, Jerry. If you're not ready to lose seven pips on a few contracts, you should go gnaw some soggy bread." I was thinking about how to answer that, when he said, "You won't be out on the street," he said, "but you ought to buy your apartment just to keep up with the market. I wouldn't be afraid of a little studio. Debt is the road to riches. You know, there's really a fifty percent chance that it's going to happen. Either a thing will happen or it won't."

"Yeah, I'll leverage my student loan into a bigger loan." For my restaurant.

His eyes widened. "That's risky."

"Not as risky as trying to live on what Mort's paying me."

Sasha's eyebrows rose to his hairline. "Go get some fresh air. See you tomorrow. You'll try again Wednesday."

I made my way down the skyscraper. It took a long time to cross the lobby. I felt so damn *alone,* I didn't know how I would get through the night. I started surfing telephone numbers. No one I wanted to call. Outside the glass doors the smokers looked like fish blowing bubbles.

I went home, took off my Jager suit and sleeveless blouse, and fell asleep in my bed in the sun. I drifted into a sweet dream about having my own restaurant on Wall Street painted white. *Terrine d'artichauts* and veggie jambalaya was the only way back into society for me. I woke up feeling like I had to take better care of myself. I stretched out my cramped leg. I watered the plants, giving the window box in the bedroom some special encouragement. The flowers in there had perked up a lot since I moved in.

I soaked my raw veggies in the sink even though they were grown on a local organic farm. There were turnips, funny yellow carrots, sprouted grains and potatoes. I was going to eat them raw in a big salad of living enzymes. *The enzymes in raw food help with digestion. You have to eat raw. Cooking destroys enzymes and forces the body to use its own metabolic enzymes to digest food. That saps your energy and leaves you sluggish. Heating also kills the vitamins and minerals in food. Cooked food leads to excessive eating in the attempt to get enough nutrition.* Saphora knew everything.

I packed my gym bag with tennis shoes, headband, combination lock, shorts and Lycra top. NYU had a gym around here somewhere. I searched for myself as I looked for the gym. I found it, the gym that is, and got a good workout. Then I soaked in a bubble bath and shaved my legs. I moved the mirror around to shave everywhere else. Self-maintenance.

CHAPTER 28
LONNIE'S BOAT

I walked down the dock during the heat wave, glad to be invited to my high school friend's boat party. Manhattan isn't the best place for a woman to learn how to give without getting something back. On this island, love is a lack. People are unaware of each other, even in bed. Others are drafted into the business of satisfying you. They're just presences sharing a distraction, whether drink, drug, or routine. I was getting away from it all. I stepped off the island and onto Lonnie's boat.

"Jerry! Where y'at?" Lonnie stood in front of me showing off her natural assets. She went on in her homey Southern drawl. She was wearing a flowered skirt and an ankle bracelet with bells on it, an outfit that Pater was not going to approve of. Where was Pater? I didn't see him in the crowd. There was a barbecue. I looked around for edible veggies and spotted a terrine of hummus. Then I skimmed the group for eligible bachelors but didn't see any men at all. Not one token scrap of man at the goddamn party? Not another futile outing. I was the only other person from New Orleans. I reassembled the façade I'd learned to put on at Harvard.

The East River glistened in the twilight. Brooklyn warehouses straddled the horizon. There were women of all ages on Lonnie's boat. "You want men, visit a prison," a middle-aged woman was saying. They're full of men."

"There are women in jail, too," I said.

"What planet are you on? Less than six percent of inmates are women, and they're usually in for non-violent crimes. You gotta go with the odds."

"That sounds absolutely vacuous," a young woman said.

The wine went to work, and their voices mingled, ". . . Nah, it's like kissing and not getting involved."

"What's wrong with not getting involved?" another one said. "No one coming home late for dinner, no one there to deny you."

I came to a young woman's defense. "*I* can't," I said. "I start missing them. The next thing you know I'm moving in."

"Then just go kiss another one," Lonnie said.

"I've tried that, but then I spend all my time hunting for the next one to get me untangled from the last one and I'm just as preoccupied."

"Then date another one."

"Hmm." That word again. I could do like other 'free' consumers and just 'date', a ritual I'd never cared to perform, always moving in on my men before they could take out their wallets. But I loathed consumerism and any form of government manipulation. I would have to skip the economics of romance and go straight for the sex without the date. "At the age of twenty-nine, the odds of aren't looking too good," I said.

"Odds for what? Men die young because they live for themselves. I feel sorry for women who marry some dolt who steals her money, bores her with football, and is mean to her while she cleans the house. Stay single. You'll live longer," Lonnie said.

The dames thought thirty was a good age. I told them that twenty-nine was hard enough. "I'll be so happy to turn thirty. I was looking hard for a man to have a family with. When I cross over to the new decade, I figure, that's it. I'll be safe. I'll say, I tried, now I give up. Now I'm free. Not only that, I've reached my sexual peak. Maybe I'll be able to just go out and have fun. But the reality is that if I sleep with a man, I get involved and want to have a baby."

"Oh no!" one woman said. "Better drown your sorrows." She passed me a bottle of Jack Daniels.

"Really?" Lonnie said. "I already had a baby, so I can afford to think that impersonal sex would be fun. I don't really remember it because I've been monogamous for five years, but the idea of having purely physical sex, mmm..." She patted the hamburgers with the spatula.

Impersonal sex. Hmph. It was cheaper than shopping for clothes. Why were women always so busy trying to find love? We could all learn from Saphora, always sticking to her ideals even if it means passing up the real world. What about everybody else you didn't love? Regina didn't want to have a baby. She wanted to be a heartbreaker. That was her dream, and here I was living it. Something clicked. I knew that the next time would be with someone I didn't love. Isn't that what men did? Hunt women? No man was going to hunt me down. I could hunt as good as any man. I was turning thirty and was gonna beat them at their own game. Hell, the soil is more fertile for women on the prowl. It was a cinch to bed down a man. Men were thinking about it all the time.

There was something unsettling about sitting around talking with a bunch of women. Not that having men around would mean protection. More women were murdered by male lovers and family members than by anyone else. I had learned not to trust any man to protect me, especially from himself. I pushed thoughts of my mother's murder down to the bottom of my personality.

Still there was this unease that set in, talking with only women. It was like being away from solid ground. The boat rocked on the water. The lack of stability came out in their talk. The conversation skipped over art and politics and went straight to superstition. The conversation would have been different if the men were there. I think I was the only one put off by the lack of men. The rest of them were happy there. At last they'd had a full three hours to talk about what was really on their minds: relationships and shopping.

The women were not alone in their worries, but they were not transported either. They delved into it, and the questions remained unanswered, buried under layers of analysis: You do it this way, but that hasn't worked for me. For you it's divorce. For me it's re-marriage. I had to live alone. Valentine was celibate ever since she turned thirty. "Valentine says that going without sex gets easier and easier as time goes on." Valentine turned red. She hadn't had sex in nine months.

"Nine months!" I couldn't go a month without it. "How long until I stop caring about men?" I said. How long until *I* was happy? When I turned thirty, my clock would stop ticking, and then I wouldn't have to move any more.

Maybe they were lying. Maybe they weren't really happy either. To me, male presence was a party prerequisite. Sex wounded me. When it was time to move on down the road, there I was staring over the edge at my familial abyss. I had lost the important connections in my life, and everything hurt me more than it should. I had to heal myself. I didn't think sex wounded men in the same way. Men had weapons. All we had was our anger and their guilt. As long as they avoided closeness, they were immune.

"Women enjoy sex more than men," one woman said.

"Yes, men don't really give themselves as completely."

"To men, it's food. To women it's love."

"At the end of the day, I'd rather be an angry woman than a numb man."

So many voices.

"They're inferior," someone else said.

"It's not *their* fault that women open themselves up completely."

"Does that make impersonal sex a war on women?"

"Yes."

"No."

"And why *not* be what they dream of?" The voice was mine. Men were all after the same thing. A stranger to have sex with. If my strangeness was all they could appreciate, that's what they would get. Walking away the next minute and never looking back. Hell, women could do anything men could do. It was time to stop feeling used. *I* could use.

This seemed like a better strategy than Prozac. Firstly, my eyes wouldn't bulge. I got to keep my job and the respect of those around me. Secondly, drugs weren't healthy. And third, maybe sex would help me get in touch with myself.

"You have to be very strict about ending it then and there," Lonnie said, "not waiting for their calls. Not even letting them know where you live."

CHAPTER 29
LEARNING TO HUNT

Regina was coming for my thirtieth birthday. She would be a good influence. The Indian queen must be in D.C. by now. Next was New York City. She was driving cross-country with two guys. On the phone she sounded like she was having a lunar eclipse.

"It's crazy," Regina said on the phone, and we both laughed. Regina said, "Ha, ha, ha." Regina, vagina, Regina, revenge: "That's what it's all about, honey. You dog him, he dogs you. That's what makes the world go 'round."

I laughed and thought about Ivan saying he regretted breaking up with me. He still called to see what I was doing. Every yin had a yang. There must be more upside to my godforsaken emptiness. I was sitting in a corner at a vegan food crawl. We were on our last place, an Ethiopian restaurant.

I felt a tinge of guilt when the waiter gave me a free glass of honey wine and said he was off in half an hour. There was no point in rushing home for Ivan's phone call. The waiter was sure of himself. He knew I was gonna do it before I did. I followed his dreadlocks around the room. If I had to learn to hunt, now seemed like a pretty good time.

He came back and whispered, "This place'll be empty soon. You can help me close up." I stayed in my seat and waved goodbye to the last vegans as they put on their coats and left the restaurant. My head spun. My eyes followed my prey around the room as he locked up.

The waiter guided me to a booth and put his hands on my hips. He pulled my skirt up around my waist. The smell of spice was engrained in the lines on his face and in the wooden tabletop.

He followed me down the street trying to get my number. "Beat it," I said, feeling my power. A cab pulled up, and I jumped in and slammed the door. No one would follow me. I stared at him, lost on the pavement. As we cruised up Eighth Avenue, I felt that there was something I'd forgotten. Not the guy, but some part of me that I had almost accessed. I would have to explore deeper. There was a strong urge to do it again with someone new. At least I never went after them online. I knew I'd only find losers there. The magic was in the hunt.

I had begun my research into this savage realm. Walking across Vanderbilt Avenue on my way home from work, I went into Grand Central Station. My skirt was short. I wasn't wearing any panties.

Be careful having sex with strangers, Jerry. Saphora tried to warn me.

I sat on a bench in the main concourse and looked up at the great astronomical mural painted in gold leaf on sky blue. My eyes wandered over the 80,000 square-foot expanse of Mediterranean heavens with winter zodiac constellations and thousands of stars sprinkled across the celestial sphere.

All kinds of men paraded through the beam of light streaming down from the ceiling windows into the station. Men in jeans, men in suits, men with long legs, men with big butts, one who was bald, one with tattoos on his arms, all equipped with the essential. This became my hunting ground.

One day I was getting off the train at Grand Central. I stopped suddenly to avoid trampling a child. A man with a suitcase bumped into me from behind. I turned around and held his stare. I liked his goatee. Outside on the corner I asked, "Are you going across town?" We shared a cab to his hotel. He put his hand on my thigh.

"Want anything from room service?" he asked.

Like I had time for room service. I'd given up on having a baby that might turn into a deranged murderer so why not get right down to business? "Why thank you," I said, "Here's your tip," and pulled my shirt over my head.

He was exceptional in bed. "Where did you learn that?" I asked. I traced the scar under his left eye.

"It goes with the territory."

"What territory?"

He flashed a police badge. I jumped, suppressing the urge to cover my breasts. "Are you on duty now?"

"Yes."

I told you! Be careful! This one is following you. I composed myself. "We should have done it with one of those hats."

"I never wear one of those hats. I'm a plainclothes cop."

"A cop. Huh. Why me?"

"I'm interested in you," he said.

His questions scared me. I didn't answer. I massaged his crotch with enough fury to rub out the past. We did it again. I left while he was sleeping. Following all the procedures for a clean break, I still felt that I hadn't seen the last of him. After that, I was always looking for that cop at bars or outside my apartment, among the half-naked on the No Pants Subway Ride, and again on the way to the Guilty Pleasure Party at the Museum of Sex.

CHAPTER 30

SCIENTIFIC OBJECTIVITY

*T*hroughout my experiments with men, the only one I kept in touch with was Ivan because he really was sick. A hundred men later, I still kept answering Ivan's phone calls and playing his little games. He wanted less and less: to talk about other women, mostly to get me to talk about other men. One night he called and tried to make me jealous with an old girlfriend from high school.

"So, how was it?" I said.

"It was great. We just kept going all night long and then into the morning. It was fantastic."

I was in shock, but as he went on, I realized he was pulling my leg. "Did you sleep with her or not?"

"No."

"Why not? It was Maria from high school."

"I was interested in her in high school, but I'm not anymore." Maria was supposedly beautiful. Could she be as beautiful as me? "Maria's not dumb, but not smart, and she's a single mother," Ivan said.

"Did you know that?"

"I found out after we'd arranged to meet. It was a courtesy date."

Bastard. I half wished he'd gotten involved with her so that I could remember him tied down with someone else's children. On the way to work the next morning, I was elated. He didn't sleep with Maria! I smiled to myself. The people who passed me on the street looked at me smiling: something good had happened to somebody in New York.

Every once in a while, Sasha would bring me another wheelbarrow of mortgages to sign. "An unpleasant job is its own reward."

Like I didn't read the news about robo-signing. Foreclosures all over America were being suspended over robo-signing. "Our bank is behind the times," I said and made Sasha promise again to increase my trading line before I plowed through them.

When would they take me seriously? I was careful not to mix business with pleasure and kept my sexual experiments outside of the bank, always cutting them short before they got sticky. One Monday morning, the whole floor seemed to be waiting with bated breath as Sasha asked, "Did you have fun at your party, Jerry?"

Which party? I decided to offer info on the most innocuous party of the recent past. "It was OK until the guy I liked started talking about having anxiety attacks. If I could only find one sane man in this town. Your advice came in handy, though."

"Which advice?"

"To be careful," I said.

"Why? What happened?"

"Nothing. Just when they were dropping me off, this one guy insisted on walking me to my doorstep."

"Wait a minute, didn't you say there would be three guys there who liked you?"

"Two."

"Was he one of the two?"

"No," I laughed. "He caught me off guard."

"Jerry is so sure of herself it's pathetic," Sasha said. "Dick!" he called, "A guy from the party walked Jerry home. Tell Jerry guys don't do that unless you give them some reason to think you are interested in them."

"That's right." Richard gave me one of his impact-assessment looks. "What did you do to this guy?"

"Nothing. I just said, 'I'm leaving. Bye.'"

"Oh, yeah. Bye, guys!" Sasha hugged the door up and down and said, "I'm leaving now!" He batted his eyelashes.

"That's right," Richard said. "That's an invitation."

"What invitation?"

"Come on," Sasha said. "He could have raped you, right, Dick?"

"Look," Richard said. "If I'm at Junior League Baseball with my son, and I see one of the mothers who likes me coming at me after the game, and if I like her, too, this is how I get up." Richard stood up, stretched, postured, brushed his hair back, grabbed his crotch and lifted his leg like he was about to pitch. Sasha got into the dance also grabbing his crotch, caressing his breast, and marching around the room like an ostrich.

They bumped into each other, to their mutual alarm.

The conversation careened into the danger zone. "You homophobes need to relax," I said. "I didn't do that. I just said, 'Bye.'" My number-one rule for safe sex was *Not at Work*. How many times had I seen them tear women apart on the trading floor?

First some guy in Sales would come on like Prince Charming promising the moon on a string. As soon as she gave in, he would broadcast the details to the rest of the boys, who would smear her reputation and humiliate her so bad that she wouldn't be able to hold her own on the floor. Eventually she would get fired. That was a Miss Calculation I wasn't going to make.

"Look, Jerry," Richard said. "This is how I do it when I don't like the mother who is coming at me." He was shifting from foot to foot with his back to the door. He looked from right to left, taking in the room, slowly moving backward. He seemed to fade into the back wall. At the door, he feinted left, and was gone.

"Watch out, Dick, she's got her spam filter on."

"I know what I'm talking about," Richard said. "That's what you didn't do. You forgot to fade."

"Yeah," Sasha said. "I can't believe you let this guy walk you home. I'm going to unfollow you, Jerry."

"Just from the café to my house. We both live in the Village. When we got to Jane Street, I said, 'I'm turning here, bye,' for the second time. Then he said he had to go to the bathroom, and could he come up to my apartment?"

Sasha stiffened.

I had to laugh watching Sasha get anxious over a guy walking me home. I'd almost forgotten about it. If he knew what I was really up to, he'd be all over me! I looked at Sasha out of the corner of my eye. He had a lot of nerve delving into *my* checkered past, standing there like a crossword puzzle. "I said, 'No,' of course."

Sasha leaned back in his chair and exhaled. "Oh," he laughed. "You didn't let him go to the bathroom!" Then he leaned forward again. "You didn't let him go to the bathroom. Poor guy has been at the party all night drinking beers, and you wouldn't invite him in after he walks you home to go to the bathroom!"

There was no winning with Sasha. He was irrational. "And if I had, he could have raped me."

"You shouldn't have announced that you were leaving in the first place," Sasha said. "Jerry, you are hopeless."

"You know," Richard said, "I feel sorry for the guy that tries to court you, Jerry."

"Why?"

"Because you're intimidating."

"That's it!" Sasha said. "You hit the nail on the head. She's intimidating."

"You should feel sorry for *me*. At least the guy can go off and court other women. I'm stuck with myself." I pulled a yen candlestick chart up on my screen. They resumed working. I got up and walked toward the exit.

"Jerry!" Sasha said. "Wait a minute. Before you go to the bathroom —"

144

"Did I say that I was going to the bathroom?"

"It's your body language," he said.

I shifted from left to right like Richard had done, avoided eye contact, turned my back to the exit and shifted some more. I took in the room, looking from Bond Sales to Money Markets, slowly moving backward. At the door, I feinted left into a backward quarter turn and tipped out the door — execution!

CHAPTER 31

BUBBLE ECONOMY

*O*nce I put on a trade, I was wrenched from all matters of the heart. Richard and Sasha melted away. I was riding on that graph, skiing down moguls, shimmying to the top again. Superstition had usurped rational thought. I began to distil a rhythm to the trading day that required adherence to routine in order to stay in the groove.

All markets were volatile early in the morning because Europe would still be open, but at coffee time, when the Old World went home for the day, things would settle down. So I got into the habit of buying volatility first thing in the morning, and selling it right before the European close. This was good for a few bucks, but was not going to earn me any promotions.

The first inkling I'd had of the magnitude of the economic crisis was that rogue trader in France who had lost £7 billion. From then on there were regular black holes in the news with $11 billion sucked under here and $19 billion imploding there. Where did all the money go? Money wasn't lost. It went somewhere. Someone had made a *killing* off the economic crisis. Who?

The desk lit up. News was coming out that Superior Bank was filing for Chapter 11 bankruptcy protection. There was an eerie silence on the desk that reminded me of when Lehman went under, back when no one could believe that the U.S. government would let a bank fail. Now we knew better. Almost a hundred banks had already failed in 2011. The exodus of Superior Bank clients, free fall in its stock, and devaluation of its assets by credit rating agencies made us fear for our jobs. No one except Mort could really fathom the massive debt underlying the world economy that was unwinding, nor the extent of the financial panic that ensued.

I watched the price of the 30-year treasury bond tick up, -59, -60, -59, and hover around the figure. There was an undeniable stickiness around the zeros, but once it burst through, it just kept on going. But when I took a pot shot at buying just before it broke through the figure again, the pattern broke down and didn't work anymore, as if everyone had seen it building up and had tried the same trade idea at the same time, only to get nailed either by 'the market', or some bigger player who was manipulating the market. Hot with anger, I picked up the phone and doubled my position, approaching my limit for the day.

I didn't hear Mort's footsteps behind me. He was

nervous with shareholders breathing down his neck. Mort could probably tell that I was losing by the urgency in my voice. "Tell me how much you're down before it snowballs."

Startled, I turned around and looked into his open mouth. I was assailed by a smell so foul I thought I saw his teeth duck out of the way. "The rules have changed, Jerry. Why don't you go for a walk and cool down while I close out your trade for you."

I was relieved that it was not my money I had lost but knew he wasn't.

As the crisis worsened, you could see the big money dumping positions just when the newscasters were talking the markets up. The TV pushed prices up to a level acceptable for the big money to sell at and then the market would nosedive. It was a new game. I figured if the media made me feel like doing a trade based on the patterns it was showing, I would have to bite the bullet and do the opposite. I put on a trade and held my breath. The strategy worked. I took profit and did it again. And again. "Ha! Take that, Mortimer. There's something to appreciate, if only you weren't already dead!"

Everyone turned away from me as if on cue.

I smelled his bad breath before I notice Mort had been standing behind me again, ready to shut down my positions. The chill of his ectoplasm ran down my spine.

Sasha quickly announced that I had made thirty thousand, then one hundred and thirty, then three hundred and eighty thousand dollars.

Richard gave me a win-win nod.

Mort wafted away, a grimace etched on his face.

Nothing could touch my optimism.

"How'jy do it?" an Irishman said. People had started to come over from other trading desks.

"I just put on this options trade."

"Pretty good for a novice," Sasha said.

"Come on. How'jy do it? Weer a team, aren't we?" said the leprechaun.

"I watched what the news was talking up and did the opposite."

"Ya did, dijya? You was coattailin' the devil, were ya?"

"I was."

Mort wafted out of the room.

'Coattailing the devil' spread like bushfire. The corniest thing about that contrarian strategy was it worked. We were on a run. We listened for clues from hokey newscasters and went the other way, betting on what the top 0.1% was going to dump next. My colleagues could trade huge amounts and made spectacular profits. The proprietary desk forgot where the idea came from. Like the top 0.1%, we had the best month in a long time. It wasn't 'til one of our clients hit their credit limit that the contrarian system went tits up. Sasha was holding his head in his hands. "Great idea, Jerry." As good as it felt making all that money, the pain of losing some of it was far worse. It was enough to shorten your life.

The phone was ringing, and after ten rings, I finally had to go pick it up myself. It was Mort. I signaled to Sasha to quiet the desk down. The CFO wanted to see me and Richard. Sasha stared at us as we walked out of the glass doors. I had butterflies in my stomach. We approached Mort's stale office.

"Come in," Mort wheezed. "Dick, this is about Righteous Mortgage hitting its credit limit." Mort winced in pain and clasped his hands together like he was praying. He tucked his belly under the mahogany. Mort had back problems due to the keg he had on tap twenty-four hours. He unscrambled his fingers and signaled to me to sit down.

The seat of the chair sighed under my butt. Its antique rim was uncomfortable. "What this office needs is a couch," I said.

Richard suppressed a laugh, no doubt imagining the yellow couch gracing Mort's empty wall. Mort coughed up a wad of phlegm and spat it into his handkerchief.

I shifted on the chair, and thought about how to placate Mort. I didn't know how to put it, since I was the last one to handle the late Righteous Mortgage. I had just been executing orders and didn't know any details about the company.

Mort turned his eyes on Richard with an unbearable intensity. "I'm unhappy with the valuation your team gave the Righteous Mortgage bundle."

Richard covered with genuine bottom-up defiance. "The Righteous Mortgage securities were sold pursuant to prospectuses and prospectus supplements that formed part of registration statements, which contained underlying mortgage loans that complied with particular underwriting guidelines and restrictions, including representations that significantly overstated the capability of the homeowners to repay their mortgage loans."

Financialese was one of the few things Mort liked. He

turned away from Richard and directed his angry stare at me. "You're the one who priced it so low, Jerry. Did you have to tell the market that?" He watched me squirm.

I couldn't even remember pricing it. Hadn't I only executed the trade? The wooden rim of the seat dug into my thighs.

Mort yelled, "We had a vested interest in Righteous Mortgage. To give you a little background, Righteous Mortgage is our neighbor, just thirty-two floors below us.

I heard chanting outside the window. I stood up for a second to get a look at the crowd of demonstrators down below and immediately grokked the situation. Some students in headbands carrying signs. A lack of leadership didn't stop activism. Revolt was in the air.

"Sit down!" Mort yelled.

But I didn't sit down. I kept standing there. It was only a matter of time. It was September 2011. I knew this trading game would only screw me for so long before it screwed itself.

"It was hard enough to unload what we did at the prices we got," Richard was saying. "The market already figured out that those mortgages were puking."

"That's enough," Mort hissed. His lips were gray.

The two men turned and looked at me as if I had betrayed them. I had only been trying to help. Now I remembered. I had executed *Richard's* trade. I realized that I was the one getting nailed for the entire bundle. Arguing wouldn't help. I sat forward in my chair and said, "They had an order at—"

"Enough!" Mort said.

I didn't say a word.

Mort didn't look up again.

Richard nodded, so I got up and padded across the carpet to the door.

CHAPTER 32
LAMB TO THE SLAUGHTER

V erry's eyes filled with tears as she wobbled around Mort's office like a lamb to the slaughter. The kids outside were making a lot of noise chanting about Wall Street. Protesting against a street seemed futile, but it took me back to my college dilemma when I wasn't sure which way to go with my letter jacket and long hair. What creature on earth could be more deliciously out of my control than this New York career woman? She tipped out of the office on those stilettos, packing the most desirable, hauntingly deranging set of equipment in human experience. It hurt to sit back down.

I had to do it, though. I was up for a promotion myself. Getting nailed with the Righteous Mortgage blowout would have been inconvenient. I tried to put the best spin on it I could. "Sorry, boss," I said. "She's got a lot of potential as a trader, but I didn't agree with her valuation, even if we had to hold most of it on our books. I was only going to let her get her feet wet. Neither of us expected the damn thing to blow up."

"I know, Dick, but it's not up to us. If that's how the customer wants to weather the storm, that's his prerogative."

I always make it a point not to argue with Mort because he is the CFO. "You are absolutely right, Mort." Then I held my tongue, trying to figure out how to merely raise the question of his wife's holdings in Righteous Mortgage stock.

Mort picked up his cell phone and called his wife. "Honey, you have your broker's number in your speed dial, right? Listen, call him up and dump Righteous Mortgage. That's right, you heard me. The whole 1.5 million dollars worth of Righteous Mortgage stock. Got it? Good. Then turn around and sell oil. Write it down. Sell ten oil futures."

Judging by the way he was looking at me, my jaw must have been resting on my chest. I shut my mouth. Our CFO had served on boards of oil companies down in Houston. He was fond of reminding me that he served on the board of Butcher-Mitchell when Butcher bought out Mitchell Oil from bankruptcy. He'd been around the block and even got mixed up in politics. They offered him an ambassadorship to Saudi Arabia.

The CFO was here today because his wife didn't want to go to the Middle East. She apparently didn't mind owning it from a distance, though. I could see Righteous Mortgage stock tanking. Heavy trading losses stacked on top of an already poor earnings statement had toppled the slippery house of cards. But why did Mort want to sell oil at these levels? Oil prices were already low. Why should they keep on plummeting? Did he know something that the rest of us didn't? I couldn't answer any of these questions, but if he was *that* sure, I guessed *my* wife should be selling *my* oil position.

CHAPTER 33
DIAL 'M' FOR MORTGAGES

*H*opes dashed, I thought Mort and Richard might fire me, but they gave me a bigger trading line. I made some of it back, so now I hadn't lost quite a year's salary.

Days went by like hours in New York. I shuffled from subway to sky-rise. The noise of the protesters outside the building steadily increased. I blocked it out and let the view of the Hudson heal me. There was talk of an ease in interest rates. The room buzzed, biding up bonds. Poor suckers, about to be weeded out of the gene pool.

"Sasha, why are bonds so high?" I asked.

He was already staring at me. "I like the way you think in prices."

Our analysis service sent us emails urging us *ad*

nauseam to sell mortgages on this bond rally. Sasha and I were arguing over it in our corner of the proprietary desk. I was saying, "If the market moves five pips and you bought $100,000,000 worth of mortgage-backed securities, you're going to make more money than in bonds."

"That's right, baby. Now tell me your dreams." He led me over to the yellow couch. "Dreams are the vocabulary of the unconscious."

I took refuge in Sasha's understanding and fell into a deep transference. "I'm out shopping," for men. "My credit card is maxed out, but there's a sale at the club."

"The club?" he said. "You have to understand dreams as if they actually happened to you."

"And what about your dreams, sugar?" I asked.

"I don't get any sleep, *malaka*. My girlfriend moved back in with me because she didn't have an air conditioner," he said.

"Buy her an air conditioner," I said, testing him to see how far he'd go.

"That's what she said."

I turned around and looked at him. He looked pathetic. He was still wearing his suit with the hole in the pocket. "Of course it's not your responsibility to buy her an air conditioner. Are you back together then?"

"No! I'm looking for a woman who is my equal."

"Pft. It's gonna be hard to find a woman who's your equal."

Sasha didn't come back with anything, and I realized he really was in a sorry state. I could tell he'd taken his Prozac. He was perky and his eyes were a little wider than usual. I was glad I'd never tried it. I wouldn't want to go around goofy like that. You could tell that it was artificial, and it didn't last very long. When it was over, he was always pretty cranky. So much for getting angry at him. It felt suddenly cozy on the desk with him like this. I yawned. I'd have to humiliate him some other time.

Mortgage-backed securities went up, as did my profits. I cleared a half a million for the month. I could do no wrong, and had my feet up on the desk, despite the miniskirt.

"Do you see what I see?" Richard asked Sasha. My skirt was unbuttoned on the side, too — it had become too tight after lunch. I was feeling pretty sexy.

"Yep."

"There's a lot going on behind the scenes, Jerry," our broker was explaining over the phone. "Stop looking at that graph."

"It's a pretty intriguing graph," I said.

"Come on, Jerry."

"It shows the spike in the income of the top .001% richest people worldwide just after Lehman went bust."

"Ooo! Where can I find that?"

"Nowhere, newbie. Journalists lose their jobs publishing stories like this. I'll email it to you."

"Great. Now go into Bloomberg and press S-T-A-R."

I pulled S-T-A-R up on my screen and read my horoscope. *During this past weekend you've had to sort through many different levels of communication and consciousness — not a small task . . . . With this coming weekend, it's back to the task of transmitting cryptic messages from another world.* "Wow," I said. I hung up. What other world?

Maybe my brother was trying to get in touch with me. Maybe it meant messages from hell. I chuckled, unaware that I was about to descend into one of the lowest places in Manhattan.

CHAPTER 34

MISGUIDED GLOBALIZATION

I had my wife selling my oil position on the way to work. I pushed my way through the demonstrators and made it into the building. By the time I got into the elevator, I was short $1,250,000 in futures. I checked my FX Alert and saw that we were up over $5,000. I stepped out of the elevator in my buffed Milanos. I padded through the tunnel of mirrors, past the Statue of Liberty watching over Hudson Bay, and off to my screens.

The number of financial agreements which derived their value from mortgage payments and housing prices had mushroomed with the housing boom when the U.S. welcomed the rest of the world's money into its homes. Rampant financial innovation enabled foreign institutions to invest in our housing market. But now that housing prices were down, the fancy products and vehicles lost their shine. Banks around the world that had borrowed to invest heavily in United States subprime mortgage-backed securities got hit with significant losses.

The floor was livid. I saw the writing on the wall. My traders were deluding themselves with their 'no problem' attitudes. They were so sequestered they still bought American as if the story had to have a happy ending. "Let the dollar get stronger. America's a net importer!" Sasha said.

I made a mental note to cut his trading line. "Who says we don't export?" I said. "The USA has become the biggest exporter of bad debt in the world." It was the hippie in me talking. "Anyone with half a brain can see which way this misguided globalization is going." Even the news had stopped calling it the 'credit crisis'. The 'economic crisis' was here. I was eager to hear Mort's take on this situation. "Sasha, cover for me. I have an important meeting with the CFO."

Mort hijacked the rest of my afternoon. In the car on the way to the golf course, I looked at my watch and broke into a sweat. I was going to be late getting home for the fifth night in a row. "And this couldn't be handled in tomorrow's board meeting?"

Mort explained that this was actually the pre-meeting. "The last place you wanna discuss issues is at the board meeting. Board meetings have minutes. Minutes get written down." Tomorrow's board meeting would be nothing more than a kabuki ritual. Management would present the financials to the audit committee for the full

161

board to approve, thereby creating an audit trail and making both directors and auditors formally liable. The introduction of new information was strictly taboo. No real decision was ever made at a board meeting. No, no, it was all arranged in advance in a quiet negotiation on the golf course. Mort would have the consultants design the fancy accounting to ensure that the audit committee wouldn't balk.

We pulled into the Forest Hill Field Club. I took off my watch, changed into my golf shoes and followed the cart. The white balls skidded down the green, and the other two members of the board ambled after them. Hacking away at a sand dune, I was thinking about our six-pack in the golf cart. Mort stepped onto the green, looking like just another golfer. There was nothing fancy about his pale green jacket. No one would have guessed from his worn golf shoes how many millions this guy was worth or what kinds of diabolical scheme he was hatching. He shepherded his prey onto the green. We ambled up to the first hole. Mort signaled for us to go first, as if he had no stake in the game or anything else. He just leaned on his club and blended into the shaven grass. Being invisible in plain sight was a consummate Mort skill.

CHAPTER 35

A ZILLION FLAKES

*i*f I had to live Regina's dream, I would at least do it on my terms: scientifically. I continued my experiments during partner exchange parties in hotel rooms, after Get Your Dance On Laughing Lotus Yoga, in a stall at the vegetarian food festival, in parks and public places giving myself up to any man who was ready. And sometimes women. It was as easy as breathing, until the weather got cold and the bulldozers piled up the snow along the streets of the West Village. I would have to move my laboratory inside.

Sasha was going to a party one night. I wished I could go. I was invited to a nudist party at a club and fantasized that it would be the same party, and he'd be there . . . but he was not there, or anywhere the forces of history might stop and let me off.

Women got in free. I was in the first room where people still had their clothes on trying to make intelligent conversation with two goons who started laughing, they were such lowlifes. It was weird for me to be talking to insects on the verge of being nude, but these maggots were incoherent.

Adding myself to the 1.3 million species already described by zoologists, I stood up and stretched my arms in back of me. The two men stood up as well. "You can't be leaving already!" one said. "Can I get your telephone number?" the other one asked.

"I don't give it out, but I'm free now," I said, looking down at them. *If this doesn't stop my clock, nothing will.*

The only thing they could figure out to do was drink. With two guys watering me, I had a lot to do. I felt my adrenalin rise, and I went for those dopes anyway. I said I was in from New Jersey and my name was Saphora just to play with them a little bit. Pretty soon I had them on the dance floor. I must have been pretty desperate to want to touch either of them, but damn could those bozos dance.

Number three hundred and ninety-nine looked like an insect. He put his tactile organs around me and led me into the next room past a ficus tree to a red velvet sofa obviously designed for my branch of arthropodology. I peeled back their shells and set to work classifying compound eyes and stingers.

"I'll hold her."

The last thing I remember is making a few entomological notes on number four hundred's segments.

He came at me with a menacing look on his face.

I stumbled backward. My big hand grasped a tiny plant leaf that was wafting by. His digits gripped my thorax as three hundred and ninety-nine took my hind.

CHAPTER 36

BAD DEBT FOR EXPORT

*T*he desk was in the red over $400,000 when I walked in from my vacation in pain from a sunburn and unable to eat my bagel. I was full of hopeful trade ideas.

Jerry was too hung over to hear about them. "Hope and trading don't mix," she said.

I looked at the profit and loss screen. It was mostly red. "What's bleeding?" I asked.

Jerry checked the trades. "The oil calls."

"The oil calls? You should have *sold* oil!" The lounge was a mess and smelled like cigarette smoke. There were scuff-marks on my yellow couch and many more trades on the blotter than I wanted to see. My staff, new and old, was utterly undisciplined. "I told you not to churn the account while I was gone!" I roared.

Jerry hung her head over her extra-large Alka-Seltzer. She had a bruise on her forearm that disappeared under her shirtsleeve and a darker one on her neck. Something had hit her hard. I figured we'd all been there and just let her feel it, what with Sasha already laying it on her: "What happened, Jerry? Didn't you get laid?"

"Maggot."

"From a woman!" Sasha doubled over and clapped his hands.

"I might have gone a little too far," she said. Her voice was scratchy.

Sasha paced the aisle. "Finally! A woman who admits it."

That kind of lack of respect for dames from a trust-fund brat gets on my nerves. Plus, it's contagious on a trading floor. Before it got out of hand, I said to everyone, "I'll bet you all the money in the doughnut store that you boys don't know ONE of the numbers that came out on Friday morning! There were five numbers out at 8:30. Maybe I should ask the head of proprietary trading. Sasha? A man should be greater than some of his parts."

The boys flinched. Sasha sat back down.

No one looked up from the screens. Finally Jerry muttered, "Retail sales were up point seven percent."

I stared down my nose at her and then ridiculed the rest of my team for the next four hours.

Sasha was on the phone with his ex-girlfriend. His salad was on the desk between him and Jerry. "No, baby," he was saying, "You'll be fine there. Every day will be a little better."

As Jerry clicked through her screens, her hand moved the mouse too far to the right and — *splat!* — the salad landed on the floor.

She kept on looking at her screens.

"*Malaka!* Look what you did to my salad! I have vinaigrette on my pants!"

Jerry looked straight ahead at her screen.

Sasha picked up the receiver. "I gotta go." He hung up the phone and sat back down. "Jerry! That was the most beautiful thing you ever did."

She glanced at him.

I couldn't take Jerry ignoring us anymore and tried to cheer her up. "It's not as bad as you think, Jerry," I told her. "The only difference between a stumbling block and a stepping stone is when you see it."

She glanced at me.

What was with her? She had a mysterious life that wasn't coming out in her diary, as if it was a secret even from herself. Where the hell was Saphora? Saphora could have made those bruises on Jerry's neck while I was busy in Vegas.

Sasha was picking up pieces of lettuce.

"Gimme your profit and loss sheet. These are good trades," I told her. "I like what you're doing here. It's inspiring me to trade, too. It feels good to get back into it. Me and Sasha just sat around for the last few years. You gotta look out for him. He's a sadomasochist. He'll hurt you just to get you to be mean to him. I'm tellin' ya: stepping stone all the way."

She didn't look away from the screen, but I saw her eyes widen.

Mort's shadow passed over my screen and I got busy with his oil sale, which had enhanced his massive wealth. I began to turn over ideas for election speeches that would grab him. He'd sold the shares off just in time. By lunchtime, he was reaping a profit of $50,000. I was convinced we were headed for the political stage.

Jerry had everything, even though she probably couldn't appreciate it right now with that red wine caked on her lower lip. I tried to tell her that it was a glorious morning for her and her men working with us here at her steady job on top of the world.

The next morning when Sasha arrived, he was very happy to see Jerry.

"Hi, Jerry." He was grinning. "It's freezing in here."

We had an air-conditioning problem. The fat boys sat next to the controls.

"Did you have a nice evening?" Sasha asked.

"Ugh," she groaned. "Did you?"

"Yes," Sasha exaggerated. "I went to a party."

"Big deal," she said.

"Good girl. Have another aspirin," Sasha said.

She sobered up a few days later and I stopped worrying about her. I watched her plunge boldly into the icy waters of derivatives, investments on investments, and swim on her own. "Look at those yield spreads," I said.

"Somebody's *really* getting screwed," Jerry said. "Who was the biggest sucker for mortgage bundles?"

"In the last five years Fannie and Freddie say they've sold about a trillion dollars worth to foreign investors. Mostly central banks." She had a knack for independent thinking. I put my hand on her shoulder. "That's gotta be just a fraction of it, though," I said. "The big bundles were in China, Japan and Western Europe."

"So we exported most of the bad debt? Debt is something that doesn't travel well. We're blowing up whole countries in Europe. What this city needs is a damn vegan restaurant on the ground where people live."

"Are you a vegetarian?"

She didn't answer.

"Come on, Jerry, what else could we do after giving home owners credit cards to take all the money out of their houses? Hopefully we're exporting enough of these puking mortgages," I said. "Remember when the British government nationalized Northern Rock Bank after its problems with SIVs."

Her eyes narrowed. "So much for moral hazard in Great Britain."

"Moral hazard! It's not just Great Britain. Look what we're doing here and now in the bastion of capitalism. The Fed is lending money at zero percent and borrowing it back at three percent. How many times would you do that trade?"

"I don't know if I would. Are *we* doing it?"

"Are we doing it! What a loner you are, Jerry. Believe me, we're not the only ones doing it. We got good company, about seven trillion dollars worth of good company. We don't produce or grow anything. We just help wealthy families perpetuate their inheritance. And corporations, because corporations are legally 'persons', too."

"How can corporations be people?" she asked.

"Not people, persons. You never heard of 'corporate

personhood'? Corporations have rights like you and me. OK, they can't go to jail, but they have all the same rights we do." I educated her about our wealthy clients and showed her how we alchemized derivatives. She was just what we needed in our club. By autumn, Mort's scapegoat was running the prop desk.

"Your profits are higher than Sasha's," I said one Monday morning after missing her all weekend.

"I know. He was put down on earth to act as a warning for the rest of us."

I looked around to see if Sasha was within earshot. We were alone. I brought her into my office and pulled down some books as dry as the Sahara on options taxation.

She said, "Don't we have a tax department for this?"

I handed her the books. She couldn't have ripened at a better time since I had to focus on the trading machine Mort had erected. The powers that be were taking their money off the table. Black holes were appearing in the market left and right. There was money to be made with all that volatility, and Mort knew how to capitalize on it.

Granted, it was a breach of Mort's fiduciary duty as CFO according to U.S. regulations to enable his family and friends to trade on proprietary information. However, there was my knowledge of his trade done in the possession of material non-public information and there was my career path. Our relationship took on a newfound coziness.

I watched Jerry walk out of my office and called Mort up on his cell phone to tease him. "There's a certain baseball team for sale," I said. "It would be good for your campaign for Mayor of New York. Look on your

Bloomberg under the ads." He didn't know how to work the damn machine, and I had to take the elevator back down two flights to punch it into his Bloomberg for him.

CHAPTER 37
CYBORG

D *on't ask your male colleagues what they do at night. You don't want them asking you about having two men at the same time.*

I squinted my eyes when I looked out the window, little suspecting that I might be incurring the jealousy of the gods only slightly higher up. Yesterday seemed like fifty years ago. I remember what I actually dreamt last night: I was becoming a cyborg. My genitals had turned into a machine. My body descended into chains and Pirelli tires. I was half woman, half motorcycle.

Oh my God! Had I ceased to be human? I watched Sasha's back as he went out to go smoke a cigarette with the protesters. He had been here the whole time, quietly waiting in the background so handsomely it killed me. I shook off the thought.

I had to call my brother to make sure he was still alive.

"When can I see you?" Raif asked right away.

"I don't know. Saphora doesn't think it's a good idea."

He didn't answer, and I knew he was still heartbroken over losing Saphora. I changed the subject. "I'm at work."

"You got a job!" Raif said.

"Yes."

"Great. How's life?"

"I have some friends, but I don't know them very well."

"Where are you?"

I listened to the phone line crackle. "It's in the same city I was in before."

"Where's that?"

I hung up the phone. I was alone with a pang of guilt. If I was going to fit in here, I would have to learn to LIKE being alone. I would convince myself that it was my solitude that was being threatened. I would start by complaining that visitors were coming. I would learn to need SPACE. I'd heard the name for it on the radio. 'Social phobia'. It had already replaced dyslexia and attention deficit disorder as the top new malaise.

I tried to feel the new phobia just in time for Regina and crew descending upon me in my tiny habitat, either next weekend or the one after that. Sure, it bothered me that there was no way to plan this out, this convergence in New York. People, people, coming in and going out, and me, processing them like a machine. I liked to think they were better going out than they came in. Life imposes its own improbable shape. The flip side of being central was being responsible for so many people with incompatible plans. I really would need space. What if I just left? I savored my peace while I had it. The truth? I couldn't wait to see Regina.

On Saturday morning my apartment smelled like smoke. I'd put water in the rest of my pack of cigarettes before bed so I wouldn't go looking for them in the morning. It was cheaper this way. I'd figured it out. I was staring at the book Richard had given me and not feeling particularly motivated. I'd memorized the most convoluted, arid sentence I could find to recite to Richard on Monday, and closed the book. It was sunny outside, another hot one. I'd had too much to drink last night, and felt like I would drift away. Sasha was probably making eggs Florentine for his ex-girlfriend.

How could the U.S. government be lending the banks more than seven trillion dollars interest free and then borrow it back at three percent? The government was letting the banks gut the taxpayers. I wished that my work would not always be pitted against my humanity. I wished for some company. I wished for my own company.

I didn't have time for things like virtual group therapy anymore. All the members were in different places in their lives. The other women were talking about how hard it was to get a boyfriend, and I wanted to talk about how hard it was to clean my juicer. The therapist sent me an email the next day. "You're not ready to leave yet, Jerry."

I would have to be self-reliant. Hell, I would have to be responsible for more than myself if I wanted to start a vegan restaurant. I stocked the fridge with alcohol-free beer and bought the New York Times classified section. I read it on the way to work and covered it with red circles and notes. Watching the boats crisscross the Hudson Bay, I called about spaces for sale downtown.

By afternoon, I had found an old restaurant that had gone out of business. "Can I see it?" It was hot, only 88 degrees, but muggy. I looked at the price and noticed that the profitability per square foot was less the smaller the rent. The owner had exclusive roof access. A roof garden might be a nice touch, but it would be hard to get the food up there. The real estate agent handed me some papers with the financials, which fell to the sidewalk when my iPhone started vibrating. I was getting nailed on my options trade. The real estate agent helped me pick up the papers while I called my broker.

"What?" he asked.

"You heard me, double up." I said goodbye to the real estate agent, and went back to the floor to find Sasha. "What are we going to do today?"

"Nothing." Sasha sat down on the couch and put an unlit cigarette in his mouth.

"Don't tell anyone that I'm looking at a space for a vegan restaurant."

"That's risky business. Sit tight. We have to have our resident business expert go over the financials with you."

"Who's that?"

"Me."

As soon as Richard left for his lunch break, Sasha and I sat down on the yellow couch and spread out the financials for the restaurant on the coffee table. I watched Sasha's beautiful lips move as he read through the legal jargon, listening to the Del Rays singing doo wop shoo bop. "Don't tell me you like this music, too."

"Just this song," said the chain-smoking Sasha with the ripped pocket. A colleague tried to sit down next to me. "How's your wife's health?"

The colleague sneered and got up.

"So the restaurant looks fine?" I asked.

"No. First of all, it's for sale."

"And? I should be looking for places that aren't for sale?"

"You don't want to buy in this market, Jerry. And it's a bad location. You can only open for lunch on that street. You're better off a few blocks west. Don't worry, Jerry! You're on the right track. In the United States, when you start a corporation, you create a personhood."

"You do?" Wow, it was like having a baby. An adult baby.

"Yeah. Corporate persons with all the legal rights of an actual person are all over the place. You might as well get with it and create a super person that will never die, doesn't need organic food or clean water, can't be arrested, but benefits from all the same Constitutional rights that you do."

I thought I saw a gleam in Sasha's eye. Very convincing. If I applied for the business loan right after I got the student loan, it would look like I had the seed capital to qualify, and neither bank would be the wiser.

"Working for an outfit like Global American Bank, you'll be approved for the business loan almost immediately." He held his arms out wide.

I would have my own business. The bank was paying

for school. School would pay for my seed capital, and clients would pay off my loans. As long as everything kept going up, I'd be happy, wouldn't I? I hugged him. "Thanks."

Strength comes from within. You don't need to get involved.

Why always look within when the grass is greener on the other side?

Don't leave the office at the same time as your male colleagues.

I picked up my things and narrowly escaped the Sasha possibilities.

Credit wasn't exactly easy in those days, but Sasha thought I was going to be able to get the loans I would need, starting with my student loan, if I could just find the right location. Nothing I looked at satisfied me, though.

I was restless. It was time to start a health kick. For breakfast, I had an alfalfa-sprout-and-spinach smoothie. I did a little Zen meditation but didn't expect to get anywhere in the beginning. I was just adding to the karma bank to get started. Not a lot, just enough to keep my balance positive like a credit in my bank account. Wouldn't that be great if we could do away with money and just exchange karma instead? I didn't really believe in money for its own sake.

The big moneymakers I knew, from Harvard anyway, were usually too smart to *believe* in money. They knew that making a fortune on bets at a bank year after year was neither here nor there. The better the position they were in financially to make a historical gash in the world, the harder it was to leave the bank. The stakes were too high to take a leap of faith. It would be like quantifying air, and they still couldn't fly. "If someone offered you a million dollars to watch a graph for a year, or a year off with no pay, which one would you take?"

"Easy answer," I'd say.

"How many times would you do that trade?" they would say.

"Five. No, eight."

"Are you sure you wouldn't do it for thirty years? Thirty million dollars is a lot of money."

"Yeah but what are you going to do with it at the age of sixty? Go back to school? Buy a business? Make more money?" Of course you give some away, I thought, but what about your life? What about your vocation, calling you, unnoticed and unrealized? What about all those years you didn't spend on yourself? What about those aces in your hand?

I had a friend in Singapore who confronted this dilemma fervently as he watched his graph every year. He read constantly, philosophy, novels, politics, history, gossip. A college roommate sent him manuscripts to read at his desk. He walked through the same Singapore streets to the gym every day. He had reconstructive surgery on his chin, a nose job, and penis enlargement. He had a black belt, five egg whites for lunch, and a model for dinner. He wasn't saving it for anything. He was just stretching it as far into eternity as modern technology would permit.

What if you got whatever you wanted 'til there was nothing left to want? If you kept trading in for new ones until you froze to death. Hung over in the gutter, who was I to say he was missing the point?

Nevertheless, his life was a little cold. There could be more love. "I would take a lot less perfection for more love."

CHAPTER 38
BLACK HOLES

I have always been afraid of heights. After watching what bank failure did to Brent crude, I'm a changed man. I can't stand to ride in an elevator higher than the tenth floor. All trading was practically halted as the boys sat there with their huge positions on the news that First Widget Bank collapsed. I took my ulcer medicine as I watched Brent crude slide from a high of $147 a barrel to $82, and nothing anyone could do about it. Ever since subprime failures cut off everybody in the chain, banks were operating on thin reserve margins. This year alone, hundreds of banks had gone tits up.

I was making so much money for my own account, I forgot to warn the boys about the bank's potential losses. The arithmetic was murderous. Too late. The boys tallied up the losses. There was no talk of who was responsible.

"This isn't going to stop," Jerry said.

"Sure it will stop," Sasha said. "You have to buy when it looks worst."

"I just sold," Jerry said. "You buy."

Sasha spent the afternoon buying up bank shares.

Life behind the scenes at Global American Bank went on business as usual, and I forgot about Righteous Mortgage as much as I could, trying to enjoy the siphoning off of less sinister insider trading profits on various purchases, moderate at first. I bought jewels: matching diamond necklaces studded with rubies, one for my wife and the other for a special lady.

This was nothing compared to the CFO's new penthouse, full of antiques from around the world or his wife's yacht. But when I heard that some of the insider profits had been donated to the university the CFO's son was going to next year, that's when I began to think that my new mistress and I could use a penthouse in Battery Park, too. I was looking through the real estate section of the New York Times, still not believing the nerve of the CFO, endowing a chair for a new faculty position at a mediocre law school.

CHAPTER 39

THE COMING OF REGINA

*A*ll that hunting for men paid off in a way. At least I wasn't out shopping for clothes. Not only did I avoid filling my apartment with purchases, I ate for free and was able to save up some dough for the restaurant.

I went to look at a couple of places a few blocks from Wall Street. On my salary I could barely afford the rent, but they were both much too small. Why did I go on hoping? Renting anything bigger was beyond my budget. *Poverty. There's something money can't buy.*

I turned the problem over in my head and dreamed about my vegan restaurant all the way home. I had to save.

Regina was coming. There was a message on my machine. Regina had called from Buffalo. She was loving it there last Friday with her new boyfriend, who was two years younger than she was. Pater had a ride lined up for Regina from New York back to New Orleans with a Frenchman. He tried to sell her on the idea of making out with the Frenchman all the way back, but Regina was having too much fun in Buffalo.

"Can I borrow your car to drive my guy's musical equipment to Manhattan and then . . . then . . ."

"Then I don't know, because if you drive my car around the city and try to hang out in New York for three days with it, it would cost $60 for parking every time you stopped somewhere, and more for tickets. Anyway, my car's not in New York."

"We're kind of running low on money," Regina said

. . . *And then we'll just drive off a cliff like Thelma and Louise,* I thought. "I don't know. This guy's supposed to buy my car this weekend. If he wants it, I have to go there on Saturday and sign over the title."

"@$¬_#!"

"How are things with the new man?" I asked. "Is it true love or just another wave of consumerism?"

"Thanks for nothing. I need a new car, new clothes, a new man before it all slips away. Where can I get a new plan before he runs off with his old girlfriend?"

"Did she follow you to Buffalo?"

"They're from here. He's a homeboy. This is his hometown. His old girlfriend owns part of a florists here."

"Let me guess. He wants to go work there and live off her."

"Of course."

"They're all the same," Regina and I said at the same

184

time.

"I'll tell you what you do: Forget his musical equipment. Take a train to New York."

"I checked into trains. It's $160 to New York. It's $165 back to New Orleans."

"You should have come here last weekend when Pater had a ride lined up for you."

"I should have come there last weekend," she said. "But I was transported."

"Transported nowhere." We laughed. "You wanted to stay there at light speed," I said, and laughed some more. "You didn't know if you were coming or going." Ha, ha, ha, we said. "Call Pater," I said. "He's got three days. Maybe he'll find you another ride." I doubted it.

"I'll call Pater."

I had seen a beautiful space for a restaurant that afternoon. The agent's number was burning a hole in my pocket, but I didn't have the money to even rent it. I had to organize the time/money equation.

I tried not to stare at the walls. If I stared hard enough, my mother's blood would scream up from the white. *Now look what they've done!* Mom was with God, finding peace. It terrified me to think about it. I felt the presence of her ghost. I had to get out of my apartment. I had to let Manhattan bombard me with stimuli and switch off my brain.

I walked through the park at Union Square where I saw an old man smoking a foot-long pipe. I stopped and looked at the man.

"A lot of people look at me," the man said. "They take my picture, too." He turned out to be an actual old guy from an elevator. I pulled out my phone and took a dozen pictures. "I dropped out of grade school to work in the mail room at one of them buildings over there." He pointed to some buildings across Union Square. "That's when I got promoted to elevator man." He worked 'over there'. He pointed out another building '. . . and over there'. He worked in almost every building around Union Square. This ninety-year-old man. "Then when I was working at a job in a building, I got another job."

I was waiting for some twist in the story where the guy made it and lost it all again. He got this new job 'over there' where he started working as '. . . an elevator man'." Now he just watches people go side to side from his bench in the park. More evidence. Life does not subscribe to Hollywood. More proof that it's all pointless. At least I escaped my own thoughts for a moment.

I went to the gym, but the gym was too hot. How could there be no air conditioning at the NYU gym in this century? NYU has billions of dollars under management, and can't install air conditioning in the gym like every other school. Someone had to be embezzling air-conditioning funds. As I was doing the splits, I melted into the mat thinking of a poem to Regina:

> 'Tis but a scratch,
> This recent pain
> Of love gone awry
> With What's-His-Name —
> Of not what was lost,
> But what could have been . . .

If nothing else, life in the city was non-stop. I made sure I had someone to see and somewhere to go every night. Running from the loneliness monster.

I had to count my blessings. I was thinking, sitting alone in the lounge at the W Hotel. Soon I would be plugged in. Plugged in, hooked up. Who was coming for my birthday? Lonnie and maybe Regina. Regina and Lonnie could rescue *each other*. But what about this kid, I.N.K. who was with Regina? Where did he fit? And if Regina was transported again, might I get stuck with *him?* My apartment was already getting crowded with possibilities. A kind of social phobia was setting in. *I'll have to hide my laptop above the refrigerator tonight,* I thought.

I followed a bald man out of the W Hotel lounge and into the elevator to see what floor he got off on. The metal doors parted. There was no elevator man in this one. We didn't really need elevator men anymore. We got in with a gay couple. The doors closed.

No man was going to hunt me down. I could hunt as good as any man. The couple kissed in the elevator and got off on the 11th floor. I was alone with the bald man.

He glanced at me.

I smiled and pressed the red button, leaning into him, "Come here, angel."

The elevator stopped.

He turned around and reached for my waist.

I caught my breath and trembled as he lifted my thigh.

When I'd had my fill, I pressed the button again. The doors opened. I pushed him out. "Hit the road, Jack."

"Hey wait!"

The doors closed.

CHAPTER 40

NO-BRAND LOVE

i was scared, throwing trinkets into drawers in case Regina's new boyfriend was a thief. I flopped down on the love seat and stared up at the eaves. There weren't enough blankets. It was really just a small apartment. There was only one bed, and one love seat, which was too small to stretch out on.

And then there were footsteps on the pavement outside, laughter. I went to open the window. Regina looking up from the street with her flowing black curls, slender curves almost hidden under baggy gray painters' clothes, to match her young friend's. "Regina!" I was so excited, I barely noticed I.N.K. standing humbly by in the next square of pavement.

I flew down the stairs and hugged Regina. At first I couldn't even look at I.N.K. It hurt to see beautiful Regina standing next to this slob with his pants pulled down telling her about all the junk in his head.

I had expected them to fit in here, but even in the Village streets, I.N.K. looked misplaced. I hustled them inside before my landlords on the ground floor saw my unlikely friends. "Look at you, Jerry! I love the blonde hair," Regina said.

It didn't occur to me that they would come during the work week. It was the evening our broker from Chicago was coming to take me out to dinner. I stuffed them in my apartment to shower and rest and went to meet the broker at Mojo Coffee. Then the broker took me to *La Ripaille*, and we drank Bordeaux 1985, which he paid for. By ten p.m., I was beginning to think he was quite an amiable fellow. Amazing what a little Bordeaux can do. He pretended it was an accident when he brushed my hand. He was unmistakably hot for me.

We wandered over to the café where I'd agreed to meet up with my friends and sat down amidst the jitterati. The broker looked amused when Regina and I.N.K. appeared like mismatched socks and sat down at the table. The broker ordered two more beers. I let them all get acquainted. I.N.K. had trimmed his goatee, and despite an otherwise careless air, his young skin looked dazzling under blue neon. It was freshly tanned from their venture into the Deep South.

Regina sat up. "Lonnie!" Lonnie from back in the day came walking up the street with a duffle bag slung across her shoulder. Regina was hugging Lonnie over the railing.

They hadn't seen each other since high school. Their black and blonde hair mingled, and Lonnie struggled to bury her East Coast accent, which Regina found charming.

The broker went on picking up the tab and took my friends in stride, saying things like, "As Mullah Nasrudin says, 'Happiness is finding your donkey after you've lost it.'"

It was something special to me, having my best friends in the same place, these antidotes willingly mixing. I, helpless, felt a tinge of inadequacy. My apartment was too small. The broker was expounding on the correlation between oil and arms. He sized up his audience and quickly moved from the oil trade to Alaskan moose stories. Tales of the wilds in the cold under the Manhattan skyline were beginning to work their magic on Regina. That was some heavy conversation we were having, downright metaphysical, about us all being connected. Wish't I could remember it. That's the price of a good Bordeaux. I was so happy to have my best friends there, I almost cried.

The waiter gave the broker another bill: expensive. When the broker picked up the tab, dollar signs flashed in Regina's eyes. I grinned at her and knew what she was thinking, just what I'm looking for, an aging man with a credit line. The broker gallantly said, "I'll cover it."

We thanked the Hong Kong Shanghai Bank for a lovely evening. The broker said, "Your friends are welcome to come stay at my hotel room with me if you don't have enough space."

That meant Regina, not I.N.K. "They're inseparable," I said. "It's not that we don't want to show our appreciation for your generosity. Why don't you come up to my place?"

I saw Regina's eyes widen.

There was no more room on the couch so I sat on the floor. The attic was too hot. The men had taken off their shirts. Sitting on the sleeping bags, we watched the passersby in the street below.

"Look at them going in their directions," I said, "all thinking they're going to make it in New York with their little pieces of reality. Even put together, they don't know it all." There was no way to know it all. It was time to make something out of what I could perceive. I stripped down to my bra.

"Let me help you with that," the broker said. He held me in back as Lonnie undressed and I.N.K. and Regina caressed my stomach.

I had thought that after three hundred lovers I wouldn't feel anymore, that after four hundred, I would become a man. The harder I collided with other humans, the more distant I felt. I watched them sleep. The clock on the mantelpiece ticked, ticked. I wept.

I woke up on top of Regina's sleeping bag with Lonnie's hand on my cheek. The broker was gone. I had come one degree closer to breaking Rule Number One, Don't get involved with anyone at work. Peaceful familiarity lulled me back to sleep.

My squatters slept on. I stepped over Lonnie, whispered goodbye to Regina and I.N.K., and made my way to work. Protestors were gathered at the entrance to the bank. A bearded man with red knuckles glared at me. He was talking into the human microphone about occupying homes. By law, the protesters couldn't use any microphones or bullhorns, so they spread the word by chanting whatever the speaker said. He talked at the people around him, who spread his words to those behind them with conviction I'd only seen in movies, ". . . freedom to own our own homes!" His words echoed through the park.

I felt his eyes on my back as I turned away and walked up the steps to the bank. As I opened the door, he booed, and an echo of boos rippled away to the back of the park. The glass door closed behind me. I caught a glimpse of his eyes glaring at me as if I were the cause of the financial meltdown.

But protestors were the least of my worries. Another fear nagged at my conscience. Had the broker spilled the beans? Sasha seemed relieved to see me. I sat down next to Richard. Another bank went under. We kicked back in our chairs in front of our screens and bounced ideas off each other. "Where is this going?" I asked.

"Remember the British student protests? Now look, the Greek and Spanish *indignados* are busting out anti-austerity protests."

"It's a socialist revolution," I said.

"Could be," Richard said.

Sasha moped around. I didn't dare look at his sulky body brooding down at the end of the desk. His friends back home were losing their jobs. I knew he was fuming at his computer screen, red with losses from his failed bank shares.

I didn't breathe a word about the happenings of the night before, and if Sasha knew I had guests, he didn't let on. Those follies were just the kind of thing a trading floor could get hold of and use to tear you apart. Sasha was in and out of the office, and I couldn't tell whether he knew of our escapade. No sooner had Richard ducked out of the office, than Sasha came back, face peeled open in a grin, with the broker. "Jerry! I had a nice talk with our favorite broker today." Sasha led the broker over to the yellow couch.

Our eyes met. He looked silly with his Burberry tie on. I could feel the heat rise to my face.

"I heard a very interesting story, Jerry," Sasha said. "He said you're a lot of fun to be with. Wonder what he meant by that."

I resumed breathing.

The boys came to lounge on the yellow couch.

"Boys, here's our broker from Chicago. He discovered the beauty of New York last night."

The boys chuckled. "Blond or brunette?"

"I think I know where you went, Dive 75, right? That place is a meat market on Thursdays."

"No need to guess," Sasha said, "he's not letting on, isn't that right?" Sasha turned to the broker, whose eyes gleamed. "Besides, there's a lady present." Sasha looked over my head. I turned around and saw the secretary standing in the doorway.

The broker laughed. "Excuse me, Jerry."

The boys laughed along — pretending to get the joke, I think — which made the broker laugh more.

The only one who wasn't laughing was me.

"Or maybe feminists don't like being called 'ladies'," Sasha persisted. "Jerry? Would you know the answer to that? You're your own woman, aren't you? You don't let society tell you what to do. And you certainly don't let men manipulate you! Any feminist knows that women don't want the same things as men. They have their own needs, don't they?"

"Yeah, like bicycles," a clerk said.

"That's fish that need the bicycles," a trader said.

The boys waited for my decree on feminism.

The phone rang.

Sasha grabbed the receiver out of my hand. "What are their names?" he asked. Before I could stop him, Sasha cried, "Bring them up!"

I think I saw it in a nightmare. Regina in ripped-jean shorts with the pockets hanging out and no bra was coming at us through the glass door.

Even Sasha's mouth dropped open.

There was my baseball hat on the New Orleans Queen. I.N.K. appeared next, paint-splattered shorts barely hanging off his butt and a 'We Are the 99%' T-shirt sticking to his chest.

I jumped up to push them back out into the hallway, but my feet stuck to the floor.

"Let them in!" Sasha shouted. "I had them sent up!" Traders peeled away from their screens. Heads turned, surprised. The fun-loving oil desk rumbled with laughter.

"Regina!" Sasha said, arms stretched wide. "The famous Regina! So this is the woman! Regina, your reputation precedes you!"

She was trying to figure out if he meant it as a compliment. "I've heard so much about you, too, Sasha," she lied and gave him such a gooey hug back, you'd a thought they went to nursery school together.

Sasha was being charming and phony, and I felt sick

to my stomach. "It's just like on South Park," he said.

"Yeah, I remember that one," Regina agreed. They kept coming up with more and more TV shows they'd both seen. "Did you like that one, too?" Regina said.

"I loved it!" Sasha said.

That's how insidious TV is. You can imagine you knew someone all your life talking about the episodes you both watched.

Traders stood up to say hello. Our Arab head oil trader smiled down on them. "Look who made it through security," he boomed pumping I.N.K.'s hand up and down. "I was wondering when you were going to start demonstrating up here."

A clerk ventured a handshake.

The President's secretary forgot what she came for and just looked at the floor.

Regina and I.N.K. dragged their mangy, paint-covered, raggedy selves across the trading floor and into the safety of Richard's empty office. "Where are you guys going?" I asked, as indifferently as possible.

Sasha followed us in before I could shut the door.

"We were out there for three hours demonstratin' with the protesters," Regina said. "Yeah, we just thought we'd stop up and see where y'at." She looked around at my digs, and then, since no one else was talking, said, "Boy, it's hot for this time of year."

"Yeah," I.N.K. said, as if he didn't dress like that all the time with his grease-stained T-shirt.

"We were sweatin' carrying those signs around the park," Regina said.

"It's hot in here, too."

"Next time you visit, take a cab, they drop you off right at the steps!" Sasha said.

"Nah," Regina said. "We wanted to scream and shout. Jerry, I borrowed your shirt. Is it OK?" She tugged on the tie-dyed T-shirt with a small hole in the stomach. Her nipples were perky underneath.

"Yeah." You should have borrowed one of my bras, too. What difference did it make now?

"Maybe that's why you're so hot," Sasha said.

"Yeah, that's what we were saying out front. We should just take off our clothes."

"Go ahead, take them off," Sasha said, having his little joke on me with *homegirl*.

"I'll gladly take off my clothes," I.N.K. said.

"Not you!" Sasha said.

Now that my eyes had adjusted to him, I.N.K. really was good looking in a ruff way. Sasha sensed the attraction and was about to resume brooding in his corner, which was about to make me happy, when Regina asked me for 'the apartment key'.

Sasha started. He watched my two hoodies stand up to go. Regina turned to me with a sorry-assed look on her face.

"You can go, too, Jerry," Sasha said. "Go march around outside. I'll cover."

"Thanks, man!" Regina said.

I took it like a poison apple, and descended with my homies into the mob of protesters.

Helicopters hovered overhead. Police in riot gear stoked tension. They outnumbered the protestors on the ground. TV cameras filmed the chaos as three young women with signs were being forcibly cuffed to the ground on a public sidewalk. The authorities wanted to escalate. As if the hippie anarchists were the enemy when it was the banks that had stolen the economy. The whole world was watching America try to dehumanize ordinary people with their legitimate concerns.

Police were corralling the demonstrators to let us pass. One of them looked familiar. I slowed my pace to see him turn his head. Yes. There was no mistaking that goatee, and there was the scar under his left eye. "Keep moving," he said.

"I thought you never wore funny hats."

He wasn't at all surprised to see me, as if he expected me there. "They needed backup," he said in a deadpan voice.

Regina and I.N.K. made a beeline down the steps. "What were you doing talking to that cop?"

"Look, I know you guys mean well, but don't come to my work next time." I felt bad telling them, especially since it was obvious, wasn't it?

Regina pouted. "I'm sorry, Jerry."

CHAPTER 41
COMMUNAL LIVING

*i*t was my birthday! I didn't tell anyone at work that I was thirty, but rushed home hoping for down-home reception. When I got home, Regina wasn't there. We were supposed to be walking to the East Village by now. Where was she? I was sorry I'd complained about her appearance at the bank. I was also sorry that Pater's best-laid plans for my birthday dinner were about to fall through. We were going to be very late. Pater would be mad at me for messing up his reservation, for monopolizing Regina, for getting older.

I forgot about all the vampires when Regina and I.N.K. walked through my door. They were excited. "We had a ball at MOMA!" Regina said. "It's great to be here,

Jerry. You made me what I am, and I love you for that. I remember when we met in Mrs. Elda's microbiology class, and how I was so impressed with you. The lady in the art museum reminded me of you. You're going to be just like her when you get old."

"Like a fifty-year-old Jewish lady?" I.N.K. said.

"Yeah," Regina said. "She was insisting that her friend cut in front of us in a thick New York accent. It reminded me of that show on TV last night—.'"

"I don't watch TV," I said. The saving grace of my fear of the murderer was that I developed an immunity to television. I missed the 33,000 murders a week, and most of television's ideological domination. In a country with more TV's than people, I escaped this trusted source of information.

"Well, you rent movies," Regina said.

"I used to."

I had no time for TV. I had to get organized to set up my vegan restaurant, and they wanted to watch TV. How could I motivate this crew to get to work? "I know what I want for my birthday."

"What's that, baby?" Regina said.

"Regina, will you call Ivan and tell him that you're going to pick up my car from his mom's farm and take it to Los Angeles to sell because you can get a better price out there, and you have more time than him to really sell it?"

"Oh no," Lonnie said.

"What difference does it make?" I.N.K. said. "All American cars are basically Chevrolets."

"Whatever you want, honey," Regina said.

"Don't do it. It won't work," Lonnie was saying as we walked through Washington Square Park abuzz in twilight.

"Yes it will," I said. "Appeal to his ego, Regina. You have to stress his failure to sell, and let him think you're trying to swindle me out of my car."

"Uh, OK I'll lay it on real thick."

"Poor Ivan," Lonnie said.

The challenge was not letting intrigue stop me from having my party. I felt that if I didn't count my blessings right now, no more good things would be conferred upon me in life.

Pater and his entourage were waiting in the restaurant at a crappy table behind a pillar. Not a scrap of Southern hospitality. They were laughing too loud at something that was no doubt not funny. "Jerry! It's about time. Let me see what you're wearing. That's not a dress. It's a bathing suit." He was happy to see Regina after all these years but was mad that we were an hour late. Of course, when his *coiffeur* friend arrived even later half way through the meal, Pater was happy to see *him*. Pater hated it when he couldn't control the women in his entourage. That phony gave me a headache. It made me sad. He berated Harvard, the Ivy League, and college in general.

"I love you guys so much. Thanks for coming," I sneered.

"How much are the other Harvard grads making?" Pater sneered back. He didn't go to college, so Harvard was always tough to swallow. He could only understand the part of me that came from New Orleans. He didn't like me 'putting on airs'.

I didn't defend myself. Judging by the worried expressions on their faces, I must have been staring at nothing again. *To hell with it. You have to sift through your own thoughts.*

Regina answered for me. "Why don't you lay off? It's her birthday."

"I'm just sayin'." Pater was subdued. "Why does she need an alias? She should just be herself. I don't think people would hold it against her."

"She doesn't hang around the kind of scrubs you do," Regina said. "One of her ex-boyfriends makes a million a year. Don't give me that look, Pater. See 'dat, Jerry? All those straight A's in high school for nothing. Being president of the Latin club, winning the International Science Fair. No use. You still end up across the table from an angry fag on your thirtieth birthday."

"No shit," Pater laughed. "What's up with your hair, anyway? That's not you."

I watched all of my 'blessings' from far away.

Just because we're celebrating the day Mom brought us into the world doesn't give him the right to blow your cover. You could easily be a natural blonde. It matches your features. No one can tell.

Pater didn't get a reaction from me, so he turned on Regina and I.N.K. "And speaking of identities, WTF does I.N.K. stand for?"

"In Nice Company," I.N.K. said.

"FYI, 'company' is spelled with a 'C'," Pater said.

"So?" I.N.K. said.

Pater's eyes lit up. "Better latent than never."

"The moment for polite banter is past. Now is the time

for asinine bickering," I.N.K. said.

It was as if I was swimming up from the bottom of a pool. Regina was shouting something in my ear. I could almost hear it. Regina was shaking my shoulder. "Pater's jealous of you, girl," Regina was saying.

"He's gay," I managed to say.

"Yeah," Regina said, "but Pater says, 'I don't know what Jerry thinks she's doing trying to start a restaurant.'"

"How old do I have to be before I know what I'm doing?"

"Exactly. Don't let him cut you down. You gotta do what you gotta do, Pater or no Pater."

"At least we didn't marry *him*," I said, still determined to count my blessings *and* get my finances in order. I went outside to call Ivan out on his mother's farm. As expected, they weren't making any headway on selling my car. I hung up. When I came back in, there was a pink birthday cake with way too many candles on it. "It looks like it's about to explode."

Regina started singing 'Happy Birthday' and the whole restaurant joined in. A warm feeling. Even Pater smiled at me.

"And now for your birthday present." This time, Regina came outside with me to call Ivan. " . . . Yeah, I'm going to drive Jerry's car out West," she said.

"Did he react?" I asked afterward.

"Oh yeah. He didn't like that idea a-tall. We'll be seeing some movement now, boy."

Saturday morning, Regina and I.N.K. ducked out of the bedroom and lounged about the tiny apartment with Lonnie, and me. I made everyone strong coffee with hot milk before the day got too hot to drink coffee. Regina and I.N.K. snuggled into the love seat with Lonnie. Lonnie looked up from the classifieds. Her face lit up as Regina described her cross-country journey. We stumbled over each other in the microscopic kitchen, maneuvering our second cups of *café au lait*. I had been lonely, and now my friends were in the way.

"Where are your kives?" Regina said.

"I don't have any," I said. "Sorry. Just break it in half."

"You don't have any knives!" I.N.K. said.

"Drop it." Regina had my back. She knew I didn't want any murder weapons in the apartment, and set about buttering a broken piece of bread with a spoon.

They didn't have any plans for the day, incongruent in the all-consuming city. "Your face looks prettier now that it's thinned out," Regina said to me.

"Who cares about her face?" I.N.K. said. Regina punched him on the arm, almost staining the sofa.

We were shrinking as we got older. I looked at Regina's shining eyes with the slightest hint of crow's feet. We were ripe at our peak, at thirty.

Street-smarts-of-a-garbage-can I.N.K. lit another cigarette. Regina put on a wrap-around skirt and some clogs, and there she was! A Nice Girl. A.N.G. and me went for a walk.

CHAPTER 42
HOLLY, GO LIGHTLY

Wandering back to the ranch, I.N.K. found a TV in the garbage. "Let's plug it in and see if it works," he shouted and carried it up the four flights.

"We have to call Wolf, remember? Your fourth grade sweetheart," Regina said. "I found him on Facebook. He's here for the weekend. I ran into him in New Orleans, and I promised him you'd call him."

"*I'd* call? I haven't seen him since fourth grade. How is he?"

"He's fat like nobody's business." Regina giggled.

"No he's not. He was always skinny."

"I'm just kidding. He's a toothpick."

"I can't believe you found a Jew from my fourth grade

class for me. That was very sweet of you. But I've moved on now."

The heat in that attic was making me sick. I took my third shower of the day to stay cool. It should be a crime to charge people to rent fifth-floor attics in New York.

Regina and I met Lonnie on the terrace of Café Gitane. We decided we would walk to the grocery store to get some beer and turn on the TV. We started down the street toward the grocery store.

"I'm getting blisters on my feet," Lonnie said.

I was happy to have them both there for one luxurious moment, and on the occasion of my risky real estate decision. I hadn't seen them together in the same place since high school. Now they'd gotten their beer and snacks, and there was a good movie on — *Breakfast at Tiffany's*. I was so excited to be sitting around with my two best friends doing something on our own when Pater called up two hours early.

"I'm back." He'd been at Coney Island. "Come over."

"We'll be over after the movie."

He seemed miffed. Again. We cackled our way through the movie, and interjected here and there. Lonnie dangled her feet over the arm of the love seat and surmised on how to catch a man. I said, no, to be a free woman was the challenge, and opened another beer. Regina waffled, and understood both sides. The room was full of smoke. I had waited nine years to be together with my two best friends, and now the movie was ending differently from the book.

In the book, Holly Golightly goes lightly off to Africa by herself and is spotted in newspapers safariing around with tribesmen. That's the whole point. In the movie, the blonde guy stops her from going away, and convinces her to stay home and marry him. All I can say is, don't go see it or you'll puke. I looked at my friends' faces. The phonier it got, the more they lapped it up. What could it mean?

"Maybe women are free only in books," Regina said.

The message was clear: I mustn't let anyone stop me from starting my vegan restaurant.

The next morning, Ivan called and asked me to call him in twenty minutes when the guy who wanted to buy the car would be there. I left Lonnie, Regina and I.N.K. on the terrace at Mojo Coffee and went back outside to call Ivan. "He says he'll pay $19,000, certified check."

I sat down at the table. "Way to go, Regina. He got an offer for $19,000."

"Take it!" I.N.K. said.

"Naw, baby," Regina said. "He's a dealer. He's gonna turn around and sell it for twenty-one."

"He can sell it at twenty-one five," I said. "If we hurry up, maybe I can leverage my student loan into a business loan and start my restaurant."

"Is that legal?" Lonnie said.

"I'd have to do it before the student loan showed up on my credit report," I said.

"She means no," Regina said.

"A restaurant!" I.N.K. said. "That's a lot of work. You would be lucky if it caught on fire."

We all looked at I.N.K.

"You better tell that business loan officer to run a copy of your credit report now," Regina said, "so you'll come up clean."

"You could help me look for a restaurant to rent," I said.

Nobody moved.

Lazy-assed mother@#%$!s. Instead, we watched Tony and Tina's wedding procession go by. When it cleared, little ol' Wolf was standing on the corner reading the street sign. Wolf was skinny as ever, tired and mangy after two nights on Pater's couch. I laughed and hugged Wolf. "Sit down. We're just having some brunch. What would you like?"

"I don't have any money."

"I'll pay," I said.

He ordered an enormous plate of eggs, sausages, hash browns, and pancakes. Wolf had just gotten fired from a job as an editor at a magazine.

"Do you write?" I asked him.

"I hate writing," he said.

"Is that why you were an editor?" Wolf asked if we had any drugs, and I started giving him a lecture. It was hopeless, and I did feel sorry for him, so sorry, I had an overwhelming urge to hand him my last thousand dollars, but a taxi driver's warning came to mind: "I can tell you are intelligent, but never let your mind race ahead of your common sense."

I'm not sure about the rest of that day. Someone ordered us a round, and the sun went down. Then Pater was there, but he left in disgust when Wolf and I were making out at the table, and then we were in the bathroom. I had all my money the next morning, though.

Regina came in around noon the next day holding the classifieds and hit me with plan z. *"I'll* help you look for the damn vegan restaurant."

I was anxious to see what she had found, and we made about fifty phone calls. Then we hit the streets.

The first agent put the key in the lock. I took a deep breath. The dining room was bright and pleasant with blonde parquet floors, and it had a slice of a view of the cityscape, because one of the windows looked diagonally onto a square. There was a dead bird lying in the middle of the kitchen floor, and a live pigeon messing up the bathroom. I shooed him out with my briefcase and closed the window. The sink was coated with an inch-thick layer of bird dung. The bathroom needed a paint job, but otherwise, it would make a beautiful restaurant. It was rather large and had a fireplace. What luck. If it weren't on a side street with only a tiny window, I would come live in it myself. "All it needs is an air conditioner," Regina said. I stuck my head out the door. "There's Wall Street. You can see your work from here."

I craned my neck to see the Freedom Tower under construction.

"I'm sure the view adds value to the restaurant."

"What view? You'll get a crick in your neck trying to see anything from here."

"That's a New York view. Why do you think everybody's in a bad mood here?"

CHAPTER 43

GENIUS

*R*egina was on the radar all right. I kicked myself for missing her appearance at the bank. They were talking about it the whole week. I would have to see her in the flesh. I found one of the ads Jerry had circled and called to see the place for myself. It was the one with the awful bird mess in the bathroom. That's when I discovered Jerry's restaurant plan. A pigeon pooped on me.

I was angry, but proud of her at the same time. I decided to say nothing about the restaurant so that she wouldn't try to hide from me more. Instead, I decided to hang out at the Suds Café across the street from Jerry's apartment.

On the surface, Regina's involvement with Jerry

seemed magnanimous. But scratch a little deeper and questions arose. How deeply was Regina in with the Occupy Wall Street movement? Was she helping with the restaurant because she wanted Jerry to succeed, or did she want to be involved with Jerry's money?

What about Jerry's sexual consumption to rival the Fortune 500? And how come her hypersexuality never came out around me? That meant there could be another jealous lover lurking in her past. I was beginning to suspect myself.

After sitting there for an hour and forty minutes, I finally saw Jerry coming out of the building with the scruffy I.N.K. kid and a woman with long black hair, undoubtedly Regina. Regina was wild, gesticulating and dancing in the street. A woman of considerable physical strength and will. Regina was obviously happy to be with Jerry, I had to give her that. I stepped out and ducked behind some garbage cans.

Hmm, where was Saphora throughout all of this? Wasn't she one of Jerry's blessings, too? She must have been some kind of hermit who never emerged from her apartment. The hermaphrodite type, squeamish at the thought of group sex. Maybe she lived above a restaurant and ordered in all the time. I'm sure she never called, but waited for Jerry to initiate. They'd no doubt grown apart since their proximity as roommates at Harvard.

I was dying to get a glimpse of this sage who knew so much more than Jerry. Saphora's high IQ must have made it hard for her to fit in, whereas Jerry had good ol' common street smarts that probably made Saphora jealous. I followed them down the street. If only I could meet Saphora and measure up her intense feelings that make socializing so awkward for geniuses. She was probably the misunderstood genius type, underestimated by peers and society, even by herself, underutilized and unable to fulfill her full creative potential.

Really smart women have it tough. I've seen it with any number of them. Guys like to be in charge. They want a woman they can trick, a woman who is willing to be exploited a little. Men don't idolize genius chicks as women, and they don't respect them as intellectuals. Geniuses can stop maturing at around twenty to hide their intellect. They're known to detach from reality and wander off on a tangent. Saphora was a psychological fit.

CHAPTER 44

STUDENT LOANS

Richard handed me a letter. I tore it open and read: I had been pre-approved for $60,000 in student loans. I had come a long way in a year and a half, establishing my credit, getting a decent job. That settled it. I was going to put down roots on Wall Street.

"Be firm, Jerry," Sasha said. "Don't take their first price."

"OK!"

I met Regina in the lobby, and we walked out into the fray of Zuccotti Park. The signs and banners were more colorful than ever. One protester had an American flag with company logos as stars flying on the back of his bicycle. Regina looked at them, then at me, and I was embarrassed that my best friend saw me, an emblem of capitalism in my suit amidst such a cool band of protesters.

I promised myself I would pay more attention to their slogans in the future. Suddenly, I was afraid of everything as if the edifice I was standing on were crumbling. There was Richard, standing on the steps with his hands in his pockets. I rushed Regina past him and distracted her with my fears. "I hope Raif doesn't come to the restaurant," I whispered. "I shouldn't say that, but it's true."

"Forget about your brother. He's not taking care of you either. It's every woman for herself. Baby, you need to stand in the place where you live and get some continuity. You can't keep changing jobs every year. You not gonna climb no man's ladder. You da boss."

Regina and I saw two spaces in walking distance from work. They were less than $13,500 a month each.

"Come on, man, the floor is slanted. Imagine your wine tilting in your glass."

The other seemed like a great location at first. It was right around the block from City Hall.

"Naw, man," Regina said, "as soon as you turn the corner, the neighborhood starts looking like an alley. The whole block's garbage is sittin' here in front of your building waiting to be picked up."

"I bet this block will come up to the standard of the rest of the neighborhood," I said. "The building will become more valuable as the rent-controlled spaces become free and are sold."

"I like the fact that owners live upstairs, but otherwise, keep movin'."

On the way back, I was about to give up when Regina

saw a sign in a window, 'Storefront For Sale'. It looked like it had been a bar some time ago. The windows and floor were dusty with disuse. I rang the bell. The landlord was an Italian woman living upstairs. When we opened the door, it was like magic.

Regina looked at the expression on my face and said, "This is it. The Damn Vegan Restaurant."

It had a charming picture window, and booths already installed around the perimeter of the room. It was filthy, but it might not need much more than a paint job. There was wood paneling everywhere under all the dust, and it had a fireplace. I knew it was 'the One'.

We wanted to hug each other, but contained ourselves. I whispered to Regina, "First we say no, then we come off it and start negotiating." We came back outside with the owner and didn't say anything. We just looked into the picture window. "I can rent it to you for $13,400," the owner said.

"No," I said. It was almost the range I had been looking in.

"What were you looking for?" the owner said.

"It's too expensive for what it is. Make it $12,300 and you've got a deal."

The owner smiled. "OK, but as is." We shook on it.

I hugged Regina at the entrance to the subway. "Thanks for helping me, man. I was so lonely 'til you got here. Don't go."

"I'll be around. I love you, Jerry." That was it. They were leaving for the West Coast that afternoon. "You take care, now, and get our restaurant going. It's gonna need a paint job."

"Thanks, Regina." The words got stuck in my throat. I was going to have to carry on from here.

She marched away yelling, "End corporate welfare!" with the protesters.

I cried in the elevator all the way up to the top of the skyscraper. They say it's lonely at the top. *It sure as hell is lonely at the bottom.*

I pulled myself together when I saw Sasha standing in the doorway waiting to hear how it went. "That was great advice, Sasha."

"What? How much did you get it for?"

"She wanted $13,400 and I said $12,300, and she took it! Isn't that great?"

"No, *malaka*, you should have started at $12,000."

"I'll do that next time, but now listen to a song. This is a song to make you happy." I put it on.

"'No Woman, No Cry!'" He looked happy when he said it. Then he started walking toward the door after me.

"Where are you going?" he asked.

"To see your friend at the Greater New York Savings Bank about a loan. I'll bring back some sandwiches. What do you want?" I asked.

"Here." He pulled a roll of bills out of his pocket and sliced off a thin $100 with 'No Woman No Cry playing'.

Sasha held out the $100 in front of me.

I reached for the bill.

He held onto it. Our fingers almost touched. I laughed and sang, "I remember, when we used to trade . . . at GAB on Wall Street."

His eyes seemed to say, Yes. The $100 bill was taut and threatening to rip.

"Those were the days," I said.

He held the $100 bill tight. He looked down at me. I almost fell over when he let go.

Sasha had a friend in business loans at a neighboring bank. The guy made it sound easy to get a business loan, but in the afternoon, he came back sounding skeptical and hopeless. "I don't know, Jerry. You might have to take a higher interest rate."

I sent him a stack of paperwork, but he wanted more. I felt a wave of panic. Maybe I could schmooze Sasha's friend. We had already agreed to go out next Tuesday, with Sasha, too. So at least I had a date with two guys.

But Sasha cancelled our drink with his friend the business loan broker. "Don't miss it because of me, Jerry. You should go alone," he said, as if it was nothing but a plot to find out how much money I had. Sasha didn't look up from his computer screen.

"Not if you're not going." *Jerk.* "He said he'd know about the business loan by the end of next week." That was a long time away. In the meantime, I started calling other business loan brokers and found one who worked with seventy banks.

"I'll do whatever I can, Jerry," he said.

At eleven, I caught Sasha at the water cooler and installed him at the desk to baby-sit the telephones. I took the meat elevator down to the ground and trotted across the street to loan broker number two. We chatted and found out that we had both been living in Boston at the same time. He was a soft-spoken Indian man, who didn't seem to let the stress of the office get to him. He looked much younger than he turned out to be . . .

My hands shook as I filled out the loan application. "One more thing." I asked him if I could apply for two business loans simultaneously 'with discretion'. He laughed and went off to make photocopies. I exhaled and slouched into the easy chair. We ran through some calculations. I wanted an adjustable rate loan because it was cheaper in the long run and with the economy in tatters, interest rates looked like they'd be pegged to the floor for years to come. It was such a good deal, and we were both happy when he gave me the checks.

"Shall we celebrate?" he asked. He suggested a bar in Battery Park.

"Thanks, but I'm engaged." Hell, he already knew my phone number and so much more. I had to get out of there!

On the way back to work, I grabbed an overpriced tourist sandwich and commuted back up the elevator to the trading room. I left an order in to kick out some more 30-year puts and ate my twenty-dollar sandwich.

"Jerry, phone." Sasha said.

I came to an agreement on the price of a storage room full of kitchen equipment. The seller was asking $12,000. I said, "It looked pretty shoddy. I don't think I can pay more than $4,000." At first the seller said he couldn't come off $12K. Then he said he couldn't come off *much*.

I told him, "See what you can do." That afternoon, I got a call from the seller's ex-wife. They were also trying to sell nineteen tables and seventy-eight chairs. "I'm willing to make a deal on the whole lot," I told the ex-wife, "but your ex-husband seems inflexible."

"You're telling *me* that my ex-husband is inflexible?"

I laughed. The woman laughed. I was on the speakerphone, and everyone in prop trading laughed.

"I'll give him a call," the wife said.

"Jerry. There is a man on the phone for you," Sasha said.

Ivan on the line saying he was worried about me.

I held the phone away from my ear.

Sasha smiled.

The seller called and said, "I can come down to $5,500."

"I'll pick it all up in two weeks," I said. "That's *with* the chairs."

"Not with the chairs. OK, with the chairs."

I was thrilled. The kitchen and dining room were mine!

I didn't have time to go see it, but she sent pictures. The chairs were superb oak with an odd design that was modern enough. Then I got an email from the seller saying, "I can come down to $6,000."

"Oh. Nice trick. Oh well. You want it. Take it." Furniture trades at $6,000.

From that moment on, I was full of energy, commuting up to the top of the skyscraper every day, settling into my projects and routine. My life was full of purpose. I was learning to predict the markets, to predict life as a market. I picked my way through Zuccotti Park with a little more confidence and stayed at the restaurant all evening cleaning. I came back early the next morning to take away the garbage.

The landlord had left me several large cans of white paint to touch up with. I decided, before I opened a single box, that I would paint the restaurant. Make the walls mine. I would get my restaurant stroke by stroke. I had a few tools. I spread the tarp out on the dining room floor and opened the paint. There was some clear stuff on top that I mixed in with the brush. I dabbed at the smudge marks on the wall, and little by little made the wall new. I painted my way into the kitchen where the refrigerator had been, and over the gray streaks there. More and more these looked like my new walls in the restaurant that would be mine. I was possessing it. When it was time for work, I washed out the paintbrush and got back into my supertrader costume.

It was actually a relief to be back on the trading floor with its smell of photocopies and coffee, rows of computer screens quietly blipping, and Sasha's back turned toward me. But I needed to be at the restaurant every day to finish the paint job. If only I could be in two places at the same time. "Bye, Jerry," Sasha said as I tried to tip out the door.

I skipped off to my new restaurant. It was everything I'd ever hoped for. I put on the superpainter costume. The white paint ran through my fingers. Maintenance. *Manu tenere*, to hold in the hand. The white paint ran through my fingers and swirled in the sink. Now it was my place.

I could feel my brain cells rearranging to fit into this new architecture. New boundaries, new possibilities, new rules, new freedom, new skeleton. There was the law and order of the exposed brick wall, which possessed me. I hoped we would stay here together for a long time and become comfortable to the bone. I imagined doing the same things over and over in my place and fell into a deep sleep.

I woke up stiff on the floor of the restaurant. The sun streamed in through the dusty window. I scraped myself up and defied gravity, going next door to the dirty magazine shop to buy an alcohol-free beer. There's something about waking up on the ground. I was alive. Above ground, I struggled to delight in things that couldn't be bought or sold. I started with myself. I knew my value. I had to face the fact that my life was not worth much to anyone but me. I was thankful for my life. It was enough, the greatest gift anyone could give. Thank you Mother, even though you will never know what a wonderful thing you did.

CHAPTER 45
KING SASHA

*E*ven with stilettos biting my feet, I normally avoid walking across the Privately-Owned-Public-Space created in 1968 that was now the site of the Occupy Wall Street protest camp. I don't know what made me tip into Zuccotti Park that day. Maybe I identified with the protesters being corralled. I'd had enough of trying to be uncool. No more being led by terror. That's how we let them steal the economy. I had to face my fears.

We had just had a snowstorm. You could feel the anxiety as protestors charged their batteries using stationary bicycles to power heaters and computers. Police escorted prisoners released from Rikers Island who had no place to go, to the park to disrupt the protest. Demonstrators were arranging for drug counselors and social workers to offer their services to the homeless, rather than marginalize these people like the rest of American society did.

A bunch of rubbernecks gawked at me hobbling by in my faux mink coat. A girl my age wearing a mail-order pantsuit was holding a sign that said, *We are the 99%*. Her eyes held mine as if to address the growing income inequality between the wealthy and the rest of the population. I glanced sidelong at the pup tents and the dirty activists who had been out there for months occupying the plaza. I wasn't about to feel bad about my one percent. It the 0.01%-ers who had stolen the real money.

The police strategy was to eclipse the issues by pitting the enemy against itself. 'Divide and conquer' — this predictable, old-world maneuver was the best the police could do since Occupy Wall Street was democratic and there was no central authority to terrorize. They would keep on emerging everywhere. But I could feel the police stratagem working as I walked across the divide.

On the west side of the park were the have-nots, with poor nutrition, dental problems and fashion crimes. On the east side were the haves, the white middle class, burning to speak for the other side but hopelessly alienating the underclass by using terms like 'slavery' as a metaphor.

One banner read, "Don't use Black suffering as propaganda for White self-interest."

The 'haves' and the 'have-nots' were in perpetual conflict, despite the leveling power of the Internet, our black President, and the tech boom. No amount of drumbeats and public urination on the part of the 'haves' could alleviate the suspicion of the underclass, since the 'haves' risked stepping into power if the movement succeeded. You couldn't say much about all of them except that they all stunk.

The crowd started to come together in a primal knot. A philosopher, Savoj Zizek, was motivating the protestors. Now the hypnotic human microphone brought fugitives and students of all colors together like church. I stopped and listened to the communal voice. "They tell you we are dreamers," the philosopher said. I could barely hear him from where I was standing.

Then the echo came, loud and clear from just in front of me: "They tell you we are dreamers."

Behind me, "They tell you we are dreamers."

You're not the only one. I had found something that would hug me back. The masses.

"The true dreamers are those who think . . . "

"The true dreamers are those who think . . . "

" . . . things can go on the way they are."

I chanted with the congregation in a single proletarian mantra. *It's in your blood.* Saphora loved Mom.

" . . . things can go on the way they are . . . we are not destroying anything . . . we are only witnessing how the system is destroying itself . . . the cartoon reaches a precipice . . . but it goes on walking . . . ignoring the fact that there is nothing beneath . . . only when it looks down . . . it falls down . . . this is what we are doing here . . . We are telling the guys there on Wall Street . . . 'Hey, look down!' "

"Hey, look down," everyone yelled.

We all laughed as if at our own joke. Some people

cheered and belted out jungle trills. The crowd fought back. The power of the movement swept me up. A man in dreadlocks gave me an approving nod. I must have been funny occupying Wall Street in a mink coat.

A tall man with a beard softened his glare when he saw me — the man who had booed me when I was going into the bank!

His eyes met mine as we chanted. "After outsourcing work and torture . . . marriage agencies are outsourcing even our love life . . . "

We were both swept up in the human microphone, repeating things before we had time to think about them. There was nothing that I didn't agree with, though, ". . . you can have sex with animals . . . ," or almost. We both laughed. "What kind of social organization can replace capitalism? . . . what type of new leaders do we want?"

I was late, but I didn't care. A general assembly meeting followed, a smart, clean, and well-ordered affair with a sophisticated process called stacking where those who wished to speak got in line. It was a progressive stack, prioritizing traditionally marginalized groups to speak before white men. Next to the beard, I felt my feet stable on the ground, a good feeling after so much flaunting it up in the skyscraper. He nudged me forward. I jumped to the side and hid behind him. I felt connected to the people as we got caught up in something bigger than ourselves.

The last speaker got us all chanting, "Shame! Shame! Shame!"

I peeled myself away from my beard and the human microphone and made my way back to the pie-in-the-sky-scraper. I traveled up the elevators to another planet. What was I doing here? My colleagues were living in the past.

All heads turned as I stepped onto the trading floor, except Sasha's.

It was impossible to tell who was phonier, Sasha or the boys. By now I'd learned Sasha's strategies with women. If he liked a woman, he would say, "Should I call her, or wait until she calls me?" He was indecisive.

And I would say, "Is she hot?"

"Yes. Very hot. I know I'll lose anyway."

I would say, "Then there's nothing to lose. Call her."

He wouldn't call her, just like he wouldn't call me, and it would go on until hell froze over.

The bank was having its Christmas party that Friday. I was counting on finally seeing Sasha out and about, but he didn't show up. The bankers had thrown money on the floor of the Greek restaurant. They wouldn't let me pick it up. I danced until three in the morning and ended up sitting on some guy's lap until they poured me into a cab. Friday, Saturday, Sunday, no call from anyone.

I didn't want to be stuck again putting in more than I was getting back, but I broke down and called Sasha on Sunday night to tell him how the bank party went, just on the chance that I caught him at home. There was no answer. I left a message on his machine. "*Hella*, Sasha," I said in a longing voice. "It's Jerry. You can call me if you feel like talking." I knew he wouldn't call.

Monday morning, after a quiet weekend, I was in my chair when Sasha strolled in late as usual. "Good morning! Good morning, Jerry! You know what? I went away for the weekend, and when I got back, there were seventeen messages on my machine saying, 'Who is that girl, Jerry?

Jerry is so fun to be with, and so nice. Where have you been HIDING HER?'"

I cringed.

Richard looked at me in amazement. "Really?" He said. "I wish I had stayed at the Christmas party longer."

Sasha waited for Richard to go back to his office. "And then, in the middle of all those messages was your message, ' . . . call me.' Jerry, you must have E.S.P."

"Sasha, SHUT UP," I whispered.

He stopped.

Richard stuck his head out, "I'm wrapping presents, so don't bother me."

"OK!" we said in unison.

Sasha shut Richard's office door. "You were dancing with Harry."

"The guy at the 50th Street branch?"

"Tall, kind of balding?"

"Yes."

"I'm calling him up." Sasha had him on the phone. "You were dancing with Jerry. Don't you know her? She works here. Yes . . . with me."

I pretended to read my statistics book.

He hung up. "Jerry. Jerry! He said, 'The one with the beautiful face?' He thought you came with someone who worked at the bank. He's a nice guy. Why don't you go out with him?"

I glared at him. "I only go out with jerks."

The mailman brought Sasha a FedEx envelope. "My tickets." Sasha said.

I put out my hand as if they were my due. "Show me." Two round-trip tickets to Athens for him and his daughter.

I had agreed to take my vacation later so he could have his Christmas in Athens.

"I'm looking for an apartment there. I'm looking for a job there."

Too late. I wished I could go, too.

He grabbed the tickets away from me. "Now you have one of my secrets. Keep it."

"No problem," I said like it was nothing.

"I have family there. There's nothing for me here now that I'm divorced. I'm dying here."

That's the thing. If some *malaka* from Greece for God's sake comes all the way to New York to have a family, it makes me so depressed I want to cry. I put all my sarcasm aside. The sincerity stung in my throat: "Oh well, I guess you have to go back."

"I want to go to California to check it out and talk to a family lawyer before my ex-wife moves to there with my daughter. Do you want to come with me to California?" He was such a flirt. He always asked questions like that, and I never responded.

He was picking the envelopes up off of the coffee table when the chorus carried me. I said, "Yes," *stupid*.

He looked up from the mail in disbelief. He was stunned. "You would go with me?"

"Yes."

My cynicism was useless now. The tragedy was imminent. He stood up. He went to his chair and sat down at his laptop and didn't look at me but seemed to address his computer instead. "Would you really go with me to California?" Then, shyly he turned to me.

I smiled and nodded my head, Yes.

He began typing. He said, "Your message sounded very sexy."

I jumped.

"You have a nice telephone voice," he said in his deep tone.

Strange coming from Sasha at work. "Thanks." I pretended to study. I looked at him out of the corner of my eye. He was sitting across from me in his swivel chair, eyes wide, seeing me for the first time. I think he was in shock. He didn't bring up California again. I wouldn't have done it anyway. The weird thing is, I meant it when I said it. Is that schizo or what?

That's when Richard came out of his office. "I wish I'd stayed. I didn't realize Jerry was a party animal."

Sasha and I looked at each other. Sasha sat up. "No one said 'party animal'," he covered. He moved his laptop to the typing table between Richard's chair and mine. I could feel him there. He felt good. We waited.

Richard said he thought it was a bit cramped, and went back to his office.

I couldn't remember giving my telephone number to my neighbor, Manfred, but here he was calling me at work and chewing my ear off. Sasha sat at my side in opposition as I talked on the phone to Manfred. I said, "Why don't you ask someone else out?"

Sasha got up and paced the aisle while I talked on the phone. "Please!" He came back, said, "Enough of this guy."

Ooo. Jealous. I had to hear what Sasha was going to say next. "Manfred, I'm in the middle of something. I gotta go." I hung up.

". . .To be honest with you," Sasha was saying, "when you called me, I was so surprised. I was shocked. They say if you try to get something, you won't, but when you stop looking for it, it comes. I do have feelings for you."

"Listen, Sasha, I—" *love you* "don't care if we are friends or—"

"Lovers?"

"Yes." Desire bucked me like a wild horse. "I don't want you to be torn apart about me. It's whatever you want. I just want you to be happy about me."

"Let's talk upstairs." Sasha and I went up to the observation deck to sneak a cigarette in the snow. The roof was the size of a city block with a gigantic satellite dish on top. We looked down at the building tops sprawled in the cold morning sunshine with the blue cloak of the Hudson Bay behind it. I could see his breath. "This is heaven," I said.

"It is," he said. He was holding the door open. Suddenly, he imitated a lunatic and went back inside without me. "What I will do to you, my goose!" Before I could follow him, he'd shut the door on me: there I was, locked out in heaven alone. I was sure that the door would open again. He opened the door and melted when he saw that I wasn't worried. I saw his face soften, a reflection of passion. It was fine with him in control. I had nothing to lose. King Sasha did laugh, a loud and hearty laugh. He looked down at me, and saw how much I trusted him.

"Come inside," he said. "You have to study."

I stamped the snow off my feet. "I study much better when I know where you are." Sasha led me deeper into the stairwell and pressed me against the wall. He lifted my butt up to rest on the banister and taught me what an uncircumcised Doric column could do.

Whenever we were virtually alone, Sasha came and messed up my hair and held my hands on the yellow couch. He massaged my shoulders and scratched my neck. But whenever we were really alone, 'King Sasha' was afraid.

A colleague from Corporate Lending came up. "Jerry!" He shook my shoulders. "You were so delightful at the Christmas party. I said, 'Who is that beautiful girl?' I didn't realize it was you until two hours later. Really. I was thinking, 'Is that a professional girl?' You were so happy dancing, and you dance so well."

Sasha shot me a gentlemanly, not-a-party-animal look.

Another colleague was having a party on Friday. The invitation lay on the table. "I guess you don't want to go to this?" I asked Sasha.

"I might," he said, and I knew he wouldn't.

I was off to take my first exam.

"I'll call you at nine," Sasha said.

CHAPTER 46

OMAR THE COOK

*H*anukkah came and went with the fanfare of a missing person. I kept my eyes on Jerry's diary and followed her after work to make sure she was well surrounded. People get depressed around the holidays.

Jerry's frantic search for a professional chef through the channels of the Harvard Club yielded one who seemed honest as well as talented. Jerry invited the chef, who had worked for a vegan restaurant, for lunch at one of her future competitors. Omar Lequeue slid into his chair and started berating the menu. She liked him immediately, which I found irritating.

I can just imagine the conversation. "No, no, no!" Omar must have said closing the menu. "You have to bring a tradition of rich, heady flavors to a refined table of seasonal vegan favorites."

"I hope we can find something to eat here," Jerry probably said. So much for my fantasies about taking Jerry out for dinner. I didn't realize she was a vegan, whatever that is.

"It's OK, I'll just have the simplest pasta," Omar would have said, twisting his moustache between his fingers. This guy must have been full of himself. "The way I see it, the dinner crowd will want to start with the lighter raw fare and drinks, including non-alcoholic beer and wine." Raw fare? What the hell is that? "Next on the menu, a variety of marinated vegetables and variations like pear salad or baby asparagus in tangy white and red gazpacho sauces. Then, main courses like cilantro lime tofu. The repast ends with a trio of gelatos. This will appeal to both vegetarians and connoisseurs."

At least Jerry thought it sounded perfect. "The way it stands now, you have to be a fanatic on Wall Street to avoid instant meals, junk food, and processed foods. Now people will be able to choose healthy things." She was so excited about the restaurant, she practically ran all the way back to work.

I asked her if she had read the books I'd given her.

She said, "Yes," and socked it to me with a deflective question: "Do we use Fas 52 to account for our options under hedge accounting?"

I drew a blank. "I have no idea. We have a whole department for that." I looked her in the eye. "Jerry, I like what you're doing. I'm giving you a raise."

"Yesss," she said. I could see that hit the spot. Jerry

threw her arms around my neck and almost kissed me. "Wow, Richard, I don't know what to say." I believe she was truly happy then, not just about the extra money. I expected her to come to work in a new suit or something, but she wasn't going to spend it. She was going to invest it in her real thing.

"Just keep up the good work." I reached up to my bookshelf and pulled down an art book on Japanese candlesticks. I handed it to her. It was a nice book. "Japanese candlesticks are a kind of graph. They show you supply and demand, as well as the direction of the market. All the information is in the candlestick patterns. If the unemployment number is a disappointment, if there's inflation, a sale at Macy's, or if you got indigestion after lunch. The Japanese invented technical analysis of market prices to analyze rice trading in the 1500s. Vegans eat rice, don't they? Be careful with this. It's my only copy. It was a present," I told her.

"Gee, thanks." She opened the red, kanji-covered book gingerly, pretending that she was into the goddamn job and wanted to be like me someday. I imagined she even felt guilty when she wrangled with me to get off at noon.

At three o'clock, the movers called to say they were in Manhattan with the moving truck. "I gotta go," she told Sasha.

"OK, I'll say you have a dentist appointment," Sasha said.

Sasha would get punished for that.

The taxi dropped Jerry off at the dock so she could get her furniture from the warehouse. A security guard opened the storage room door and the smell of mold assaulted her nostrils. The furniture was rotten. It was completely ruined. There was no way to clean it up. She had paid $6000 for a heap of trash. She sat on the dock and cried.

CHAPTER 47
TORTURE CHAMBER

*T*he weekend was beautiful. I strolled through the crisp mornings wearing a skirt that looked more like a belt. I tried not to think about the furniture or the fact that I was paying rent on a place that wasn't generating any income. Or my transgressions with Sasha at work.

I didn't want to be alone. I hadn't seen anyone, although eleven people had called. It mattered how many people called when you were alone. I counted them, but didn't feel any better. Life was a market, but more wasn't enough. Why was I lonesome? There was a message from Wolf on my answering machine to greet me when I got home. "Let's get together."

I opened a can of lentil soup and ate it trying to figure out which way to go. My first thought as I dunked a cracker in was, In another life, I would have been interested in a relationship with Wolf from back home. But now I'm busy with machines. I can only afford transient relationships with people who don't know me.

A bird flew from the sky to my bird feeder. He looked at me and said, "Beup, beup." At least I wasn't stuck saying *that* all the time.

My iPhone flashed. I knew the boom-and-bust churning of the machine was intended, even though newspapers insisted that the economic crisis was the result of an unlikely mix of high-risk financial products, undisclosed conflicts of interest, and the failure of regulators to rein in the excesses of Wall Street. I could feel the whole corrupt edifice crumbling beneath my feet. One day I wouldn't be able to rely on the bank's virtual money anymore.

I did my laundry at the Suds Café across the street where I could drink coffee, and watch the news during the spin cycle. The market was scary. There was no safe haven. Credit rating agencies failed to accurately price the risk involved with mortgage-related financial products. No matter, investors praised the emperor's new clothes and validated those prices with every losing trade. I started to worry that it had been four months since I'd had an AIDS test.

There was a message on my answering machine: Regina. "We started working in I.N.K.'s girlfriend's florist's and got into a fight. I'm on my way back to New York."

Regina was coming back! I was waiting for her to arrive again. We would tear up the town. That was the great thing about living in a Mecca. Friends were always going and coming. I washed my clothes and maintained my life as I waited for my girlfriend. Between cycles, I went back upstairs and added a red streak to my Ash Blonde #6A hair. I got my laundry and discovered that someone had stolen my favorite jeans.

The news had me worried about my job again, and that made me worry about my brother. I wished Saphora was still in touch with him. I called Raif but he wanted to argue.

"No," I said into the telephone, "It isn't safe to see each other. Someone could be following me. Anyway, I can't come to New York right now. It's too far away." There I was, lying into the mirror with one of my mother's expressions on my face. Some things could not be told until they were forgotten. Like how beautiful my mother was. Sitting at the kitchen table. Dancing with me. Demonstrating in that photo from 1969. They still came up. And I pushed them back down. I had a lot to drink about.

Regina was very late. My journalist friend, Manfred, called me for the second time. "Where's your friend?" Manfred was turning out to be a Hispanophile.

"She's late, I guess." I looked out the window at the tire marks in the slush. "There's a taxi."

"Of course there's a taxi. It's New York. That's like looking out at a harbor and saying there's a boat."

The taxi door didn't open. "Wait there's another taxi behind this one."

"Don't do this to yourself, Jerry."

"No, really. There's another one."

"It's all going to end in tears," Manfred said.

The buzzer rang. "I'll call you back!" Regina looked

glamorous with her long, dark hair framing her smooth face. She staggered up my four flights with her wardrobe in a huge suitcase on her back. "Hi." I threw my arms around her and didn't ask for any explanations, just carried her suitcase up the stairs.

"It's great to be back," Regina said as she looked around.

"Look what I've got." I popped the cork off a bottle of champagne and poured Regina a glass. Regina said she wanted to meet Manfred. I called him back, and we agreed we would meet at a bar later on.

"Here's a present," Regina said. It was a wrap-around skirt that opened wide on the side. "It's not even a slit!" I said.

Walking down Seventh Avenue over the subway grating, the wrap-around skirt blew wide open, and I was wishing I hadn't worn such plain underwear. As I tried to pull my skirt back together, I walked right past the bar and Manfred standing outside without noticing him. Regina and I wandered around the crowded bar and finally found him sitting in the window watching the show: "Jerry!" he said. "Was that you?! I saw your skirt flying up to the sky, but it covered your face.

I held my skirt closed and introduced Regina. Manfred looked overjoyed to meet her and suggested we go directly to The Path Café. Regina and I were relieved to cede control to a man, and marched off toward Greenwich Street where we found the crowded hole in the wall. There was every variety of funk at Le Zoo, and Regina and I made no attempt to hide our surprise as we watched the weirdoes saunter by. Our waiter brought a bird's nest of fried noodles with vegetables inside, followed by an exquisite fish entrée, which I couldn't eat, with sparkling wine, after which he came to our table with a towel neatly folded over his arm and chatted with Manfred about the photos of movie stars on the walls. Manfred finally got the waiter to agree to break the rules and allow him to smoke at the table. The waiter scraped the crumbs off of the pink tablecloth with a silver knife and placed a tiny ashtray in the center.

Manfred was fully aware that he had scored some points already with his restaurant pick and started pulling a bunch of shreds of paper out of his pocket. "What would you girls like to do tonight?" His hands shook as he smoked. "You have three choices. Here's Dial-a-drug. That's a service you call up, and they come 'round in a car. You get in the car and pay for your drugs. Or there's a night of simple debauchery."

"What about number three?" I asked.

"The latter was number two and three," he said.

"Fine," Regina said.

We wandered out of the Village, I'm not exactly sure where. The streets can be tricky around there. We went to buy some beer and walked along the warehouses of Greenwich Street in the dark until we came to a staircase going down. There was no sign, nothing. Obviously, Manfred had been here a number of times. A bald muscleman stood there with his arms crossed in front. "You have to bring your own beer, and it's thirty bucks to get in." It smelled like the undead. Manfred paid. Me and Regina breezed past a myriad of men and entered the musty club. There were two large rooms with bars, and a maze of small chambers for love and torture. Maybe I would run into Sasha in here.

"What's that sound?" Regina asked me. "I think it's over here," she said and disappeared around a dark corner. I followed reluctantly, not wanting to be left alone, always averting my eyes. I didn't see Richard appear around the corner until he bumped into me.

"Richard!"

"Jerry!"

"What are you doing *here?*"

"What am I doing here?" His best-practice smile froze on his lips. "Yes, well, uh, that's exactly what I wanted to know."

I almost peed.

"What are we doing here?" He said and faded back into his dark corner trying to look like just another pervert, only in a J. Press blazer and old-money tie.

I did an about-face and bolted with Regina through the dungeon to a piece of wood with stools around it.

"This must be the bar," Regina said. She opened our bag of beers.

A young man came and sat on the next barstool like a gargoyle perched on a ledge. He pointed his Jewish nose at me and smiled as if to say, *I'm here,* with his chin sticking out. "My name is . . ." *Angel.* Then Manfred was there talking to him, and then Angel drew me into his monologue. He was a painter.

Manfred offered Angel a beer.

"Where are you from?" he asked. All I could see was Angel's teeth beaming at me. I sneered and looked away. There must be a way to avoid this oncoming double date.

"Come on," the angel said. "Negativity is a waste of time. Sing it out. Me and the rest of the world want to hear the irresistible truth."

I opened another bottle of beer and guzzled half of it.

Manfred stood up. "Regina and I are going to take a walk."

Angel filled the void at the bar. He said things *I* could have said. "My paintings usually don't go the way I planned. I'm sure I'm not the source of my actions when I paint. The ancients didn't consider artists to be the authors of their works. An artist recognizes beauty in accidents. You have to ask yourself, to what extent am I the source of my actions? It might not even be *me* doing the painting. When an accident happens on your canvas, and it looks nice, you think you are doing a good job, and the temptation is to continue painting *that* part of the canvas. It takes a lot of discipline not to mess it up! You have to recognize that it's beautiful and *leave it alone*. Don't paint over it!"

Angel's words evaporated as soon as he said them, but I knew he was free and had said something healing. He asked questions and kept me company. I heard myself relating my hometown tale of torture from the bottom of my consciousness. Even though I was done with trying for another relationship. I studied him writing something down, perched on his barstool like a gargoyle? or like a guardian angel? I hiccupped. "Angel, will you stand behind me and put your fingers in my ears? That's the best c-cure for the hiccups."

We stood up. He put his fingers in my ears, and I held my breath. The hiccups went away, but Angel's fingers in my ears had attracted a crowd of perverts. The perverts stood around us in a circle. They watched for a while longer and then dispersed. I saw Regina and Manfred in a corner making out. They came up for air and faced another group of perverts that had crowded around to observe their innocence. I thought I recognized my plain clothes cop friend, but Regina skirted me away before I could be sure.

"Come see this," she said. She pulled me away from Angel and led me to a naked woman, her arms spread-eagled, wrists tied. A man was whipping her with a miniature whip no more than three inches long, and she was squealing with delight, saying, "Oh. Ohhh."

"Excuse me," a man said into my ear. "You're blocking my view." A whole crowd had gathered behind me to watch this spectacle. I moved over one centimeter and continued watching just to annoy the man behind me until it occurred to me that the naked woman's mockery wasn't working on me. I went back to the 'bar'.

"See anything you liked?" the Angel asked me.

"No."

"This stuff doesn't do much for me, either."

"I have enough pain."

"I know how that is." He hung his head, no doubt thinking about something in his own past. "How long ago did it happen?" He asked.

"It was the year after I graduated from Harvard, 2002."

"Almost a decade ago."

"Yes." I lit another cigarette and slugged my beer.

He stared at me. "What happened?"

CHAPTER 48

DELICADOS

i had spent the summer after Harvard in Mexico with Regina and Raif. Our bright futures rolled out before us, we tramped off to an artist colony in San Miguel de Allende. The bus ride was long, and the Mexican bus driver wouldn't even stop to let us go to the bathroom. People were peeing into Coke cans and throwing them out the window. We got to our town, rented a villa and settled in. One day, Regina and I were sitting in the square trying to quit smoking, and this white guy with no hair crossed the square smoking a cigarette.

"Hey you!" I said.

"Shut up," Regina said.

"Hey!"

The guy turned around and walked over to us. "Got a cigarette?" I asked.

"Yeah. Here's two *Delicados*. These are better than Camels, and they only cost twenty cents a pack."

I looked at the oval cigarettes. That's how we met this painter. Raif was furious losing Regina to the painter. He did everything to get her back and catered to her every whim. They lay in the bathtub looking at each other together for a day, but she still wanted the painter.

We decided we had exposed my little brother to too much and had to get on a health kick. We found an old Mexican gym that looked like a torture chamber. Raif followed Regina and me to the medieval gym. The equipment there was so old, the barbells were bent from the weights. The stone steps had troughs in them from all the abused feet that had passed there. On the way back we had milkshakes with two eggs in them to build our muscles and ran into the painter again.

The painter inhabited a large apartment with a balcony overlooking a garden fountain. We were all eating dinner at his house. Raif was swearing, and Regina was falling in love with the painter.

"This is cool," Regina said. "Where'd you get this skull?" On the painter's desk was a human skull with a philosopher's red candle stuck to the top of it, and wax streaming down it.

The painter pulled out the drawings he'd done of it. "Do you know how much this skull would cost if you tried to buy it in America?" he said. "Two hundred dollars. I got it for free. The caretakers dig up the bodies and leave them out in the open if families don't pay the rent on graves. I just snuck in at night and took this."

"I must have one," Regina said.

We began to plot a romantic skull theft. We summoned the courage to visit the graveyard at night with the painter leading the way on a skull hunt. We climbed the fence and hunted for bodies. We found two heads. They still had some hair on them.

We brought them back to our villa. "Where's a bucket?" the painter said as if from another dimension. "We have to bleach the hair and skin off these." He dumped the skulls into a bucket, and we all left to go to a bar.

I fell ill and lay in bed for the rest of the vacation. Every night, I was left at home sweating out my fever with two skulls. I got up once on Regina's birthday. She and the painter had bought two piñatas. In a delirium, I watched Raif blindfolded swinging at the colorful bird and horse to repetitive Mexican music. The piñatas burst. Bright bits of candy flew everywhere. I dreamt that the skulls were flying across the room, back and forth, flying skulls and pieces of color. I hate candy.

Weeks passed in the Mexican heat and dust. When I felt well enough to stand up, we made plans to leave the sunlight of San Miguel de Allende. Regina needed a suitcase for the skulls. We went to all the shops, but no one had suitcases. It seemed that the locals had never left the town before. Finally, we found a bridal shop that had everything a bride might need for a simple wedding. On a shelf up by the ceiling was one powder-blue, cardboard suitcase. We bought it for three dollars. Both skulls fit perfectly. Regina decided that when we got to the border, I would have to carry the powder-blue suitcase because I was the most innocent looking. At the border, I marched across the border with Regina's bridal suitcase. Sure enough, on U.S. soil, I turned around to see my two friends being searched.

We brought those skulls back home. I thought that I was bonded to Regina after that. I figured I would never lose my two friends after skull robbing in Mexico together. We had to stick together. That's why I got sick and had so much bad luck afterward. I had felt the power of the skulls.

CHAPTER 49
CORRUPTION FROM WITHIN

So Raif was corrupted by his own sister and her best friend! And it was Regina he had the relationship with, not Saphora. Or maybe Raif was involved with *both* Regina and Saphora! They were all a bad influence. Look where they led me, and I swore off the Vault years ago.

When I saw her looking like Marilyn Monroe with her skirt blown open over that subway grating, I had to follow.

I couldn't sleep and skimmed through Jerry's diary again. It looked like Raif was, indeed, involved with both of Jerry's friends. It began to make sense that Jerry was frequenting places like the Vault.

Where did the mother fit into all of this? It felt like I might have all the pieces, but how did they fit together?

CHAPTER 50
HI, I'M JERRY

*A*ngel peered at me like a gargoyle listening to me saying, "I think I brought a curse down on myself and my family."

Angel laughed. "Nah. It goes back further than that. It's not your fault. You're just paying. These things are ancestral. They go back generations."

I looked around at the dungeon, trying not to breathe in the mold. I dropped my eyes, but they drifted back to a small chamber for love and torture. I heard the unmistakable rhythmic slap of whip on flesh, and found myself among a crowd of people watching a fat, naked, middle-aged man tied ass up. It couldn't be Richard! The man was in nothing but his socks and shoes, being whipped by a blonde in a skimpy maid's outfit. I covered my mouth with my hand. I had to get out of here!

I had lost my courage and was ready to go, but the others did not appear to be ready. Manfred paddled Regina on the butt, and she ran screaming. They disappeared leaving me and Angel with two small whips. Angel picked up a whip and tapped me on the knee. I didn't enjoy it. I tapped him with the other whip. No effect. We put the paraphernalia on the bar.

Regina was nowhere in sight. I turned on my barstool to find a new spectacle, which Angel must have been watching set up behind me. The fifty-year-old man sat there bare-naked except for his socks and shoes. It couldn't be. I looked around for Richard, but he was nowhere in sight. The man's hands were cuffed behind his back, and he was sitting on a milk crate. People walked by without stopping to look at him. A woman adjusted his bonds. There was a string tied around his unimpressive organ. The string went up to the ceiling, around a pulley and held a paper bag on the other end.

I looked again to make sure. Yes, it was Richard, and he was way out of his depth for someone who was usually in control, being forced with a paddle to do something with the paper bag, only he couldn't figure out what he was supposed to do with the paper bag.

Angel smiled, pretending to ignore the installation. "What happened after that?" he asked.

"Uh, after that?" I didn't want to remember after that. I just wanted another beer. Angel opened it for me and let me stare into space, and I remembered that I went back to New Orleans. My brother was living there, and I wanted to be near him and be like a family again. We were still too young to be on our own.

I didn't want to remember turning around to look at mom's eyes full of fear. I had said, "Don't worry," and laughed a little as if it was nothing.

Mom walked out across the front lawn.

The days passed. I took the dogs out for walks. Mom was supposed to come back by now, but she didn't. *No meaning can escape the blackhearted chorus. Surely the millennium approcheth.*

That was the last time I saw her. And then there was no space in the Jewish cemetery, and there was only a Catholic priest available. At the funeral the priest wouldn't shut up. I had asked for a moment of silence. We were all different religions, and no one wanted to listen to a Catholic priest's formula.

The priest broke the moment of silence. "The strain is too much for me," he said.

"No!" I said. I reached out my arm to stop him. "Can't we just have a moment of SILENCE?!"

The priest stepped back. Everyone was silent, language barriers melting, souls coming together. Mom was with us.

Too short. A cup clattered against a saucer, breaking the silence again. Coffee was served. The prayer broke into movement. People stood up and hugged me and held my hands. A friend of Mom's said, "That was the right thing to do."

I remembered my mother every hour of every day. Four years passed. Time was a balm. Sweet forgetfulness. Years later it was only three times a day, and then twice a day.

"That's a lot of beer you're drinking," Angel said.

I stopped staring and looked at him. "There's a part of me that's frozen. The part that wanted to find its calling. Now it just has to survive. Surfaces are enough for me. I don't want to be reminded of how things are supposed to be. I have to fight just to be pleasant and comfortable."

"That'll make you age," Angel said.

"It already has. I'll never be safe, never trust anyone, not even myself. I'll always be on the defensive. I have to have certain things, money, anonymity, a healthy body, people to talk to." I stopped talking.

Angel had stopped listening. He was watching the perverted scene behind me. I turned around again. That couldn't be Richard with his hands cuffed behind his back, wearing only his socks and shoes, looked more helpless than ever. A crowd gathered, and he hardened with the woman's ministrations. The string tightened, and the empty paper bag dangled uselessly from the ceiling.

"And here we are," Angel said.

"How old are you?" I asked him.

"One year younger than your brother," he said with a twinkle in his eyes.

I recoiled and halted him with my hand. "I am not getting involved with any younger men."

"Why not?"

"You always have the upper hand. I end up with a broken heart."

"Why?"

"Because you have more resources. You're younger, physically stronger. You can get more. And then I have to watch you turn all those heads. And all the destruction you do. If I hit back, you run and tell. No more. No way."

"Tell who? I'm not your brother."

"Look, Buddy—"

"Everyone's different."

"Have I learned nothing from experience?"

"Why not be open to a new experience, Buddy?"

"There are no new experiences. Didn't you go to college? We're always in this dungeon."

Manfred and Regina came back. "We're ready to leave," Manfred said.

I turned to Angel. "We're leaving." I stood up and turned to go, exposing him to a cakewalk of perverts. The moment of separation had passed so recklessly that I was surprised when I started to miss him. I came back to his nesting place on the barstool. "Would you like to come?" I couldn't believe I just said that.

"Yes," he said.

It was delicious changing my mind.

CHAPTER 51

HARLEM AFTERNOON

*W*e walked outside as it was starting to get light. I could see Freedom Tower looming over the brownstones of Greenwich Village and panicked for a moment thinking that I should be up in the clouds getting quotes from the brokers. But it was still the weekend, and I was free to slop around in the snowy streets with the perverts and the garbage cans. We went to an all-night convenience store to get some refreshments. Outside in the street again, I looked around for Manfred and Regina. They were up on someone's porch making out.

"Hey, you guys," I said, "Come on!"

At Manfred's apartment, Manfred and Regina snatched the ice cube tray and disappeared into the bedroom. I shut their door and put on a CD. Angel pulled me closer to him on the couch and kissed me. We had been together for six hours, already longer than most of my recent experiments. Angel kissed me. The new man pushed Raif to a cool spot in the back of my head. I could feel the opposition between family attachment and sexual desire. I clung to Angel to abolish my family. *A family mired in the curse of ancestral defilement, a family that must disperse in order to survive.* Tears were streaming down my face. "I'm like a broken piece," I said and passed out in his arms.

He wrote a story in the half-light. It was the first time in a long time I woke up next to a man. We were lying on the floor. I said, "I know there's another bed around here." I found the empty bedroom and climbed up to the loft. Angel followed me. At noon, we woke up again. He kissed me and tugged at my shirt. "This is a neat top. Can I take it off?"

"No."

He laughed and rolled off me. We lay side by side until I couldn't stand being together with a man any longer. I sat up. As I climbed down the ladder, we looked at each other with embarrassed smiles through the rungs. He was lying prone, and I saw his face in the daylight for the first time. It was then that I realized I had been blind. His green-blue eyes stared out from dark curls. His face looked more noble than devilish now. I was surprised to see that his body was long, tan and muscular. "Angel, you are handsome."

"Thank you," he said.

Regina and I met for a conference in the bathroom. "How was he?" I asked.

"Jerry, that man is such a good lover, he makes you want to disappear into his world." Regina was victorious, and wanted to know what was wrong with me. "Go ahead, Jerry. Why not have a little fun? Would you like me to recommend a shrink?" she asked.

"I already tried that."

At Mojo Coffee, Angel mixed juice with his water. Regina always laughed at *me* for doing that. I watched snowflakes melt on the windowpane. Angel said something so beautiful, I was trying not to cry. I was about to memorize it, but it slipped beyond my reach. "What were you doing at the Vault?" I asked.

He took it as a rhetorical question.

How unlikely to have met someone so nice in such an awful place.

We took the metro to North Harlem. Walking to the Cloisters, I told Angel about going to see a channel last year. "The channel talked to a guardian angel, Jeziah. Jeziah said I'd grow out of a lot of the people I was friends with now, like Ivan, and meet more evolved and healthy people. The next day I went to synagogue, but I didn't meet anyone."

"And then you found me."

"Yes." Our feet crunched in the snow as we walked up the hill. "And I started crying when you kissed me. Why did you bother?"

"When you said you were like a broken piece . . . I knew you would do the work to get through it. It's more than wanting to date non-stereotypical Jews. I've decided I want someone who can understand the kind of pain that I went through when I watched my father die. I want someone who knows what loneliness is."

I hugged him.

Through the trees on the hill, we saw a black man in the window of a gnarly Harlem tenement building. "I don't know how people can stand it here," I said. "I have so much more luxury, and I feel like I can't take anymore pain."

"You probably can't take anymore pain," Angel said walking toward the Cloisters abbey, which belonged to the Metropolitan Museum of Arts. "You have this tragic quality." He put his hand on a pillar and turned to me. "The hardest time to be alive must have been the Sixth century B.C., at the end of mythology and the beginning of tragedy. That's what tragedy is, broken myth. It was a break with the past that lasted a hundred years. That's how long it took tragedy to transform society. After that, the city sublimated tragedy. Now we have the city."

"The machine," I said.

"The metropolis."

"The –polis," I said. We turned up a winding path through the woods. "Here it is, the path of life. Are you sure you want to get on it?"

"Yes," he said.

"I don't know. It's risky."

"Come on." Angel took my hand and led me up the path. He pulled me aside and kissed me under the arches and in every medieval room of the Cloisters. I stood before an illuminated book. He put his hands on my waist and kissed my neck from behind. I had never met such an affectionate man. We wandered past the Unicorn Tapestries and out to the abbey's herb garden where we sat on a wall facing each other, knees touching. He pulled me closer. I felt myself falling.

The Cloisters were closing, so we went outside and lay on the hill and made angels in the snow. Angel climbed on top of me and kissed me again.

CHAPTER 52

STAND UP

Another trade blew up while I was deep in Jerry's diary. Let it. I was onto something.

I had to really dig through her stuff to find this. It was buried among her daydreams and sexual escapades. It wasn't an entry in her diary or even a specific email, but rather several fragments that I had to piece together.

Her brother finally talked her into meeting up. She made a big deal about taking the trip to New York and how much the ticket would cost. I hypothesized that this was to throw him off the trail.

They were going to meet on a Sunday at Rockefeller Center. She was in the arcade underground looking out the bay windows when he arrived at the top of the steps where he was supposed to wait for her. He paced up and down on the steps and checked his watch every five minutes.

She just stood there looking at him as if that's all she came for. "He looked like my old self, before I dyed my hair blonde," she said in an email to Regina.

It was a clear day, she wrote. *The flags were flying, and there were lots of people. He kept going away and coming back to foil the police officers who were moving people along to keep the steps clear.* For some reason she got spooked and bolted out of there.

He called her on her 800 number as she was getting out of the subway near her apartment. "I'm sorry," he kept saying.

That just didn't make sense. Why wasn't he mad at her? I would be extremely pissed off if anyone stood me up. Especially my sister. I had to get to the bottom of this.

CHAPTER 53

INCANTATION

*A*ngel had a friend whose restaurant was shutting down. All the furniture had to go. Walking to the restaurant to get the deal done, Angel said, "That was pretty disgusting watching you drink all that beer at the Vault."

"I know, baby. I really must stop drinking. My restaurant will be open in a month. Then I'll have so much work, it'll be easy to stop."

"Why stop when it's easy? Why not stop now, when it's hard?"

The furniture was fine and the price was right. The failed restaurant owner lit a cigarette as we closed the sale.

The next morning Angel walked across my apartment naked. "So now we're on the road," he said. "Let's get on the highway."

Wow!

I asked Regina that night, "Do you think he really meant it?"

"He's a man," she said. "He meant it when he said it. I'm glad for you. There aren't many angels left. Maybe only one or two." She was heading back to Manfred's place.

At our next interlude, Angel said, "You *called* me." He sat down on my living room rug and picked up my laptop.

"What do you mean?" I said, lunging for the laptop.

He held it out of reach and began reading it. "Look here. You wrote this entry that night before the Vault. I don't usually go there. I had just told a friend that it would be a long time before I got involved with anyone. Then I took the train to Manhattan and walked all over the city. I walked up to Central Park, and back down to the Village. You called me. That's why I was there."

"You were scouring the city for me?"

"I was. I noticed you the second you walked in."

He began reading my diary.

"Don't read that!" I said.

He didn't look up. "You just let me go all through your body and I can't read your writing?"

I'd called him. I wrote about him and conjured him up. My diary had accessed another time at the beginnings of art, and he was . . . what? *Had* I crawled back into myself with my incantation like a cavewoman painting animals on cave walls to bring about a successful hunt?

Maybe art could be useful, like a rain dance ending with a clap of thunder. He sat there as perfect as any statue on the other side of the chessboard.

"What kind of painting do you do?" I asked.

"Graffiti art. Political slogans on buildings and overpasses, and sometimes reverse graffiti. Writing on walls by removing dirt."

I looked at his eyes and felt his spirit, and cringed at the thought of him seeing my colleagues.

"What are those green and yellow things hanging up there?" he asked.

"Old dresses." I got up and took the yellow dress down from my makeshift closet that covered one wall of my bedroom. "It's from a play I was in down in New Orleans."

"It's adorable. I love frills. Put it on."

I laughed and went into the other room to put the dress on. I opened the door and appeared in my Southern belle role, tossing my head and rolling my eyes at Angel over my shoulder.

"Jerry! You're marvelous."

I put my foot on his knee. "The *finest* women in the world come from New Orleans."

He hesitated for a moment and then slid his hand under the daffodil hem.

I snatched myself away. "I thought you wanted to play chess!" I said, and moved my knight. Lying on the bed with the chess set between us, my cleavage visible between my pawn and my king, I watched Angel pull his shirt over his head. "Taking your clothes off on my move is cheating."

"These are the new rules." He fumbled with my zipper knocking over my pieces.

"Hey, Angel's can't move that way!"

"Dark Angels can."

The chess set clanged to the floor. His body covered mine like a slow rolling wave that never crashed. He was a good lover, too good. I felt lost. Soulless and out of love, I wrapped my legs around him in agonized passion. I tugged and pulled at his body. There was no tenderness, just the re-enactment of a nightmarish scene, a kind of masturbation rather than love. I couldn't take any pleasure in it. But my untouchableness made me twenty times more desirable to him.

And then he was gone.

The next night, my brother called my anonymous 1-800 number. I ran to the phone to pick it up, then hesitated when I saw it was Raif. "Hello?"

The sound of his voice made me jump. It was strange having him just call me up whenever he wanted to. I tried to control my apprehension and started pacing the floor as he apologized again. I carefully said I had changed my mind about the trip to New York. "I don't think it's a good idea. Someone could be following me."

"You think so?" He sounded alarmed.

I changed the subject and told him how Saphora was doing.

"You sound distracted," Raif said.

I had the September blues. Mom was born and died in September. I worried that Raif would be able to find out where I was with my 800 number. I called the phone company to make sure the block on caller I.D. was turned on.

I was down all day, even though I had a beautiful Angel for a lover. Saturday night, I felt so sorry for Angel telling me that he loved me all the time, I tried to feel if I loved him at least a little, with his statuesque form and dark curls. He seemed lovely enough. I tried to imagine Sasha saying it. What I really felt was that I would fall in love with Angel eventually, and if I didn't, there was something wrong with me.

He led me into his oversized studio in Brooklyn. I followed his jeans as he showed me his paintings. Maybe my heart had hardened. I decided I would *have* to fall in love with him. I wrote a note to him in a book I gave him and ended it with, "I love you." I had to write it because I didn't think I could say it. I handed the book to him.

He traced the cover and then opened the book. His eyes skimmed the page. After he read it, he said he loved me again. By now I *had* to say it. "I love you," I barely whispered.

He knew right away that I was faking it. Such a smart angel. The next night, he was going to come over, but he decided to stay home and work. He called me to say, "Even though I feel passion for you when we're together, I don't sit around daydreaming about you. It's strange. I usually get lost in fantasies about people I'm involved with, especially in the beginning. But with you, I can still focus on what I am doing when I am away from you. At first I was worried about it, but then I decided it was a good thing. I think it's because I'm so comfortable with you. Do you know what I mean?"

"Yes," I said. *You mean you're a nut.*

"So if I don't see you tonight, or tomorrow night . . ." The next day, he extended his absence for two more days. I was in agony all day hoping that the love I felt for whatever object would finally reveal itself for what it was, an essential self-love, the basis of a healthy personality.

The crowd outside the bank made it hard to get in the front door. Once I made it up to the trading room, Sasha was cranky, and the yen moved 100 tics against me. All of last month's profits: wiped out. From cloudsurfer to roadkill in one night. I'd done everything wrong. I looked over my shoulder to check for the CFO. No one but Sasha, almost asleep in his chair. The problem was me. Why must I pine over this man or that? It was transference. What true emotion would I be left with?

My phone rang, probably Raif trying out my 800-number. I answered on the first ring and immediately regretted my eagerness.

"Jerry!" Ivan, saying how much he missed my cooking, which consisted of opening a can. "How do you make your famous tuna fish salad?" He probably just wanted to see if Angel was still there.

I turned on the radio to let him hear some background noise. "Well, do you have the can opened?"

"Yeah."

"You have to boil an egg."

"You do?"

"It takes eight minutes, and while you're at it, you might want to boil a couple more so you'll have them for next time."

"What am I going to do with all these hard boiled eggs?"

"Put them in the refrigerator."

"Will they last long?"

"Yeah, they last a while."

"OK, the water's boiling. Don't I have to poke a hole in these eggs?"

"No! That's how you make a baby."

"But you're supposed to poke a hole in them with a pin to keep them from cracking."

"That's at Easter, when you want to blow out the stuff inside and have a hollow egg." I hung up the phone and turned away from the screen gone red with losses.

Sasha laughed, trying to disrespect me while I lost money, but I fought back.

"Relax," I said. "You're not doing any better."

"No comments from the peanut gallery."

"Oooo." I didn't expect Sasha to come out with his dukes up. I looked at him sidelong and decided he meant it. "You're sadistic," I said.

"Mmm, that's better," Sasha said. "There are places for people like us, Jerry, in fact, right in your neighborhood."

"I know," I said.

"Uh oh." He was being possessive. "Don't let anyone talk you into going to the Vault."

"No comment."

"Ohhhh! Too late!" he cried. He looked at me a little differently from then on and was content to immerse himself in our work.

Angel called on the private line. Sasha rolled his eyes and handed me the phone. He tried to listen as I turned my back to him. "For someone who doesn't think about me when I'm not there, you sure do call me a lot," I said.

Angel was angry for the first time. "You know, you're a pain in my butt. I mean that."

Just what I needed. Some guy from the Vault telling me I was a pain in the butt while I lost money in front of my boss. "I'm in pain."

"See a therapist. That's what worked for me," Angel said.

"Why didn't painting work?"

"In the world, I'm a human being. I'm a god as a painter. I think there's an inherent problem there."

"Yeah, the world." I had to yell above the noise. The prop desk knew that one of my male friends was on the phone. They drummed up an argument over football so I had to hang up. "Keep it down! I can't hear the phone." Myrmidons. They loved to wind me up.

As soon as I hung up, Ivan called.

"Oh! A double!" The boys started cheering supposedly over a game of wastepaper basketball.

"You sound satisfied with your life there," Ivan said on the phone.

"I am satisfied," I said, imagining Angel's perfect physique. My plate was full of everything life had to offer. Angel would make a wonderful father. I wasn't even half listening until I heard Ivan crying.

"I'm not saying I want to get back together, but— "

One of the boys pressed speakerphone.

"I miss you," Ivan said over the loudspeaker. "I miss what we had." He sniffled.

I tried to press the button for a private conversation, but Sasha held my wrists. The receiver fell to the floor.

"I'm dating now," Ivan said, "but it's not the focal

point of my life. I'm in a good position to reassess some things. It's just hard. I wish we could still keep contact and see each other sometimes."

The boys clapped and cheered.

I wrenched my arm free from Sasha, un-pressed the speaker button, and said, "I'm not big enough."

"What do you mean?" Ivan said.

"It would be too frustrating. Look, I just think you could be more ambitious. With what you have, you could be a lot more ambitious."

"In what way?"

"In every way. You could move out of your mother's apartment, for starters."

Sasha started laughing. The prop desk clapped.

"Do you think I can see your new place sometime?" Ivan asked.

"Yes."

He called me back seconds after we hung up. "Thank you for telling me I could be more ambitious."

CHAPTER 54

"MY LAST GIRLFRIEND WAS MARRIED"

*A*ngel cancelled seeing me Sunday, Monday, Tuesday, and Wednesday. He thanked me for giving him his 'space'. It seemed to me that that's what you were supposed to give guys these days. He was painting. He wanted me to leave him a message saying where I was going to be Thursday night.

After my options class on Thursday, I blew Angel off and went out with Pater Familias, *et. al.* Manfred dragged me, Regina and Lonnie to yet another bar, and I didn't get home 'til after midnight. I was walking across Greenwich Avenue alone. As I approached my door and looked up, I noticed there was a dark figure standing on my porch. The hair on the back of my neck rose. I froze and then re-gained control of my legs enough to turn around and run.

"Jerry!"

Angel. I stopped. It was Angel waiting for me on my steps. What do you know? I twirled my keys and caught them. The specks in the sidewalk shone in the porch light. I leaned on the railing and put my head down on my arms. "I was just thinking how nice it would be if you were waiting here for me," I said.

"I've been here for two hours."

"Two hours! Why? You are the sweetest person in the world." I reached up and put my arms around his neck.

"No, I'm not."

"I've been drinking. I smell like beer."

He hugged me. We went upstairs and lay on the couch. "You were scared," I ventured. Or maybe that was my baggage from Ivan? I ran my fingers through his dark curls. "You got cold feet and disappeared all week."

"No. I wasn't scared," he said.

My baggage. I let him listen to a song Ivan and I had written. I jumped into the shower. When I got out, Angel handed me my red velvet dress.

"It doesn't fit anymore."

"Leave it unzipped."

My shoulders were bare in the velvet corset.

He leaned back on the bed. "I guess I am scared," he said.

Not my baggage. "I need you," I said, forcing the issue, and even half believing that I loved him. A blonde lock fell onto his face. We kissed, infinity. Indecision gave way to desire.

"You're devastating. It's like all the bad and awful things about myself are coming out, and I have to annihilate myself. It's such a humiliating thing."

I looked down at Angel.

And then there was his physique, stolen off of a sculpture, tall and beautifully proportioned. I could still see his muscular chest turning. His back tapered into that slight derriere. I scratched his back.

He was aware of my desire and worried that I loved him for his looks.

"You do look fine." I almost let him win at chess.

"Two bishops are worth more than a bishop and a knight," he told me. I changed my move, and he captured my knight.

I changed my mind and took his queen. "Checkmate."

Angel's tongue tangled with mine. He lay on top of me.

I looked at his pure lips and kissed him with the power of a broken atom.

He stopped, surprised, and looked at my lips. "I want to do this slowly." It sounded rehearsed. He hugged me and sank into me. We lay in each other's arms. "The Italians say this little nap is the sweetest part of making love," again, rehearsed.

Cut! I wanted to say. *Take it from the top.*

He drew away. Angel awoke to me looking at him. "You don't sleep much, do you?" He asked.

Life in hiding had a price.

"I want to punch the guy who did that to your mother," he said. But to my relief, instead of pursuing the murderer, he drifted back to sleep. When he woke up again, he said, "I keep getting these strange pictures. I see this alcove. It's an arch, and it's dark in there."

I'd stopped wearing my wedding ring but couldn't erase the memory of the arch in the old house I'd lived in with my husband. *Remember, all the arches we made? Knocking out those three-foot walls in our house in France. Remember the dust all over everything in the kitchen?* I lay silent. *My baggage.*

"There's an appliance in it," Angel said.

"A refrigerator," I said.

"Yes. I think so."

"That's my kitchen in France. We'd tucked the refrigerator into the arch under the staircase." My baggage. Now I was the one falling asleep.

"And there's this brown paper on the walls."

I struggled to keep my eyes open. "Yes. That old wallpaper was in our bedroom, remember? It wasn't really brown. It was just old." Memory was healing. Angel was healing me. Dragging up my wallpaper and other things we'd forgotten from the depths, making us new.

"Yes! And a barn, or a big room."

"The attic. It was unfinished. Do you remember the beams on the ceiling?"

"Yes. It's so strange. I don't know what I am doing in this person's house." His body stiffened. "You're still married, aren't you?"

Illegal question without an answer. I had lied before, even though the truth was so much more interesting.

"You're not married." Angel said, leaning on his elbow, realizing it for the first time.

I opened my eyes. "I haven't seen my husband in four

years."

"Why did you split up?"

"He became a pilot, and we flew apart. I came back to the U.S. and asked him for a divorce. He wanted to stay married, but never wanted to visit. He sends me airline tickets. I flew to Japan and Hawaii, first class. I flew to Los Angeles three times last year, first class. Regina lived there. I needed to see her. My friends are my only family now. Hiking with Regina was like going home. Mount Rainier hovered like a planet just behind the trail. The snow crunched underfoot with the sky full of stars. Just the right setting for a ghost story. My legs hurt for days after that. Life is funny. I never thought I'd be married for airline tickets. I never even wanted to be married at all.

"You *are* married?" Angel didn't try to hide his irritation. "I just ended a relationship with a married woman. I promised myself I wouldn't get into another one. She didn't have free airline tickets, though." He looked at me. "You *are* drawn to tragedy."

"I suppose."

"You're free with your airline tickets, but you are fettered."

"I am. And you? You said you had an affair with a married woman. Was she older?"

"Forty-three."

"Hmm." Everyone had their baggage these days, another year, another suitcase.

Tragic woman and 'other' man fell asleep in the arms of the past. We woke up and walked down Greenwich Avenue, hungry in search of brunch. His blue eyes caught mine from beneath dark curls. Those two blue pools rendered me useless. I slipped my thumb into the belt loop of his jeans.

The next night, he called me around midnight and woke me up. I said, "You were going to come over here tonight."

"Yeah, well I'm staying here. I've been painting, and now I'm exhausted."

"Are you interested in someone else?"

"No. I don't have time. That's funny that you think I'm interested in someone else. I am having a love affair with my paintings." He said he felt like he was with his paintings even when he was with me.

"Fine," I said, having graduated from the Ivan School of Flakery, "I've got work to do, too. I'm not going to be jealous of a painting."

"You should be jealous of my painting. I can't give you everything you need. I feel bad about it."

"Nobody can be everything to another person. Everyone has places only they can go."

"But I don't want that. That's not for me."

"I'm not going to argue with you."

"When I go down into my painting, I disappear, and I don't think about you. I feel ambivalent. I don't think you're the one for me ultimately. When I'm painting, I don't know what I feel."

I knew it! He had been too passionate and over-zealous. I was glad I hadn't trusted him. And to lose a man to ambivalent paintings done with little skill on brick walls. "Maybe we should take a break," I said.

"No. I don't want a break. It's just that when I paint, all the dirt and self-disgust comes out. I'm devastated."

Not my Angel. What about your wings! Not you, too.

"I can't be consistent, and you need consistency," he said.

"Did you feel this way with your last girlfriend?"

"My last girlfriend was married. She would go home to her husband, and I would be free to do my work. I didn't mean to tell you this over the phone. Well, what do you think you need?"

Keeping my needs pared down to the bare minimum as Ivan had trained me to do, I said, "A monogamous relationship."

"I can't guarantee that. We can still be friends, and lovers. But I don't know how long that will last. It won't be a lifelong thing."

"You can know that after three weeks?"

"Yes."

"Why were you so set on jumping into a relationship in the beginning?" I asked.

"It's what I needed to do."

I started to think about what I needed to do. "I don't think I feel like coming to your party tomorrow night."

Silence, then, "I'm surprised. I didn't think this conversation would turn out this way. Do you want to keep seeing each other, or do you just want to break it off."

"The latter."

"OK I guess this is good-bye."

"Bye." Easy come, easy go. It was better to move on.

Pater called right on time. "Hey, Jerry. Where y'at? We're all comin' to Angel's party!"

Ugh, I had invited the whole Southern crew, and now I had to call it off. "OK," Pater said, "Let's go to the Union

Square market."

Sitting over a plate of chocolate éclairs, I said to Pater, "I can't believe I blew off that good-looking guy."

"You don't need any head games," he said.

Regina and Manfred came up with a bag of groceries, and Regina invited me for a girls' night out. We went to an NYU party given by a Turk. Belly dancing, Regina pulled off my clip-on belly button ring and put it in her nose. One minute we were drinking beer in the cab, and the next minute we were in a dyke bar. An old dyke put her hands on my waist. "Hey, that's my girlfriend," Regina said. "I don't think she likes that. You can dance with her, but don't touch." The dyke bartender bought us shots, which I didn't touch. We danced 50's style. There were a lot of fat Hispanic and black women. There was a strip show. There was a lovely woman next to me, who turned out to be the bartender's girlfriend. I asked her "Is there anything in particular you didn't like about men, I mean, from your past relationships?"

"No. In fact all the men I've dated have been wonderful. It's just that the sex is so much better with women."

"The sex? But they don't have dicks."

The bartender laughed.

Regina and I walked home arm-in-arm pondering the peaceful ending to procreation, the human race, thinking how to do it as we wandered through the Village toward home. "Up until the twentieth century, people mostly died in their thirties, a woman's sexual peak," she said. Life was like a praying mantis devouring its mate at the moment of ecstasy.

CHAPTER 55
VEGAN CURE

A dozen of Jerry's friends came for Vegan Cure's grand opening. I mined her diary for news of the fanfare and wished I could have been there, but there was no way. My wife had a detective taking pictures of me with his cell phone on the way home from work.

The restaurant's wood paneling gleamed. The clientele loved the big bathroom and wouldn't come out of it, so Jerry brimming with Southern hospitality, lit candles, turned off the lights and served champagne in there! I felt proud of her for opening the Vegan Cure, and I'm sure she must have felt glorious. From her journal, it sounded like the ambiance was sublime, and Omar came through with the complicated menu.

The next night the restaurant was empty, and the night after that, only two couples came in. Then it was empty again. Jerry resumed worrying about losing her job and her brother.

"You've always got your job," I reassured her.

She had to get a restaurant reviewer in there. She had opened in the heart of an area real estate agents had dubbed 'Power Lunch Alley', in a building that dated back to the 1870s. Her Italian widow landlord, who had been living in an apartment above it since 1930, came down for dinner on the second day. "I remember when this place was a longshoreman's bar, and in the early sixties, it was a Latin night club, the Rumumba." The landlord tasted Omar's olive oil mashed potatoes and agreed to reduce the rent if Jerry would have the landlord's dinner sent up in the freight elevator daily.

The restaurant was expensive to run, and Jerry was operating at a loss. She knew she had to open for lunch or die, but she had to be here at work, too. She invited a journalist. She seated him herself and made sure he got everything he needed to write his review, which he said would be good. Two days later, she cut out the review and hung it in the window, "Gleaming wood paneling and exposed brick walls lend a stately air to the rich space on the Wall Street neighborhood thoroughfare."

A couple from the Hamptons wandered into the restaurant. The cool of the evening crept in after them through the open door, the woman said, "I'll keep my jacket for a few minutes." She made the couple feel welcome. Omar's wife, dressed in a spandex top and frilly skirt, led the clients past the dimly lit piano bar to a spot by the warmth of the fireplace.

Local business people, residents, and newcomers alike found that the Cajun vegan cuisine in a luxurious, relaxing setting made Vegan Cure the ideal place to socialize. She invited more journalists. Another reviewer wrote it up in the newspaper as "a new age enclave with understated velvet banquettes, providing the perfect space to enjoy outstanding healthy cuisine."

Jerry urged Omar to spice up his vegan and raw cuisine with a hint of Creole. A reviewer panned the one-layer lasagna as "heavy and complex". Jerry had Omar cut it from the menu. His peach cobbler was there to stay. The wine list was hand picked by Jerry. She made sure it was varied, with Opus Ones as well as a number of bargain treats, such as Oregon's tasty Benton Lane Pinot Noir, and chilled red *Côtes du Roussillon* from the French Pyrenees. She had people wandering downtown through Battery Park for Cajun vegan jambalaya. On Saturday night there were quick-serve hurricanes and jazz bands played during Sunday brunch. Jerry was always there herself.

CHAPTER 56
NOT PUTTIN' UP WITH IT

i saw First Love in the dwindling crowd outside the bank one freezing cold morning. I felt a surge of embarrassment dressed to the hilt in my suit and black stockings. I tiptoed past a bunch of radicals carrying 'Occupy Homes!' signs.

I stood still for a moment when I reached the entrance. There was Angel's unmistakable graffiti on our front door: *"YOU'RE FIRED!"* I guess I made an enemy, I thought as I dove into the lobby and let the door slam behind me. I tried to rationalize away the shame. The problems on Wall Street were bigger than me. The people chanting outside couldn't possibly realize how enormous the crisis was. They hadn't experienced the sheer size of the market like I had. All the kids in the street knew was that housing prices had tanked.

During the boom, financial innovation had spread like fast food. For the first time, the rest of the world could get in on the U.S. housing market. People forgot that the rest of the world was bigger than America. Foreigners who had borrowed and invested heavily in subprime mortgages suffered serious losses. Now that the big boys had taken their money off the table, we were still measuring the crater that was left in the world economy. News of more home foreclosures flooded the trading room daily. The number of home owners who had borrowed to the hilt seemed endless. The only difference this year was that people were getting angry. Not just foreigners. Even now, in the cold of winter, Americans kept taking to the streets.

Upstairs, deaf traders were laughing. "The Big Board isn't going to cave in because of a bunch of kids with no message."

And scoffing. "It's a huge waste of taxpayer money to pay all these police overtime for two weeks."

There were no jobs for the newly graduated, but there was no arguing with a whole trading floor of men either.

The bank needed a strategy to keep up its image in adverse market conditions. Sasha announced the strategy: we were going to go through the motions of recruiting.

"What's the point of that?"

"To get our name out there. When they do get a job, the newly-minted MBA's that we couldn't afford to hire will at least remember the GAB campaign."

"That's the dumbest idea I've ever heard of."

"Thank you. You have been chosen to write the recruiting speech for the President. I'll help you. It'll be teamwork." Sasha tore himself away from the volatile situation in the street and took turns with me typing and editing. I cringed as I watched the new company video playing like a bonafide TV commercial with fast clips of the activity on the trading floor. The video cut to me on the phone checking the computer screen for a price. I looked convincing. I felt nauseous.

Mort called us down to his office and explained the strategy to us. "Marketing a bank is big business, and there is no more receptive audience than a group of newly minted MBA's looking for job." Mort winked at Sasha. "This brilliant devil has come up with the idea of selling ourselves to these future managers."

"So we're recruiting for our management training program and marketing? I mean, are we really hiring in this economic climate?"

"We're grabbing market share. Never mind that we aren't really hiring."

Those poor kids! I hated myself for snowjobbing graduates. I knew what Saphora would say, and tried to justify myself. "This bullshit would have gone on without me, Saphora. There's nothing I can do about it."

Trading had died down before the end of the fiscal year. I followed Mort's lousy orders and did my small part to grow the bank in the corrupt direction outlined. Thus began the godforsaken Global American Bank marketing tour.

Our MBA recruiting sham was held at the Terrace Restaurant overlooking Central Park. I'd dressed correct, in a red ascot and blue wool, except for the long slit up the back of my skirt. The newly-minted MBA's showed up in their business suits sporting more qualifications than any recruiter could reasonably ask for. I felt awful looking for excuses to rule out the bright-eyed grads.

There were a hundred men and two women. We had to reject one because she had not sent her résumé in advance. "Sorry, this dinner is only for those we had time to screen. Thank you. Goodbye." There went fifty percent of the women with a look of horror on her face. What was I doing there?

"The training program is only for the fittest," Sasha said. He shuffled their business cards and threw them in the garbage can under the reception desk. Then we passed out our business cards, and rewarded the survivors with a cocktail.

I went through the rehearsed introductory conversation with the hopeful MBA's one after the other explaining, "Global American Bank is a worldwide operation concerned with hiring bright, analytical talent such as yourself, people who demonstrate outstanding character and an international perspective." The group around me thickened, until the lights dimmed and everyone took a seat.

I took the microphone. "Welcome ladies and gentlemen to the Global American Bank (GAB) career opportunity night. We are here to show you that young people are powerful, too!" In order to keep them from guessing at Sasha's marketing ploy, I avoided eye contact with the eager MBA's as I recited my tongue twister on the non-existent jobs: "Despite the global trend toward consolidation in the financial sector, we need your help to retain our competitive advantage and build our clientele. That's why the bank is offering more complete one-stop-shopping product packages and structuring capabilities covering the spectrum from origination to distribution." I nodded at Sasha, and he pressed 'Play'.

The video started. Images of the ultramodern trading room flashed across the screen to eyewitness news music. The clips of traders interacting with sales people, making prices, calling brokers and making loads of money impressed the MBA's. I watched myself, larger than life on the silver screen yelling a price at Sasha, who yelled the price into the phone and then said, "Yours at seven!" holding his hands up in the air in triumph.

I sat down among the MBA's, and raised my glass. "To our new candidates," whom the bank wasn't going to hire with money disappearing into black holes in the economy. It was too easy to preach to this innocent chorus, this next generation of bankers, assuming that some of them made it into banking elsewhere. Deep down, I dreaded seeing them in the springtime in Zuccotti Park in front of the bank.

At midnight, we said good-bye to the MBA's and until tomorrow to each other. Our cab flew through the hills of Central Park. "You were excellent tonight," Sasha said. The city lights gleamed through the trees. We rolled down our windows and breathed the night air. The taxi driver watched Sasha caress my thighs in the rearview mirror.

Most days Sasha and I stayed late at work on the momentum of the road show. I was supposed to be starting business school, but missed the first half of my statistics class. I was completely lost for the rest of the lecture. A classmate let me copy his notes. I did my grocery shopping on the way home in the dark, the only exercise I'd gotten all day. I went from store to store looking for Choc full o' Nuts Decaffeinated Coffee, to no avail.

As I turned the corner, I got a strong feeling that someone was there on my doorstep again. I looked at the steps, no Angel. I climbed the stairs. There he was in front of my door. "How did you get in?"

"Magic."

"It was not. Somebody let you in." I put the groceries away, got changed, made us some tea.

"I was disappointed at your letter," he said. "I guess you have a lot of anger."

"I have a lot of anger! What about the door to my bank? You decided you didn't want to get involved with anyone. You wanted to see another older woman, right?"

"No I did not. I'm looking for a real relationship."

"Good, I'm glad."

He still wanted to 'be friends'. "Your being white one week and black the next hurts," I said. "I don't want to join the harem."

"I didn't say I *didn't* want to see you. I still wanted to see. I said I didn't know."

How many women didn't he know about? "You did not. You said you knew I was not 'the One'." Men will say anything.

"That's true," he said. "Well, I feel bad that you are hurt," he said. Not, *I'm sorry I hurt you.*

"I still think you're an Angel," I said.

285

"I am."

"What went wrong? Did you see a limitation in our relationship?"

"For me, yes. You might have a lot more assets than I do. But what I have is this artistic insanity. I need someone who has that same insanity. You probably don't view that as even desirable."

Touché. The last thing I was going to work toward was insanity living in the shadow of a murderer. I had to keep my bearings. What if the murderer came after me? Ivan was mainstream compared to Angel. Angel was a bona fide nut. "I'm sure you can find an even more neurotic Jew in New York who will give you plenty of stories to tell without any of the boring dependency. A really weird Jewess who will make you look normal and open up opportunities for group pity."

I threw myself into my work. The next day, the market moved violently against me, just like in a nightmare, and I stopped trading for the rest of the day. I just watched the graph quietly and daydreamed about Angel.

I grasped for guidance like a cat clawing at a leaf falling from a tree. My horoscope cautioned me not to alienate an important connection in the second half of the month.

CHAPTER 57
'B' AS IN BELL CURVE

My blonde head was in my hands in front of the computer screens. It was the day Richard exposed me to Engelbert for the first time . . . *Ahh ahh ahh aaaii* — He *needs* her love? I lifted my head. "A woman must have written this song," I mumbled.

Sasha and Richard looked at each other.

"No man could ever think this up," I said.

They turned around and stared at me. "I can't believe *you* said that, Jerry," Sasha said. "I didn't expect that coming from *you.*"

"Excuse me," Richard interrupted. "I've been married twenty-two years. I don't think I'm that bad of a guy."

"OK, I'm the idiot. You two have been fair with me, and I have to ruin a beautiful thing by resurrecting the

287

battle of the sexes. It's a beautiful song." I blushed. "I just meant, guys never say that stuff."

"You just haven't met the right one," Sasha said.

"I haven't. And if I did, my reverse sexism would probably scare him off, right?"

Sasha and Richard didn't say anything.

On the way home, my train stopped underground between stations. The passengers all stood there, stuck, trying not to look at each other. A black man's voice came on the loud speaker saying that we were going to have to change tracks. ". . . Ladies and gentlemen, train 'B', that's 'B' as in BELL CURVE is making all 'F' stops up to 7th Avenue."

"You got the mike," someone said. "Say it, brother. You don't have to be a Harvard professor to say what's on your mind. Everybody get on the bell curve." I got out at the closest F stop and ascended into the street. I walked the rest of the way. As I approached my mailbox, I sensed that there might be a letter in it from Angel. Sure enough. A postcard of Wall Street. It said, *You are an interesting woman. I would enjoy a correspondence. Perhaps we could write to each other SOLELY as other selves. Will this encourage schizophrenia? Should one be wary of mental illness? Or should we dabble under the guise of art?*

I folded the card. I didn't believe in mental illness. Anyone looking for mental illness had to be a poser. I hadn't even had time to memorize his phone number and would have had to go find it on a shred of paper in the garbage can. Angel called at that instant in a funk. I didn't feel like talking. He called again and read me the Dial-A-Poem he'd written.

"It was disconcerting watching you check the yen with Wall Street complacency as you got into bed. . ." Everybody had something wrong. But he had failed at detecting my problem.

The quicker I could see through him, the better. Another mutable man, the kind you marry and grow not to know. High turnover was the best solution.

Angel invited me to a movie, as 'just friends'. Maybe it wasn't such a bad idea. Ivanoldovitch was on his way over to see my new place.

"Hi, Jerry!" Ivan said. *Oh well, let it flow*, I thought. He was about to leave when Angel rang the bell. "I've got to go," Ivan said.

"We're all 'just friends'. Would you rather run into him on the stairs, or meet him up here?"

There was a knock at the door. No time to decide.

Ivan paused. "I guess I'm meeting him here."

When I opened the door, Angel went stiff.

"Hi," I said.

Angel was despondent. "I'm so tired, and hungry. I've been going since five a.m."

"Want me to order some food?" I suggested.

"I don't know what I want," Angel said, stepping into my apartment.

"I'm not really hungry," Ivan offered.

"I'm starved," Angel said.

Ivan's eyes skimmed Angel's statuesque form from head to foot. An embarrassing silence ensued, which I thought would be Ivan's cue to leave. But Ivan just stood there with his hands on his hips facing Angel.

"Let's order from 'Zen Palate'," Angel finally said.

I left them there posturing and went to get the menu.

"I'm not really hungry," Ivan said again.

"Great," Angel said.

Angel couldn't eat half of the things on the menu because they had meat in them. The three of us looked at each other until finally Ivan said, "Well, bye," and opened the door.

"Bye," I said, and closed the door. I heard him say 'Bye' again through the door.

"I didn't like Ivan," Angel said. His food didn't arrive until the movie had already started. "I don't care," he said, "I just wanted to see you. I like hanging out here."

I hadn't seen a movie in a long time. "Want me to get a log for the fire?"

"Yeah."

I lit a Duraflame log. Next thing I knew, Angel was lying under my blanket, trying to lick my ear. "I don't feel that way," I told him. "Now we're just friends."

"What does that mean? 'Just friends'?"

"There are friends, and 'just friends'. 'Just friends' are not lovers."

"I don't make rules like that. I go with my emotions."

"It's not a rule. It's the way I feel. You said you knew I was not 'the One'. When you stopped believing, I lost interest."

He threw the blanket off. "I can't believe you invited me over here to waste my time."

"I didn't invite you over here. We were going to see a movie. Anyway, being friends was your idea." Now he was hopping mad. I once had a treasurer who used to hop when he was angry. It was hard not to laugh at the little guy turning red and jumping up and down, but our jobs depended on it, so we managed. But my job didn't depend on not laughing at Angel hopping on one foot as he put his sneaker back on. He had been hiding a bad temper all this time. When he opened the door, I felt relieved. "Bye," I said as softly as possible.

"Fine, but I don't have time to get together! When I'm this tired, I'd rather stay home and sleep than waste my time!"

"Well, I hope we can be friends," I said, "Write me a postcard." I bolted the door after him, then leaned my head against it and exhaled, really laughing for the first time in a long time.

CHAPTER 58
PROTOTYPE

*A*tta girl. Two birds in the hand make it hard to blow your nose. I was glad when the relationship with Angel was over. I crossed him off my list. Angel was just a prototype that Jerry imposed on a series of sexual relations. Not much scientific objectivity there, I might add.

I did my best to ignore her relationship follies so I could focus on the more serious work of investigating the murder. I suffered so much every time I spied on Jerry.

Not that I would have minded being Angel for a day, even as a mere distraction from her family darkness, or maybe as a tool to help her feel she was in control and could keep the murderer from coming into her life at random.

I had accepted the fact that she was out of my league a long time ago, but nothing could protect me from the feelings of betrayal that would come with the next turn of the screw.

CHAPTER 59

OBJECT

*R*egina was stirring a pot of French onion soup when
I got home. "Hey girl," she said.

I chuckled.

"What's up, baby?" she asked.

"I had a nice day with Sasha."

"As expected. Now *he* won't disrespect you. You'll get him."

"He disses me every day," I complained.

"Does he, now?"

"How will I keep him?"

"Who cares about keeping him? Start at the start."

"What start? He's been waiting in the wings since I got here. It took all this time to appreciate him."

"Woof woof. It's romantick. Come oown, now."

"Sasha's always telling me how his ex-wife betrayed him and how his girlfriend went mad."

"I know whatcha mean," Regina said. "You can only trust him as far as you can throw him."

"I can't trust anyone," I said. "Not even myself. And especially not Sasha."

"Honey, you got a bad attitude. If everybody's the same, you could get stuck trusting the devil."

"I trust them as far as it gets me, but ultimately, I'm the only one who's going to save my skin. Sasha was something I took for granted. He was there, like my job. Then I started dreaming in color, with the whole Freudian family at work. Richard in front, and Sasha in back. They were always there. Like furniture. And then he wasn't there at the bank's Christmas party, and I realized it was already too late. He'd crept into my dreams."

"What about Richard? You didn't see *him* at the party."

"Richard? Pft. Come on. You've never seen him." I finished my soup and went to the gym. My body hardened. I bought another Greek language series and listened to it on the Exercycle.

". . . *Icoyenya e ki?*" Is your family there? *Icoyenya? Family.* No, my family is not here. This is a city of angels. I love machines. I cycled faster. *Icoyenya.* Family.

I pushed him out of my thoughts. If I wanted to keep those student loans coming, I had to be a student. I had to cram for my exam. It went well. I would have been surprised if he had called. But he said he would, and when he didn't, what could I do but go to Mojo Coffee? My waiter sensed my dilemma, and instead of cutting me off after two free drinks on a work night, he said, "What difference does it make?" and filled my glass over and over.

I got home to no message at midnight. I dialed Sasha's home number and left a message on his machine. "I'm sick. I'm not coming to work tomorrow." Out sick. A first. Bastard. I rolled into bed, done with Sasha. I woke up done with Sasha at around ten a.m. to the phone ringing. He would have to call me five times before I'd reconsider.

"Five times?" Regina stirred from her snooze on the couch. She was beat after her first day at her new job at a sperm bank. "That's asking a lot," she said. She should know.

The fifth time he called, I said, "Hello?"

He said, "Are you alone?"

"What?"

"Are you with anyone?"

"What are you talking about? Of course I'm not with anyone. I'm alone." I didn't tell him Regina was here. I just said, "I had a rude awakening from my fantasy."

"What's that?" Sasha asked.

"I don't think this is going to work."

"There is nothing to work," he covered.

"I'm not as half-hearted as you," I said.

"What do you mean?"

The recorded line beeped. "How can I tell you what I mean on a recorded line?"

He called back on his cell phone saying, *"That* wasn't why you missed work."

"Yes, it was, baby."

"No! Hold on, let me get the other line." He was

talking into the other phone, "Nothing today." He came back. "What are you doing?"

"I'm making some muffins, and then I'm going to the gym."

"Nice. What kind of muffins?"

"Corn muffins."

"I love those. I made those once, and said, 'Look, I can bake!'"

We laughed. I hugged the phone and laughed from the bottom of my tummy.

"Talk to me," he said.

He felt so close, I suddenly felt sad and pouted that he took too long to call me back. He tried to console me like a baby. We talked in raw emotions. "They say that women have a higher pain threshold than men."

"Do they?"

"I don't."

He laughed adoringly. "We'll talk about it over dinner."

"I'm talking to you now. I can't wait." And I can't go out with my colleague!

"OK," he said.

"OK, buddy."

"See you tomorrow."

"Bye."

Regina and I were lying on our respective couches staring at the ceiling, when the phone rang.

Sasha's deep voice: "I want some muffins."

"I'll bring you one tomorrow."

"One?"

"I'll bring two."

"You threw me a curve ball. I don't know how I feel. It's like something hit me and I'm saying, huhya huhya."

He called two more times that day. "Are you coming in tomorrow?" He called five times.

I told him, "I could really get sick hanging around here pretending I'm sick."

"Don't get sick. I need your company here."

Tall, dark, and getting handsomer by the hour. He invited me to his house over the weekend when he knew I had to stay home and study for my second final.

Back at work. "I'm not going to ask again," he said.

I pretended not to hear him. "This economy is going to tank."

"Nonsense. It's time to buy!"

"Get outta here," I said. "Look at our model. Artificial intelligence trumps natural stupidity." The spaghetti on our screen pointed the way to hell. "We're headed for a recession. Seven billion here, twenty billion there. The whole thing is going up in smoke."

"It's up to the citizens to fix it," Sasha said.

"They're not citizens. They're consumers."

"I'll betcha things turn around."

"OK," I said. "I'll sell dollars and you buy them. We'll see who wins."

"Hmm, and if I win, you have dinner with me."

"Uhh, and if I win, you clean up the residuals for the next three months." I was sure I could beat my rudderless colleague.

"OK," he said. "It will be really nice. It will be wonderful."

We put on the trade. I sold a million dollars worth,

and Sasha bought a million. The whole aisle chose sides and watched in suspense. Richard thought I would win and said, "Avoid eliciting jealousy, Jerry." The deadline was the Wednesday after my final. I went through anxiety running the restaurant while cramming for the exam. It went better than expected, but I wasn't getting an 'A'. Then, I came home and scoured my apartment. It was clean. I was free. No more exams. I was so excited about Sasha, I didn't sleep.

We were going neck and neck on the bet. The week started off with First Commerce blowing up. There was a nine-day bank run with people withdrawing billions in deposits. The Office of Thrift Supervision had to take action. The FDIC was arranging a fire sale of most of the bank's assets and liabilities to one of the surviving banks. I won!

Everyone teased Sasha. "You were reinventing the flat tire with that trade." I'll never forget his face. It was the darkest red. He fumed all day.

Richard said, "Don't feel the least bit sorry for him, Jerry. Sometimes you're the bug, and sometimes you're the windshield."

I wasn't thinking about beating Sasha anymore, though. I was dreaming about sleeping with him. I was thinking, 'DINNER!?' I want to get it on, and you want dinner.

I whispered in Sasha's ear that we could still go out for dinner. "Don't tell our colleagues."

"OK," he said.

I thought it was rather big of me. I was feelin' pretty good 'til I got to the restaurant ten minutes late and, poof!

— no Sasha. I got drunk waiting an hour and a half for him. I couldn't believe he stood me up.

Ouch. Now he had me. I thought I was gonna be cool about the dude. I even won the bet, hah! Help!

CHAPTER 60
MORNING AFTER

*T*he next morning, Sasha walked in saying, "I've really been thinking about this a lot, Jerry."

My heart sank. "Don't shoot." I stuck my hands up.

But he did. "I don't think we should go out. It could get ugly around here."

I played it off as best I could. "Now I am free to pay my bills." I wrote a check and stuffed it into an envelope. I made a phone call to my organic food co-op. Everything was clear for delivery for a Vegan Cure detox.

"Jerry, if we didn't work together, I would love to go out with you."

"I quit," I said.

He looked startled. "Let's go into Dick's office," he

said.

I smiled and followed him into the empty office. Just then my phone beeped. An SMS from Ivan.

"I just got fired," Ivan said. He called, and I had to pick up. "What happened?"

Sasha started to walk out.

"I don't know," Ivan said. "I couldn't get them to give me a real reason."

"Hold on. Sasha, give me one of those cigarettes."

"Jerry! I didn't know you smoked."

"Just give me one. This is what happens when I don't sleep."

"Here, take as many as you want." His hands were shaking as he held open the packet for me. The same hands that had dismantled the smoke detector. He lit my cigarette.

"I feel awful," I said. "Isn't that the worst? It's like a big hammer coming down on your head. It's like running into a brick wall. I feel sick." It was probably the cigarette.

I told Sasha that my ex-boyfriend had just gotten fired. "I'm really worried that he's going to try to come back," I said.

"Yes, Jerry! He's now packing his bags to come and stay with you this weekend."

"If he calls again, I'll say there are people staying at my apartment."

"No, say you're going away."

"I'm worried that if I say I'm going away, he'll want to borrow my apartment while I'm gone."

"Then say there are already people staying there, too." Once again, Sasha had tailored the most appropriate lie.

"What are you doing this weekend?" Sasha asked.

"Are you asking or are you just asking?"

"I mean, where are you going? Are you going to the Hamptons?"

"You said I was going somewhere, not me. I've never been to the Hamptons."

"Never been to the Hamptons! Jerry, you're a novice."

A novice? I hadn't been called a novice since I'd learned to ski. Maybe I *should* go nicer places and meet older people.

Sasha was in a bad mood all day. I, however, was going out. I applied 'luscious rust' lipstick. There was a party I'd been wanting to go to for a month that I'd thought I'd have to miss for this non-relationship with Sasha. Three more guys called me at work. " . . . No, not tonight . . ."

Sasha turned green and cursed at his laptop.

"I can't tell you how happy I am that my exams are over," I told him.

"*You're* happy," he said.

I read the newspaper, and he tried to figure out how to get his Excel macro to work. "To hell with the newspaper," he yelled. "Come over here and help me."

I didn't move. He looked at me, deep brown eyes in outrage saying telepathically, COME HERE.

"I don't like being yelled at."

"I'm being nice," he said.

I moved my chair next to his and could feel him close to me again. We tried all my ideas and all of his, but the macro wouldn't work. He left early, and there I was alone, calling the support desk.

303

I couldn't even get it on with a thirty-five-year-old divorced father. Oh well. As Cicero said, friendship is the highest love. I'd always liked the unrequited stuff myself. It cut steel.

We calmed down by midweek.

"Look at this," I said. "The assumption of ever increasing housing prices is a fundamental problem in our model, but there are other statistical problems, too. Here's an error in estimating the aggregate probability of default. You can't estimate interaction effects with any accuracy as independent."

Sasha said, "I don't know why you see a big conspiracy everywhere. You're talking apples and oranges."

"What if a homeowner has auto loans on top of his mortgage? What if the mortgage default triggers defaults in auto loans? And then our model adds assumptions like 'the future will be similar to the past, and real estate goes up ten percent a year'."

He didn't answer. He was looking at my breasts.

Richard came in at lunchtime when I was eating my salad and reading the news. "I don't understand you," he said.

I chewed my lettuce and braced myself for another gooey encounter with Richard.

"If you want a stable relationship . . . " He pulled Sasha by the arm. " . . . Sasha is right here." Sasha looked at me with big rabbit eyes, pretending he was available.

"Spare me," I said.

"He's a nice guy," Richard said.

"Mercy!" I said.

It didn't occur to Richard that it might be Sasha who was stopping the progression. If he'd a known, Richard would have already taken Sasha outside and slapped some sense into him.

He's nuts! I thought, but could only say, "Mercy. Mercy. Mercy."

"And if you just want to fool around," Richard explained, "there's me."

"MERCY!"

"I can't believe it," Richard persisted. "Sasha I can understand, but I can't believe you refused me."

"Easy, Dick," Sasha said. "Jerry is a mathematical visionary. It would be a waste to match her genius with TV-watchers like us."

CHAPTER 61
JERRY TRADES WORLDS

Z oo York in its heyday was the place to make a deal. Love boiled down to trading needs. People were packages all looking for the right synergy to improve their product. I knew everyone had appraised me as the only woman on the floor, with a view to enhancing his own qualifications. I knew they all fantasized about doing the transaction.

A letter came from France. I hesitated before opening it. *"Tribunal de—"* Divorce! My divorce had gone through. I was free. It was the best day of my life. I didn't realize what a downer being married had been. Why on earth did I want to get married again? I whistled all the way to the bank.

An auditor came up to visit. I blew him off. He talked to Sasha and Richard. "He's come up here more times in the last month than in the last ten years," Richard said.

"He has the hots for Jerry," Sasha said.

The president of the bank came up to wish us a belated Happy New Year. He gave us a bottle of champagne. "Happy New Year." He shook Sasha's hand. I went to shake his hand too, and he yanked me into his arms, "Come here." He kissed me on the cheek. "Other side," he said. He kissed me on the other cheek. It felt different now that I was truly eligible.

When he was gone, Sasha called Mort. "The President was here . . . No, no presents. He kissed Jerry!"

Sasha was sitting next to me at his laptop. "Today I'm in the mood."

"Done," I said.

"I'm having a hard time picturing you naked."

"I can help you with that."

I went home and vacuumed in case he called. He had me in a constant state of readiness. I was in the business plan. I was part of the machine. I cuddled up with my glow-in-the-dark MBS Alert.

What a welcoming sight, that little black box with prices flashing across it. The Fed was lending banks money at no interest. No time value for money seemed impossible. Unless you were Arab.

In Arab countries, interest was illegal, so it wasn't unheard of. You could borrow without having to pay any interest. How are they gonna keep 'em down on the farm, mamma after they've seen *gay Pariiii?*

"I want to kiss you," I told Sasha.

He looked around the trading floor. "No," he said. "We'll wait until I get back from Athens, and if we feel the same way, we'll go out."

Work didn't encroach, it subsumed. Life became a market. "I love my job," I told a broker on the speakerphone. Waiting for him to come back. Then we were waiting together in Zuccotti Park for our Town Car. Sasha was talking to a protestor. "I've been camping but never glamping," Sasha said. "It looks luxurious with all that expensive equipment you've got there in your tent. Whenever I see you guys on the news, I always see a lot of junk, I mean, material belongings and only a few people milling about."

I turned my head so the protestors wouldn't see my face and dove into the car as soon as it pulled up. It took us to another recruiting presentation. Ms Modernity, I collected résumés, and handed out one more round of champagne before slinking back to the inert reality of my brick wall.

On the way up to the bank the next morning, I stopped at the doughnut and coffee cart on Wall Street. There was a long line. This was the last chance to get a reasonably priced breakfast on the way to the tourist trap. The coffee guy was rushing through everyone's order, and it was finally my turn. "Can I please have a large, black coffee, a small coffee with cream, and one of those long doughnuts."

The Middle-Eastern man started pouring a medium coffee.

"Don't you have a large?" I asked.

"This is large. We have small, large and extra-large.

Nobody in America wants a 'medium'. Do you want extra-large?" He showed me the extra-large cup. That was the one that Sasha always got.

"Yes. That's the one. Thank you."

Rushing through the order all the while, he poured the coffee into the extra-large cup, and we conversed about the name of the long doughnuts: they were bowties. A short, balding man behind me groaned and said, "Jesus Christ!"

I turned around and said, "It isn't taking any longer."

"Yes it is!" he said, fat, sweating, and exasperated.

"Relax," I growled.

A heartbeat later, I handed Sasha his doughnut bag.

Sasha looked in the bag. "He gave you two doughnuts," Sasha said.

"Did we pay for two?"

Sasha inspected the change in the bag. "No. One. He likes you." Sasha ate one of his doughnuts and said, "I'll do the doughnut run next time. You take too long." At the end of the day, Sasha said, "Today went pretty well. What would you do with the ten-year on the close?"

"If I had to go home with a position," I said, "I would sell it five minutes before the close. Traders start to leave the floor for the day five minutes before the close, and the ten-year loses some of its steam."

Five minutes before the close, Sasha called up and sold the ten-year. This was his own, personal position, not a trade for the bank, and he wasn't supposed to do it. It seemed to me that if I wanted to keep up with the Joneses, I would have to set up my own trading account.

"Now that you have all the prices on your iPhone, you don't worry anymore."

"Fine with me. It's better than sleeping with a boyfriend." I had stopped missing Angel now thanks to my overnight position.

"Jerry, I'm losing my confidence in you."

"You sure are short a lot of ten-year for someone who's losing confidence in me."

CHAPTER 62

FUZZY

I 'd spent months fighting to make the restaurant profitable. I ran to Vegan Cure at lunchtime, stripped off my suit and barely made it into my New Age gauze when someone knocked on the restaurant window. I looked up from my lunch.

Three protestors were standing there asking to come in. "Can we use the bathroom?"

It was soothing to see these folks. I unlocked the door and let them in. They were so scruffy, they probably thought it was normal that I wasn't wearing a bra. The revolutionaries smelled like a barnyard. They must have been living in the street for weeks. I was proud of my giant bathroom when they filed into it and said, "Wow! This is enormous!"

The bearded one was hardcore. "Mind if we wash up." It wasn't a question.

The hair on the back of my neck stood up when I recognized his voice. It was the man who had talked about freedom and made the human microphone boo me! The one who chanted with me. I made use of what Sasha had taught me about the nature of man. "It's only for polite society. I was just about to put the sign up on the door."

He looked into my eyes like a baby whose rattle had been taken away. He recognized me. "Please."

"There's soap in the dispenser."

The three of them came out of the bathroom looking polished. "Can we see the menu?"

"You can take a look in the kitchen. I don't usually open for lunch." We stood around the counter eating leftover falafel burgers.

They wanted to know why I wasn't open at lunchtime. I didn't want to confirm that I was one of the enemy working for a bank, so I ignored the lunch question and turned the microscope on them. "So what axe are you grinding on Wall Street?"

"The banks took my job," the fierce one with the beard said.

What a tough. And they called him 'Fuzzy'! "Is that your real name?" I asked.

He ignored the question.

"Look what happened to Martin Luther King," one of his friends said.

Fuzzy almost smiled. "In Iraq, they trained me in riot

312

control, horrible choreography to keep gaps from opening in the military frontline. I threw stun grenades and zip-tied the enemy. I threw canisters of pepper spray— bam! You know what that feels like? It feels like the hair is being plucked off your face."

Fuzzy's friends stuck up for him. "His wife divorced him. And what does he do? He tries to save her house from foreclosure."

I couldn't look directly at Fuzzy, he glared so hard. "Does he have kids?"

"Two," the other hippie said. "The banks suck. They charged me six percent for my student loan when they got the money at zero percent from the government. That $700 billion bailout was *at least* $7.7 trillion of taxpayer money."

"That's just wrong," Fuzzy said, unmovable.

Wrong? I was surprised to hear righteousness being taken into consideration, I had been hanging around traders so long. It felt good to be with a man who could still discern what was right and not right. *You've gotten lost.* My head swam thinking of morality.

"Yeah, but $7.7 trillion is just what the kleptocracy is admitting to now." Fuzzy sank his teeth into another pita. "These falafel burgers are great." His chest hair peeked out of his T-shirt. I catalogued this piece of information. When he left, I leaned my back against the door, looked up at the ceiling, and closed my eyes.

Why should these protesters have to fight alone? *Because you have to go sign mortgages for Sasha. Because a cop and a murderer are following you. Because you have to stop Wall Street from crashing.*

CHAPTER 63
SADIE HAWKINS

O ne morning, Sasha was the second one in. He put his beautiful mouth in front of my lips. I held the phone at arm's length and my lips barely touched his. The kiss was soft.

"Mm!" he said. "Mmmmm!"

"What's that?" the broker said over the phone. "It sounds like a beached whale."

The desk was empty again at noon, and Sasha came back while I was eating my lunch for another kiss. My tongue touched his briefly. How would I ever get enough?

"Jerry, you taste good. Really. Sweet, that's what it is."
He towered over me and threw his head back. "You taste

so sweet." He was struggling as if he would believe it if he could just get his big lips wrapped around it again.

I'm sure someone must have seen us, but no one mentioned it. Sasha sat next to me through thick and thin, greeting me first in the morning, these days in freshly pressed suits, asking me how my evenings went. There was plenty of romance from nine to five, but nothing ever came of it. Why was he fooling around at work with me and then disappearing into the subway at five? After office hours, I was left to my own devices. Then I would report back to him in the morning.

"So, where did you go last night?" he was asking me, chest thrust out, clearly hoping I would notice his new Herod's tie.

"SoHo. I showed my classmates a friend's art show. I said 'Look, my friend did those paintings.' And one of my classmates said, 'I could do that. A child could do that.' Then we went to Mojo Coffee, and who was there but Kate Moss."

"Kate Moss!"

"Yeah, like a porcelain doll, and a geek at my table said, 'She's not pretty.' There was no escape: my classmates were bored and boring."

"Wow," Sasha said. "I want to live in Manhattan, too. Did you say anything to Kate?"

"I thought about it, but . . . I was embarrassed about the people I was with. I didn't want Kate to find out how boring my friends were."

"I love it. You thought they would ruin your chances with Kate."

"Yeah. Anyway, tonight I'm going grocery shopping.

Doesn't that sound glamorous?"

"Yes. I made sure I got the refrigerator pretty well stocked." Sasha tried to keep my attention on him. "I went to the market yesterday."

I ignored him and skimmed the headlines.

"You are so cold, Jerry," he said. He looked upset. He pulled my chair close to his. "You are so angry when you don't get what you want."

I hugged him. "I have what I want."

"You do?"

"Yes."

His lips were close to mine. I watched his full lips. "I don't like violence," he said into my mouth. Is that what my impatience was to him? Violence? He was so precious.

"I love you," my lips whispered before I could stop myself. We looked left and right and then our tongues touched and stopped. I sat back in my chair biting my lip. Did I just say that?

He grabbed my shoulders. My hair fell across my face. He kissed me again and hugged me. "Jerry, let's try."

"What?" My heart quickened.

"Let's make plans. Let's disappear together. We'll take a big roll of money and slice it real thin."

I didn't dare to dream of a married life with kids again. It would be too much to ask for. We hadn't even had a date, and now he had me dreaming about quitting the rat race and settling down in a house on the ground.

His deep eyes implored me.

I felt like I was made for him. I had finally met someone I knew I would never stop loving for the rest of my life. Where? I wanted to ask. As what? And for how long? As 'just friends' or . . . . But I held my tongue and didn't spoil the moment.

It was time for action. That Saturday, I appeared at his front door. "Jerry! What a surprise!" The heat wasn't on, and you could see our breath in the foyer. Sasha's apartment was Spartan with one fork, one knife, and only one chair. He invited me into his bedroom. There was no furniture except a mattress on the floor and a rope next to it. For a moment I thought I was back at the Vault. Sasha was into self-flagellation. "This is how I have fought off the desires of the flesh. My desire for you. Now I will possess you. You do it." He stripped off his clothes and bowed his head to the floor. I drew in my breath. There were long cuts on his back. He tossed me the rope. "First catharsis." He knelt down and tucked his chin into his knees. His skin shone like an eggplant.

"And then?" I asked, as the rope came down on his back.

"Argh...," Sasha moaned. His face knotted in agony, and then he sighed, relieved to be on familiar ground inside his ritual of pain.

My nervousness about whipping my colleague was dispelled with the first meeting of flesh and rope—Crack!

"Awuulll."

Before he could raise his hand to cover his back the next crack fell. "Is this how you welcome your guests? We will all take turns whipping you!"

"Yes. I am bad." Sasha peeked at us.

"Stop counting, you bastard."

"Beautiful pain! Hummmm," he concluded.

Sasha's obsession put things into perspective. We

didn't have a traditional relationship, but the important thing was that it worked. The next morning in the office, the sun had burned all the mist off the horizon by the time I realized that if I were really going to disappear with Sasha, I was going to have to take the lead. I was going to ask him to marry me. I looked at my reflection in the computer screen and said to myself, "You are crazy."

My reflection smiled back, as if to assure me that my family was alive somewhere in the future. *Your children will not be exiled much longer from their mother.* Surely the rightful man would break the irons. He always finds a way.

It was settled, then. I had to keep trying. I went back to the trading floor and heard myself mutter, "Looks like we made it to Sadie Hawkins Day."

Richard did a double-take. "Did you say what I think you said?"

"What's that?" Sasha asked. He was sitting between us as usual.

Richard and I laughed.

"Come on. Talk to me. Who is this Sadie Hawkins?" Sasha said.

I thought it was some ancient myth, but Richard said, "It started with the cartoon Li'l Abner."

"American traditions are ungrounded," Sasha said.

"That's what makes us Americans."

Richard fought pre-destiny. "Don't start playing out a cartoon, Jerry. You're still young."

"What is it, Dick? Tell me!"

Richard turned to Sasha. "It's the day when they shoot a gun in the street, and all the men start running, and then they shoot it again and all the women start running after them. You're brave coming to work on Sadie Hawkins Day, Sasha."

"Jerry!" Sasha said, "Are you going to pop the question? Who's the lucky guy?"

I stared at my oil chart.

"Sasha," Richard said. He covered his eyes and put his head on Sasha's shoulder. "I feel sorry for the guy she's going to ask."

"Me too," Sasha said.

"Why?" I said.

Richard was trying not to laugh. "I'm just kidding, Jerry."

I waited until they were out of earshot, and called Information. I got the coordinates for Tiffany's.

"Guys," I said, "I've got to take all this garbage over to the tax man." I held up my tax folder. "Do you mind if I disappear for an hour?"

"I'll do your taxes, Jerry," Sasha said. "We have a program. We do everybody's taxes. Why pay three hundred bucks when I can do it for free?"

"No, this stuff is way overdue. I'm taking it to the tax man to get it done right away so I can forget about it."

"Sasha," Richard said, "She doesn't want you to do her taxes, and she doesn't want to marry you."

I was very excited, and Sasha could sense my mood. All day long, he said things like, "Nobody's ever asked me to marry them."

CHAPTER 64
"DROP IT IN HIS DRINK"

*i*t was a beautiful blue-sky day for a romp at Tiffany's. I grabbed my purse, commuted down in the elevator to street level and walked out onto the plaza in the frosty sunshine. "Taxi! Tiffany's please."

On the way over, I checked my position in my personal account. My oil puts were sky high. I fought the urge to buy more and called my broker to sell the whole thing. "That's right. Take profit. I know they're still going up. Close the account." Now we would have a nest egg. I was going to need it to pay off my credit card after this little shopping trip at Tiffany's.

I looked out the window to see if anyone was following me. It was impossible to tell. I didn't see the plain clothes policeman. The taxi driver counseled me on how to buy a ring. "And make sure you get the karats in writing."

I opened the wooden door to the gleaming diamond shop. It was like in the movie. Tiffany's was still entirely wood-paneled inside. Jewels dripped from every shelf. It was more modern than in the movie, I noted, walking down the aisles, brushing my hand along the counters. Case after case of diamonds gleamed upward at me. There were big, yellow diamonds, small white ones, bluish diamonds changing colors as I glided by. The stones were sunken into the settings in the fashion of the day. I found the androgynous wedding rings over on the left. "Can I see that one?" It was a fat gold band with a curve in the middle and one tiny diamond set far enough into the gold so as to appear flat. What was the price of happiness? "How much is this?" I asked.

"$12,870."

"Only? And how about this one." I pointed to a man's gold wedding band with a fiery white diamond wedged into its side. One side of the diamond was exposed, so the light would enter from the side of the band and bounce off. The saleslady took it out of the case and held it up to the window. "There is only one like this one. Isn't it magnificent? $35,780."

Only $35,780 to be happy for the rest of my life. "I'll take it."

"Of course."

I wrote the check and watched the lady wrap up the little blue box. I was so giddy I had to laugh. I was getting married again! I hid the tax papers in my empty metal briefcase — I'd thought of everything. I strolled down Fifth Avenue with Sasha's ring. "Taxi!"

Back at the desk, Sasha looked at me funny, trying to figure out what was up. He seemed disappointed that I wasn't holding the big plastic bag with my taxes when I walked in.

"Nobody's asked me to marry them," he said again. We tiptoed around each other. He called me out into the deserted hallway for a feather light hug. "You forgot something," he said.

"No I didn't," I said.

We kissed.

He invited me down to a colleague's office for coffee. Something he had never done. When we were alone on the desk again and he was sitting across from me, he seemed to be waiting for something.

"Are you going to do some work tonight?" I asked.

His eyes widened. "Yes." Then he looked doubtful. He started talking about his friend the cook.

"I liked him. What's the name of his restaurant?"

"McDougal's."

"An Irish restaurant with a French chef?" I asked.

"Yes." He was on to me. I could tell he was wondering what I was planning.

I could tell he wasn't sure if he was imagining it, or if I was up to something. "I've got to go," I said.

He looked at me sadly. I kissed him on the forehead, once, twice.

"I'm going, too." We took the elevator down together. Now he was clinging. On the ground floor, he touched my shoulder.

I ran into the subway and raced uptown, my train following his taxi underground like a cartoon to Grand Central Station. I bought a ticket to Sasha's station in Greenwich, Connecticut, and wondered if I was going crazy. I usually didn't talk to myself, and now I was telling everyone I met that I was going to ask my colleague to marry me. The guy in the ticket line said, "Do you know how you're going to say it?"

"Yes. 'Will you marry me?'"

"Don't say that. Just drop it in his drink."

"No knees? No proposal?"

"No! You don't want to start your new life suppliant."

On the train, I was scared. Rather terrified. But I'd been in much tighter jams before. I could deal with whatever was coming. And something was definitely coming. The die had been cast. The chorus had spoken. It was decided. Harlem floated by in all its squalor. When we got to his stop, I stepped out of the train and hid myself on the staircase, but I didn't see him on the platform. Walking down his street, I didn't see anyone in front of me, either. He had not gotten off this train, not here anyway. I rang his doorbell. No answer. I went to the neighborhood restaurant and asked for Sasha's favorite bartender. "He's not working tonight."

"Then we're going to have to become friends, because I need someone to talk to."

"We're all pretty friendly here."

"Hi, I'm Jerry."

"Nice to meet you. Jerry. So what brings you here?"

I explained my predicament and showed him the ring. The *maitre'd* came by and said, "No way! That's so cool.

He'll say yes. And if he doesn't, we'll marry you. Just hang in there. Don't get nervous. You can stay here 'til he gets home, use the phone, whatever you need. I think you're wonderful."

I went back to Sasha's and rang the bell. The house was dark and silent. I waited for a while and then went back to the restaurant, a little embarrassed.

"Still not there?" they asked.

"Nope." I sat down, and ordered another beer.

"Well, you know," Hawk said, "You can't just go ask him to marry you like that."

"I can't?"

"No. You need a bottle of champagne to celebrate."

"I do. Where am I going to get a bottle of champagne?"

"You'd have to go into Old Greenwich for that. But the liquor store closes in a half an hour."

CHAPTER 65
BLACK ICE

I painfully followed this prescription and arrived again on Sasha's dark doorstep, this time with champagne in hand. Was he going to come home with some woman on his arm? I went back to the restaurant and called McDougal's. They said he'd left a half an hour ago. Did I miss him coming back? Was he already inside his apartment? I rang the doorbell again. Nothing. The gamester. I went around back. The light in the upstairs study was on. I went back to the front and rang the bell. Nothing.

I looked over my shoulder, wondering if anyone could have followed me out here. At midnight, the next-door neighbor came out. "What are you doing here?"

I told him the whole hard-luck story standing on Sasha's cold doormat. The neighbor tried to convince me to come inside. "His old girlfriend spent a few nights on my couch." A clue.

"No, thank you. I have to know for sure if he's lying." The neighbor gave up and handed me a blanket. Then he came back with a cup of tea and some cookies. I wrapped the blanket around myself, drank the tea and ate the cookies. I stared up at Sasha's window. The light upstairs went off. Sasha had to be inside. I rang the bell again and again. He must have an alarm system. It was possible that the light was on a timer. It was late, and he had to wake up at six a.m. I rang the doorbell again. Was he hiding? The coward!

I knelt on the mat and huddled in my blanket, but the cold was too much. If I were snow camping, I'd be in the bottom of my sleeping bag now. I wrapped my silk scarf around my legs. Kneeling, I kept my legs from freezing with the heat from the rest of my body. I pulled the scarf tight around my thighs and covered myself completely with the blanket. I pressed my head against my knees, Japanese style. Except for my toes and fingers, I began to warm up.

The hours went by one by one. I burned on the inside and froze on the outside. It was one a.m., then two. I lost track of what I'd been thinking about all that time, but I did not sleep. A noise interrupted my daze. A tapping on metal. I looked out from my blanket, but there was no one. Only myself and the streetlamps. At 4:30 a.m. in the cold morning, the metal lampposts contracted with a 'CHINK'.

It sounded like a submarine on the bottom of the ocean, "chink, chink". At 5:30 a.m., the sky began to get light. A word leapt into my thoughts, *icoyenya,* but I couldn't remember what it meant. I remembered only that Sasha had not come home. I huddled in my blanket and tried to make it warm again, but it had been dark for too long, and I was freezing. I could not feel my hands or feet.

I did not notice when daylight had come, but there was no denying that it was going to be a beautiful blue-sky day. Another neighbor appeared and glared at me as she clacked down the walkway to her car. I folded my blanket. Other neighbors alit from their condos and drove off to the train station parking lot to start their commute by train into the city, many to Wall Street. An airplane soared overhead full of fortunate business people leaving on the redeye flight for Europe. Millions of people were up by now.

At 6:11 a.m., Sasha opened the door. "What a surprise!" he said, as if he hadn't known that I was there. Some man. He was drinking ice coffee. "You're late for work!" he said. The morning light shone razor-like on his living room carpet. I looked out the picture window at the misty river. He sure did live in the Styx. All remnants of magic were gone. *The goddess of the flashing eyes, Athena, has gone.* We were both over the edge in a madland. The relationship was smothered in anxiety. Nobody was responsible for this mess we were unwillingly in together. I tried not to see the strained expression on his face. "I was going to ask you to marry me," I said anyway. He was gnawing his fingers.

Sasha looked at me and took another sip of his ice

coffee. The ice hit the sides of the glass. I shivered. "It sounds like an ending," Sasha said, handing the ring back to me.

I looked up at the white expanse of his living room ceiling and tried to believe that the world would go on without him. "Keep womanizing if that's all you can understand." I had spent the night on a doorstep in February. I could get through this, too. I had to get back to reality. I stood up and tried to shake off the malaise.

Running by my side toward the train tracks, Sasha said, "I don't remember the last time I ran." My thigh-high stockings fell down around my ankles. I pulled them up, and they fell down again. I ran like a five-year-old. On the platform, Sasha rubbed my arms up and down, trying to warm them. The train made a helluva racket. It smelled like someone had tossed their breakfast in our car. The world seemed to have come to a stop, now that I knew that Sasha was irresponsible: there really was no Sasha. There was *no one* to rescue me. I would not be escaping to greener pastures with Regina, or anyone else. I was not running off to an island to get married. I had made it to Tiffany's and come away with Cracker Jacks. This was my cartoon, and I was the only one in it. If I had frozen on his doorstep, I would have been the only one to suffer the loss. *Icoyenya*. "What is *icoyenya?*" I asked him.

"'Family', *malaka*." He said, almost to himself and looked out the window at Harlem. "I don't know if I should move back to Greece."

We got into a taxi and headed into the graveyard of skyscrapers. My stomach turned at the thought of repeating our courtship. "You *will* do the right thing, darlin'."

"You're messing me up," he said. "I nearly missed my train because of you. I can't believe you wore those. Roll your stockings back down below your knees." It was difficult in the car, and the seat was cold on my exposed thighs. He unbuttoned my blouse, and I leaned forward thinking he wanted to kiss me. Instead, he opened a pen knife and cut my bra straps. He felt under my skirt. "Take off your panties." I wriggled out of them. "Good girl. You're not to wear panties to work anymore. Offer yourself freely and always wear a skirt so we can have easy access."

He must have meant the royal 'we'. The seat stuck to my thighs. I hoped the driver wouldn't turn around and see my naked breasts. "Tell me you love me," Sasha commanded.

"I love you."

CHAPTER 66
MISOGYNISTS ASIDE

P ride is expensive. Prostitution is more expensive. Breaking my code at work shocked me into sobriety. It was clear that the Sashas of the world had no use for a wife. Yet I knew I couldn't survive on the trading floor without Sasha's support. This still didn't make me hate him, well at least not the idea of him. But I knew that eventually one of us would have to go, and when he was gone, there would not be another master to replace him. No more misogynists. Male constructs, aside, I had my own needs, and one of them was to be my own boss.

I wished Sasha would accept that we weren't together, but he continued to taunt me. I stopped wearing makeup and tried to be as repulsive as possible so that he'd be the one to break up. If he closed the door, I wouldn't be able to go back to him out of weakness.

I dreamt that the door to my apartment slowly swung open, and a big black hellhound with green claws was standing there in the dark. He started to come in. I said, "Shoo!" He slowly stepped back, and I closed the door. I was still standing there when the door swung open again. I realized it was a recurrent dream. When the door swung open and the evil hound appeared for a third time, I was confident that he would back away again when I threw up my hands and said, "Raaaar!" He moved one paw back, but this time, push as I might, I couldn't close the door.

It was as if the dream had actually happened to me. It changed me. I fortified myself against any canine seduction and was disciplined from then on. While most of my colleagues were still buying American, I stuck to my view and went against the dollar. I forced myself to cut my losses and let my profits run. And run they did. By spring, I had the highest profit on the trading floor. It was time for promotions on the prop desk, and Sasha and I were the only ones eligible. I was determined to get it.

I overheard Mort hissing something at Richard.

"They're incompatible," Richard said. "She's a Mac and he's a PC."

I carried on with business as usual. I was waiting for the dollar to reach a breakout level so I could sell it forward against the yuan. I paced up and down the aisle in my knee-length skirt trying to get Sasha's attention. The dollar sat there all morning. When I came back to my desk, Sasha was sitting at my workstation tying up my phone.

Of course, the yuan ran up to -25. The broker's speed dial number was only programmed into the phone that Sasha was on, blabbing to London in his imitation British accent.

"Sasha, could you put them on hold and use the other phone?"

He ignored me.

"Son of a — get out of the way! Where's the phone number?" I was dancing around him looking for the broker's phone number. "Where's the $@#%! phone number? Never mind!" I threw the phone back into the cradle. BANG.

Sasha looked at me. "What's wrong?" he blinked.

I knew he saw everything I did. "I wanted to sell the dollar. You ruined my trade!"

Sasha whispered in my ear, "Are you naked under there?" Before I could answer, he'd turned his dark figure away and gone to sit on the couch.

I pulled up a point figure chart and showed Richard where the dollar-yuan was going to top out. I was pretty sure Richard was on my side in the promotion competition, but this time Richard ignored me.

Fine. Take Sasha's side, I thought. He's been here longer. When Sasha moves back to Greece, I'll be the one taking his place on the trading desk. He was jealous. I felt kind of sorry for him. An hour later, the yuan began creeping again. I got on the phone. "How's the dollar-yuan?"

"You sold 'em."

"Thank you." But it turned out that the price I'd sold it at was the low of the afternoon. "Thanks, for screwing up my trade, Sasha."

Sasha was sulking about his losses and pretended not to hear.

The glass doors of the trading floor slid open. Mort stood in the doorway looking like Death himself. Heads turned. The boys' shenanigans simmered to a lull. Mort was on the floor. Head down, he walked slowly through the aisle in his black suit. Everyone hoped he wasn't coming for them. He stopped in front of Sasha. Sasha dared to whisper into Mort's ear. My heart filled with dread.

He came over to my desk. "Jerry, there's a problem with those mortgage notes you signed." The shareholders had turned up the heat on Mort, and he was going to turn on his scapegoat.

"*I* signed? Sasha signed them, too."

"Apparently there's only a problem with the ones you signed."

I gave Sasha a hard stare and asked Mort, "What problem?"

"It seems that not all the paperwork was in order when you signed those notes. We can't prove that we owned those mortgages."

I must have turned white. I think I was ranting, "You knew that!" Sasha — or was it Mort? — lifted my feet up onto the desk. I was too dizzy to notice my hemline. At least I was no longer following Sasha's no-panties rule. "It's not *my* fault that the legal department didn't check that paperwork. Pretty soon you're going to be blaming me for the wrong assumptions in your convoluted mathematical models or for the housing market falling apart!"

Everyone was looking at our own bank's shares on Reuters. GAB was tanking. Mort wheezed. "U.S. watchdogs have decided thousands of Americans have been evicted illegally because bank employees rubber-stamped repossession documents without checking the paperwork. Jerry, you've done a disservice to the bank."

That was all it took. 'Disservice' was the signal. The money market desk sneered. *They'd* had nothing to do with my treachery, the snobs. Sasha stood there with his arms folded in a buffalo stance. Mort had removed himself from the conversation and was sniggering with the boys on the Equities desk. I couldn't believe my eyes. It was Mort who was taking cues from Sasha! Who *was* Sasha?

One of the boys said, "Why would she dye her hair blonde if she has a redheaded pussy?"

". . . and she has a mole on her twat?" another one asked.

"She should get that removed."

"Jerry, why don't you get that mole on your twat removed?"

"It's for sentimental reasons, lads."

"She thinks it's attractive!"

"The first time is for love. Next time it's a hundred dollars."

"Do you think she'd make it as a prostitute?"

"We could try her out."

"Nothin' to lose."

"You can go in the hole and still come out ahead."

I had broken Rule Number One. The boys went on about Sasha's doorstep victory. Each new piece of information pushed me further outside their world.

Richard's attitude toward me changed. He couldn't believe I'd picked Sasha over him. He snorted like a bull every time I entered his field of vision.

The TV blared, "Oil prices plunged this morning with worries about the global financial crisis. There was news of an emergency OPEC meeting to discuss cutting output and defending prices." Mort watched light sweet crude fall 2.36 dollars. He was making money on the plummet in oil, but he still wanted more. "Did it occur to you to check that all those mortgage documents were complete before you signed them?"

Richard and I looked at each other, not sure which one of us he was talking to. Richard said nothing. Finally, I answered. "Wasn't that the Legal Department's job?"

"Legal! You're supposed to be going over and above. It's *your* signature on those documents. You should have verified what you were signing! Now we've got our first court case contesting our claim to a home in foreclosure proceedings."

"They don't have any ground to stand on," I said.

"The hell they don't! What about all those mortgages we bought from Righteous Mortgage right before they went bust? The clods moved out of the building three months ago. If we didn't get the mortgage notes before they left, how are we gonna get 'em now? How many of those bogus mortgage notes did you sign?"

Thousands.

Richard mumbled that it wasn't my fault. "The whole system is rotten. Hell, even the rating agencies' credit assessments are worthless. They took a cut in the sales of securitized bonds they themselves rated."

My colleagues went back to making me pay for my indiscretions with Sasha. They wouldn't drop it. I was the butt of every joke. Everyone was encouraged to attack my sexuality or use me as an excuse for a bad trade. My self-esteem went to hell.

Two more homeowners filed cases contesting our unjustifiable foreclosures. Richard got another phone call from Mort, and seemed to enjoy breaking the news to me. "Jerry, Mort's suspending you from trading."

I felt dizzy. "Because of the mortgages?"

"You got it."

"What does that have to do with trading?"

"It's a question of integrity."

I glared at him. "Oh yeah, Mort's got lots of integrity with his shabby legal department and everybody in on those signatures. Who else is suspended?"

"Look, I'm sure it's just a formality. When this blows over, you'll be back in your seat." Richard gave me an industry-standard smile. "But for now, just come in to work and watch the markets." He took the opportunity to rub my back.

CHAPTER 67
FREE RADICAL LUNCH

*T*he mailman came up with a bouquet of yellow roses and set it down on my desk. "Who's this from?" I asked. There was no envelope.

"A secret admirer!" Sasha said.

Richard whistled.

I looked at them doubtfully, feeling a little sick. I moved the flowers over to the corner of my desk and tried not to look at them. I didn't like anonymous flowers, except that Sasha liked them even less.

The next day, Richard's secretary came in with a message for me. Written on pink paper were the words, "Saphora called, call her back." I stared at the paper.

"Jerry, what's wrong?" Sasha said.

"Nothing." I wanted to ask Sasha to read me the message to be sure it really said what I thought it said but crumpled it up instead.

Who could have sent that message? Did Raif know where I worked? This couldn't be happening now! I had to focus. I was supposed to be planning a masquerade party at Vegan Cure.

I tried to ignore the feeling that someone was following me. I forced my body machine to grind toward productivity. It churned out more angels. I watched them flake away through dusty streets.

One balmy day at the coffee cart, I stared into my brown bag at a single bowtie doughnut. I looked over my shoulder at the people in line behind me.

"Hurry up!"

I was depressed walking through the crowd of protesters, even more so being surrounded by people. I arranged my paperclips along the side of my desk and logged onto my computer.

Angels didn't even fit on one's résumé — 'Managed MBS Risk, 2010-2012; bedded angel'. The only satisfaction seemed to come from the promise of more money. There was a huge market out there in the reorganized qualifications of the chronically dissatisfied, clothed in Escada. Anyone too flaky to buy into it could rent. And people were still getting promoted! What hypocrisy. Not democracy, demo*crisy*. We all became temps after the rest of the world's liposuction of American debt. Real estate plummeted, banks foreclosed on the floorboards and people moved to Zuccotti Park.

"Jerry, are you sitting down?" Sasha said.

"What does it look like?"

"Jerry, there's an investigation going on. It's about the mortgages you signed."

"Come on. I don't know anything about them."

"You'll have a chance to tell them that. Jerry! Put that vase down!"

I let out a deep sigh. We were under investigation. The dopes called me into a meeting room. I know all the finks on the trading floor took aim at my back as I left for the interview. In a conference room off the floor sat two investigators, both a little overweight, humbly writing out their questions on legal pads in front of them. "Jerry, please sit down." I sat in the seat across from them and buried my hands, which had begun to shake, in my lap.

It proceeded methodically, and we all feared for our jobs. Sasha didn't like it any more than I did. It didn't occur to me that I was responsible for anything that turned up sour at the bank. I still hoped that nothing would be pinned on me, since I had done nothing especially wrong. We had all been in the know since the beginning.

"Is this your signature on all these mortgage notes?" they asked.

"Only on half of them. Sasha signed the rest."

"Can you show me his signature?"

I flipped through the piles of notes. They were all signed by me. "Where are the ones Sasha signed?"

"These are all of them, and your signature is on them all."

"That can't be! I wasn't the only one signing them." Sasha's must have been dupes. I slumped back into my chair. He'd set me up.

Mort was lurking around my desk when I came out. "You need a vacation, Jerry."

My heart skipped a beat. My first thought was that the idiots wanted to search my desk, check the phone tapes and ask questions about me on the trading floor while I wasn't around.

"Thanks, Mort, but I feel fine. I'm not tired at all."

I kept a stiff upper lip and tried to compare notes with Sasha, but he ignored me and continued his routine. Our communication had been reduced to the absolute minimum, although these days he coattailed my trades, never commenting on how much money our positions were making.

When Mort called me in a second time, I panicked. When I saw his big iron door, I knew that hell was on the other side.

"Jerry, sit down." He waited until there was no risk of my knees caving in. "The investigators are holding you responsible for the robo-signing."

"Me?"

"It's your signature on all those documents." Cigar smoke seeped from his nose.

"I was following your orders."

"I want you to take a break, Jerry. One week while we investigate further. You can go now."

I collected my things and snuck out of the bank without saying goodbye to anyone. The ride down to the ground seemed to take forever. I walked through the village of pup tents the occupiers had erected and went and unlocked the Vegan Cure. I walked around the restaurant with my hands in my hair.

There was a knock on the window. My three radicals waved at me through the glass.

The one with the beard had stopped glaring, and said, "Hey." He seemed as upset as me. I knew he remembered booing me as I went into the bank. He knew, but he didn't seem to hold my day job against me. None of them was surprised when I told them I worked for a bank, but I was surprised to hear that Fuzzy had been laid off from a bank. I told them the whole story and was relieved to find Fuzzy sympathizing. "Imagine being accused of signing bogus notes that your boss ordered you to sign! Welcome to the machine."

"What kind of machine bails out banks and not homeowners?" Fuzzy's friend said.

"The whole city's a machine," the other friend said.

"The whole country's a machine," I said. "You wake up with your forehead pressed to the gutter as the wheel turns." Self-reliance is a hard enough lesson, but in a city with no gravity, where the unwary peel off and blow away! Sleet fell on the oiled streets outside the window. Someone's purple tie was flattened in the bus lane.

"These sandwiches are great!" Fuzzy said. I had a warm feeling of security standing next to him. I could feel his years as a family man. "You should open at lunchtime," he said. He pressed his tummy against the counter. "That's when everybody's down here." His eyes twinkled. "We'll bring our friends."

"I usually don't have a lot of time in the middle of the day."

"We've got lots of friends."

"That's nice of you." Other people were as dependable

as cloud. What was I saying?

"I'll set up, and you come at the end of the day to count the money."

"Hell, what do I have to lose?" We could try it this week, now that I was suspended from trading, and after that, well, the bank didn't need me to sit there *all* day. It could take months for the restaurant to turn a profit, though. How could I afford to pay them? "When's your wife's case in bankruptcy court?"

"Soon."

"Maybe we can make a deal." I explained my plan to them.

"It's a date," Fuzzy said.

"OK, I'll go grocery shopping tonight. How many friends can I expect for lunch tomorrow?"

"At least twenty."

The next day at twelve-thirty, Fuzzy came into the restaurant with about twenty friends. "Hey, can I shave?" he asked.

"No!" I said. "I mean, you look fine like that."

He smiled and went about taking their orders. Seven sweet potato and black bean chilies, six Vegan Decadences for $6.95 — that was creamy basil spread on warm focaccia bread with Kalamata olives, roasted red peppers, fresh tomato and garlic, and fourteen Zoomazooms for $6.50 — falafel burgers with spicy vegan spread, spinach, tomato, onion and black olives wrapped in a brown flour tortilla.

Eight more protesters came in asking apologetically to use my oversized bathroom. It must have been hard to get local restaurant owners to let you use the bathroom. I figured it into my marketing budget and bought extra toilet paper and soap. On their way out, I handed them restaurant flyers with a picture of the oversized bathroom and asked them to tell their friends about Vegan Cure.

They smiled and took a dozen flyers each. "We're experienced at this," a girl wearing an American flag said. She came back the next day with more friends. I gave the girl in the flag some more flyers and the leftovers from the day before to feed the movement.

The next day, I got a call from a lawyer. "Jerry, we'd like you to be a witness in our foreclosure case."

"Gee, I'm honored." I was going to save Fuzzy's ex-wife's house, even if it cost me my job.

CHAPTER 68
FLOWERS

What if Jerry knew that I was reading her diary and she was messing with me just to get even? I couldn't see straight and had to know. That's why I'd played the trick on her.

I was the one who put the flowers on her desk, to see who she would call and thank. It was an act of desperation, I know. I meant to add a little volatility. But she foiled me again, not calling anyone. Just gloating over the Gerbera daisies and looking at Sasha down the aisle. I shoulda fired the both of them!

None of my theories about her friends bore fruit. I was

left with the question mark of Saphora, who remained the most likely by virtue of never appearing. That's why I told my secretary to leave the message that Saphora called. But, Jerry just gave up her move.

The fact that Jerry didn't call anyone did give me one clue, though. She was extremely discreet about her personal life. That kind of overprotection suggested that Jerry might be covering up for Saphora.

CHAPTER 69
THOUGHT CRIME

*O*ne chilly morning, I was waiting near the Manhattan Bridge for Fuzzy and his ex-wife. I waved when I saw them drive up. His ex- was prettier than me, medium build, no makeup.

Several blocks away, Occupy Wall Street protesters gathered to block the streets around the New York Stock Exchange. I thought they were coming off duty when I saw them walking toward us and turned my back to them. Before I knew it, thirty police officers had surrounded me and the car with Fuzzy and his ex-wife, still inside. I looked around for my cop with the scar under his eye. He wasn't there.

I thought they would pass us by, but suddenly they

were on us. "You're under arrest," a policeman said as he shoved me against the car and handcuffed me.

They pulled Fuzzy's lean body out of the car.

"What are you arresting us for? Thinking?" Fuzzy yelled like a famished Bolshevik. "You can't arrest people because they might be thinking about exercising their rights!"

"Yeah, is thinking a crime?" I yelled.

We were all taken to the East Village police station, where they separated us for questioning. After an hour of exhaustive probing, the black woman officer stood up and said, "Would you like to make a telephone call?"

I couldn't think of anyone I'd like to notify of my imprisonment, and I certainly couldn't call Raif from a police station. "No."

"Take off your shoes."

I was too tired to object.

She took the insoles out of my shoes and said, "Put your clothes in this bin."

"Excuse me?"

She proceeded to strip-search me.

"I have a right to a lawyer." Now I wished I'd gotten that cop lover's telephone number.

"Would you like to make that phone call? Maybe a family member can find a lawyer for you."

"No!" Were they trying to get to Raif? "Why are you keeping me here?"

"You are being held for obstructing governmental administration and elbowing a police officer in the face." She led me to a cell. "That's a felony."

Fuzzy and his ex-wife were in the cell. Man was I

happy to see them! Unbelievable that they put us in jail together after all that. We became hardened 'thought criminals'.

"*They* steal the country's money and then put *us* in jail," Fuzzy's wife said.

"They've gone too far," I said. Fuzzy's wife was very down-to-earth. She was confident. Was she past getting jealous over Fuzzy? We talked about bank foreclosures and her house that was being repossessed. The bars were cold, so we huddled together in the middle of the cell, bonding. Nothing would dissolve us.

That evening, my cop with the goatee and the scar under his eye did appear in front of our cell. "Seems you were breaking the law," he said.

I jumped up. I hesitated before approaching the cold bars. It must look to the others like I was responsible for our imprisonment.

Fuzzy and his wife looked at me quizzically. I didn't know what to say. Maybe I *was* responsible for this. *The ancients had no word for 'will'. Actions were dictated by the gods.*

I tilted my face toward the cop's. "There is no absolute law," I said in a low tone. "There are layers and degrees of law. Tragedy evolves with law. The more civilized we are, the more tragic we become." Saphora was coming out.

The cop whispered with his goatee touching the bars, "What do you suggest, anarchy?"

"I'm just trying to survive," I said. "These are my friends. I don't have much family around here." *And what you do have is mired in curse and ancestral defilement for a crime that attached itself to your whole lineage and now to your friends.*

"I know better than that," the cop said.

It *was* my fault that Fuzzy and his wife were in here.

The cop put his card through the bars. "Call me."

"How?"

He took the keys out of his pocket and let us go. We ran out of the police station and into the subway.

I saw Fuzzy the next day at the restaurant. We were scared for a while, but in the end, nothing came of it. The Manhattan district attorney's office dismissed the case.

CHAPTER 70
YOU ARE NOT A LOAN

*F*uzzy's ex-wife's lawyer got us our court date. The bank had to be notified. Good, I thought walking into the courtroom, all eyes on me, let them know. I passed a wooden alcove harboring a white statue of Themis, titan goddess of law and order. I prayed that the law of the – polis would find us today.

We'd had good luck so far. The lawyer had to pull a few strings to get me entered into the proceedings as a witness. He put Fuzzy's ex-wife in the front row on my left. She showed no outward sign of knowing me but managed to greet me with a furtive smile, which I took as a thank you for coming to her defense.

The judge appeared in black. I looked at Themis overseeing the room again and silently asked for her instruction in the primal laws of justice and good conduct of assembly.

The foreclosure proceedings began. The judge addressed me, asking how many foreclosure documents I'd signed.

"I have no idea," I said. "I think I signed as many as 700 foreclosure papers a day, and the bank bought at least $70 billion in mortgages from outside originators over the last two years. The mortgages didn't meet our guidelines and had flaws like incomplete appraisals, missing insurance documents or miscalculations of income, but they had to be packaged and sold to the rest of the world. They needed me to sign them right away and said that the defect rate was only around eight percent."

"What was the procedure for verifying that the documentation was in order?"

"The only thing I checked was whether my title was correct. Some of them were no-documentation mortgages. At the time, I thought our bank's legal department had reviewed the documents."

"Did anyone pressure you into signing?"

"Lots of people, from our CFO down. They humiliated me in front of everyone and intimidated me into looking the other way on serious flaws. We were so overwhelmed with paperwork that the mortgage department couldn't handle it. They said we had to cut corners, and all the new people were being asked to do it. Then when we were investigated, they said I was the only one. That's why I'm blowing the whistle."

"Can you give us a sworn deposition saying you did not verify the principal and interest the bank claimed the borrower owed?"

"Sure." *Decision without choice, responsibility without intention. You were the human sacrifice to the gods.*

There was a recess, and then the judge came back and ruled that, in a shocking display of corporate irresponsibility, Global American Bank had fabricated the amount of the homeowner's obligation out of thin air. The court held that the bank's behavior violated both federal and state law. The court fully discharged the debtor of her mortgage and awarded her $160,000 in damages and attorney's fees. "Because of these bad titles, it is apparent that the bank cannot prove it has the right to foreclose on the house."

Fuzzy's wife hugged Fuzzy. I pretended I didn't know them and tipped out of the courthouse. Reporters gathered around me and peppered me with questions. There was no rice at this ceremony. I looked at the cameras dead on and delivered my message: "The banks told you it was fine to take your money out of your homes. Now they have bought and sold your mortgages so many times, they don't know what they have and what they don't have. Homeowners, FIGHT BACK! Banks don't have their paperwork in order to come forward in court and legally claim orphaned loans."

A reporter stepped in front of me. "Jerry, can borrowers use this robo-signing case as a precedent to get their mortgages legally erased?"

"Damn straight. Borrowers with mortgages as far back as 1998 can use this case in bankruptcy court. Several have already used robo-signing as a crowbar to force lenders to reduce their principal or payments."

"Jerry, are you saying homeowners can challenge not

only the foreclosure, but also the legitimacy of the mortgage?"

"Precisely. This is a very important legal tool, and people should use it. Banks plowed through the paperwork when they were buying and selling these mortgages. A blizzard of lawsuits is coming. It's going to be a mess for the courts. Millions of faulty documents have been filed in land record offices across America, a situation that has led to calls for Congressional hearings. Now it's time for judges to plow through, and they're tossing out the flawed foreclosures. Homeowners can make the allegation that they don't think the bank is going to be able to prove its ownership. You pull that thread, and the sweater unravels."

Fuzzy and his friends were assembling in a human microphone on the steps. Fuzzy led me back up to the top step. I yelled, "Fight back!"

A TV news camera turned around and pointed at me.

The crowd around me said, "Mic check," and I repeated, "Fight back!" They echoed in the human microphone, "Fight back!" My words rippled through the park.

"You are not a loan."

"You are not a loan," spread to the extremities of the crowd.

"Don't let them take away your homes!"

"Don't let them take away your homes!" they chanted in chorus.

The message passed in waves: "You can fight them in court . . . they've bought and sold your mortgages so many times . . . they don't have their paperwork in order . . . to come forward in court . . . and claim those orphaned loans!"

Among the crowd echoing my message was F.L., bronze face peeled in joy.

CHAPTER 71

STRUGGLE, JERRY, STRUGGLE

When Mort got word of my activism at court, he switched off the light at the end of the tunnel. My feet felt glued to the floor as I clenched the phone. "You need not come into the office again. Your things are in a box with the doorman." He slammed the phone down to dramatize the ending of our boss-employee relationship.

I'd lost my job.

The next morning in the lobby of the bank, I looked through the box. "What about my laptop?"

The doorman shrugged. "There was no laptop."

I was in emergency mode. I felt the rush of adrenalin. It eased the weight of the box as I carried it across Zuccotti Park. I pushed the door of Vegan Cure open with my butt, and put the box on a top shelf in the kitchen. I longed to call Raif and tell him everything, but it was too dangerous. How long could I keep fighting off the urge to run to my brother, the only one who ever got close enough to destroy everything I ever wanted? There was no one to turn to.

They say bad luck travels in threes. The second tragic stroke had to be that I was still single. My social experiment had failed. Looking over all the data, my investigations of men were inconclusive. The best lay from a purely scientific perspective was a forty-nine-year-old who couldn't dress without tying his shoes before he put on his pants. He really knew how to command me. I'd had over five hundred lovers, and my goddamn clock was alive and ticking.

Had I also missed the love of my life, my own self love? The instinct to have children with a man who didn't want a family was still there as raw and bottomless as ever. But now that I'd passed thirty, time rolled out before me. The urgency had gone. Raw solitude was still there underneath, but at least I had a place, my business, my routine, my community. I was plugged in.

My iPhone vibrated with dismal news. The huge inventory of foreclosed homes weighed on the economy. I worried about my business and struggled to make my mortgage payments as the fifty state attorneys general negotiated a settlement with banks while they tried to squirm out of their responsibility for robo-signing. Was the third stroke of bad luck the economy? I hoped so.

CHAPTER 72

-POLIS

*A*t the break of dawn, a cop was out in the metropolis writing fifty-dollar tickets and sticking them on the windshields of the cars along one side of Saint Mark's Place. A half-dressed woman in bathrobe and curlers got into her car and moved it to the other side of the street just before the policeman got to her car. –Polis skyscrapers shone behind the horizon of townhouses along Third Avenue.

Look there's a policeman across the street. Saphora noticed the police officer first. Saphora was wide awake.

I turned around, afraid that I might see my mother's murderer. The sun glared through Freedom Tower as if to make apparent the harsh reality that still floated beneath my grasp. The heels of my go-go boots clacked on the bright pavement. I'd dreamt the murderer was free. No, the murderer *was* free. I was going to meet the murderer. I was afraid I would see him coming out of the potholes in the street. I was trembling.

He was waiting for me at a table for two in the window. The smell of his unwashed hair assaulted my nostrils. I accepted the habitual neglect that surrounded this boy-man who could only bite the hand that fed. His jaw was stiff, fists clenched: side effects. *He's been taking his medicine.*

"What hides from its father, runs to and from its sister, and becomes its dead mother?" Raif asked the lion's head carved on the arm of my chair. No meaning could be derived. "This society is rotten to the core. It's family fondue."

I was caught between the thirst for justice and this dogged need to protect my younger brother. The anger deep inside me threatened to come out, but it was Saphora who held his hand in the café window, not me.

Next to us, a musical table was talking about their next CD.

"I like this place," I said. "This street is colorful." Me and Raif looked out the window of the café. It was warm.

A man holding a boom box on his shoulder pedaled his bike and made circles in the street.

"You know Lou Reed mentions this street in one of his songs. It goes, 'Blah, blah . . . on St. Mark's.'"

"Really?" I said. Lou Reed used to be Raif's favorite singer.

"What do you want for breakfast?" Raif asked in a motherly tone.

"Just oatmeal. I'm a vegan since Mom."

Our eyes locked. He was getting angry.

He raised his voice. "You mean, since I killed Mom."

People at the other tables turned and looked at us.

I will deal with that. I could feel Saphora struggling against my soul for consciousness. She was coming out. That mean, subterranean, rational personality I had suppressed to put up with regular people and work with myrmidons in a company. Saphora was swimming to the surface. I braced myself for her hatred.

Raif prodded. "You have a bootstrap problem."

Saphora said in a calm voice, "I didn't say, since you killed Mom, although we both know you did."

"They told me to do it."

The other tables were silent.

"Yeah, and you always do what you're told." Saphora could be very sarcastic. It would be all right. She would handle him from now on. "What are you going to do about it, lamb?"

He put his head on our hands. "I don't know what to do."

We had been to hell and back. In a metropolis like this, it was easy to lose your mind. I gave up trying to understand it. A memory came flooding back, and I knew that Raif was thinking it, too. *We are neither wild beasts nor gods. For us, taboo is forbidden. We see tragedy in acts of parricide through the lens of law under the weight of the −polis.* "We both know what to do," I said, "even if we don't understand. Among gods and wild beasts, parricide is not forbidden. Only man outlaws defeat by nature. You're not alone. Orestes was alone. *He* was the first to see the old ways of mythic power clash with the law of the metropolis."

"Orestes went to prison," Raif said.

"Orestes was *the first* to go to prison. Civilization turned logic against instinct. Civilization mutated man into a tragedy and put him on trial before the metropolis. Orestes was dragged before the –polis for his unholy act. When Orestes killed his mother, prison was born."

"Are you saying I should turn myself in?" Raif said.

"I'm saying the prison is in your mind. The –polis tore Orestes and all humans from their animal inheritance. Its law divided man against himself. Consciousness is the bars in your mind. The city lays down the law, you step into the machine, you feel remorse. The prison of the mind. In the Sixth century B.C. law was new. It transformed the –polis until myth was sublimated. Guilty and innocent, parricide and incest, nature suppressed seeks her deserts."

The room was silent.

Raif looked nervous. "I wish't I had a cigarette."

The musical table at ritual next to us picked up on this and started talking about smoking. "Yeah, this is a new experience for me, recording a whole album without smoking," the oldest one said. "Usually the studio musicians and technicians rip through packs of cigarettes."

Raif started laughing hysterically. It wasn't funny. Not only did I not have cigarettes, but I had to listen to ragamuffin musicians talking about nicotine withdrawal.

Raif leaned toward me. "Do you know who that is sitting next to me?"

"Who?"

"Lou Reed."

360

"No!"

"Yes! Look."

I looked at the man's bony back, two inches from Raif, and then into the mirror above the man's table. Our teen idol really was the aging man talking to me and Raif through the mirror. He knew Raif killed Mom. The mirror was tilted downward reflecting the contents of the dishes and cups on the table. Raif's profile was framed in Lou's face behind dark glasses. There were teacups hanging on the wall. Just an ordinary lunch, framed in gold, among a mural of diners at ritual, sipping coffee, speaking murder.

"Mom appeared to me as the devil. It was a decision without choice," Raif tried to whisper. "I had to kill her."

"The ancients had no word for *free will*, no word for *will*, or for *duty*. All was duty. We *must* live, eat and die. *Phonos akousios*, murder committed despite oneself."

"The voices ordered me to kill her." He had the whole room's attention. Lou turned and stared.

"And you passionately desired what they forced you to do, even though you weren't obedient on other occasions!"

"Yes. And then I saw what I had done. I saw Mom—" Raif was crying.

Lou's table was dumbfounded.

The defilement of crime attached itself beyond Raif to his whole lineage. I was bound to this murder as his sister, our childhood turned inside out. Flesh recoiled upon itself, the ultimate corruption. No ray of meaning could escape the black-hearted chorus.

New York offered up its transitory society. Customers left; new customers filled the table. Family was kept invisible. "Now there's no family," I said. I wished I could tell my brother I lived here now, near him.

I controlled my outer self and tried to keep Saphora from spiraling back into the dark past. I searched for the light. "How are you managing in New York?" I asked. Getting along, being pleasant, not reaching for the apple of knowledge in Saphora's hand.

Raif looked out the window. "Sometimes it's lonely."

It was always lonely. His hand was hot. The café was safely crowded. I dug into my pocket. Empty. "Can you pay for lunch? I'm broke." Everything had gone into the restaurant venture and paying off my credit cards. Raif paid, nervous at the thought of supporting his ex-Harvard sister on his disability.

"I'll be all right as soon as I get my next pay check," I lied. There were no more paychecks.

The waitress took the money. We looked out the window. "Lou Reed! Now what do we do?" Raif whispered. He was excited.

"We should say something to him," I said.

"He's probably tired of fans."

We waited.

"I guess that's why we didn't get a good waitress," I said.

"Yeah," Raif said, geeked. "I don't care about us either."

Raif finished his dessert and said, "Do you want to go?"

"Hell, no! I mean . . . might as well wait for Lou."

Lou told the waitress he was having eggs today. I winked at Raif to say, Lou comes here all the time. Raif looked like he was about to burst, so I calmed him down by telling him about work. "I couldn't get a job 'til I lied to the interviewers and said that I wasn't married." Lou's table fell silent and listened to my story. "You know," I said, "it's illegal to ask someone in a job interview if they're married. But the phonies ask anyway. The first time I lied, I got the job. The men are all married or divorced-with-kids. Marriage supposedly stabilizes them. But for us, it's a liability, it's taboo. It's a bitch."

"You can say that again," Lou's reflection muttered. His lackeys agreed.

Lou Reed was talking to me through the mirror! His lackeys repeated him like a human microphone. Mom was certainly with us now.

At last Lou's table put on their leather. I grabbed my jacket. We all got up at the same time. When Lou turned around, I whispered, "Lou. Lou!" into his ear.

He pretended he didn't hear me. I bet he used to wait on tables.

I said into his ear again, "Lou, my brother admires the hell out of you. Let me introduce you to him."

Lou turned around and looked at Raif.

"This is Raif. Raif, Lou."

They shook hands.

"Nice to meet you," Lou said.

"When's your next album coming out!" Raif said.

"I'm working on it now. By next year."

"Cool," he said, stuffing his hands into his pockets. We all went outside.

Lou and his band wandered off. Me and Raif stood on the curb. Wow, there goes Lou Reed. We looked over our shoulders at the shrunken man.

"You know," Raif said as we wandered uptown, "I used to really admire him."

"You can play every song he's written."

"Yeah, but now I don't think he's that great. I mean, his handshake was kind of limp."

"He's probably sick of meeting fans. And they were probably worried we were going to follow them back to the studio since we got up at the same time."

"No way. Nobody does that."

"I have."

"You have? Who did you follow?"

"Camper Van Beethoven. I climbed into their van after a show in Boston."

"You did?"

"Yeah."

We crossed 21st. "You didn't have to talk to him," Raif said. "You didn't have to say that I admired him so much."

"Hey. I introduced you to Lou Reed!"

Raif smiled. Ha, ha, HA. We felt so FREE, we were ready to walk all the way to Central Park.

"Meeting Lou Reed in New York is cool, but it's not as great as meeting you in New York," Raif said.

That was so sweet. I remembered Raif visiting me at Harvard. We used to wish that we both lived in New York. If we had known the price, we never would have wished for anything.

"Yeah, but meeting me in New York is not as great as meeting me and Lou Reed!"

"Yeah!" he agreed.

It was a sunny day.

"Saphora, I'm going to turn myself in."

"I'm going by 'Jerry' these days."

"Whatever."

We walked in step.

"I'm not going to be pushed around by the spirit world anymore. I'm going to take control of my destiny."

I had to say it. "I can't do it for you because you're my brother, but I know you need to accept the punishment and atone for murdering her. I know you loved Mom."

Of old, parricide was the will of the gods. Now you say, 'No,' a psychological mutation, and take responsibility yourself as the final scapegoat of the gods preferring jail and punishment to predestiny and loss of control.

I was afraid he would break in half if he admitted his guilt before the law. I was watching the tragic birth of his inner psyche. I could imagine my younger brother in front of the judge explaining that something had snapped in his head, that he was possessed by a *daimon*, but was also responsible to the metropolis. A good citizen who turned himself in: better to take responsibility than let life slip into the hands of fate. "It's proactive, something to do." Confessing to murder.

"OK," he said.

Nothing would make up for killing our mother.

Central Park was in sight up ahead waving in the wind. Panic opened a pit in my stomach. I looked around. I had the feeling someone was following us a half a block behind on the other side of the street. When I turned around to look, there were just a few hipsters on the sidewalk. A glint of metal shone in the morning light up ahead.

I looked at Raif's profile. He seemed tense, too. Then I heard the footsteps running toward us. Raif covered my eyes. I struggled to peel away his fingers, but in truth, I didn't want to see. In a heartbeat, five men appeared on all sides and closed in from the front, side and back. The third stroke.

We turned our backs to each other. The men surrounded us. We tried to break through and run, but they caught me and wrestled Raif to the ground. They flashed police badges and did their ritual.

"Wait!" Raif's voice cracked. "I'm gonna turn myself in!"

They ignored him and slapped handcuffs on him, his body sprawled in four squares of sidewalk. They pulled him off the chessboard. He turned and looked at me as they dragged him away.

"I'm coming, too!" I cried, and followed them down the street. Pawn to king five.

A police car pulled up.

I recognized my plain clothes lay, scar and all. He had been following me the whole time, just waiting for the endgame when I met up with Raif.

Is this how you end it? I shook my fist at the sky, laughing in cloudless blue. The godgame was up. The cop didn't say anything to me, and I would certainly never speak to that sonofabitch again. He pushed Raif into the car head first.

The sheeple were probably going to say it was a case of 'temporary insanity', *just as the first court acquitted Orestes, guilty of premeditated murder of his mother because he acted on order of Apollo. It was a 'justifiable murder'.*

I tried to get in back with Raif, but the cop shoved me aside. There was only one way open for me. The passenger seat. Once in the seat, I felt avenged. I adjusted the visor to look in the mirror.

I screamed.

I couldn't see myself or even Saphora! Just an empty space where my head should be. There was the family face of my little brother, *innocent and guilty.* Plaything in the divine hands, a scapegoat for parricide. *Spirit in a cage.* His stiff embodiment an incarceration of my soul, each trapped by the other. The face was pale.

CHAPTER 73
PARRICIDE

T his shred of social fabric makes me long for Mother
Russia. WTF happened to American culture? Now
they are murdering their parents. What have we come to?
It never crossed my Russian mind that Raif could have
murdered his own blessed mother! But looking at the
banks' parricide of the US government, I can't say I'm
surprised.

This makes me worry for my livelihood. There hasn't
been a single indictment of a Wall Street banker, but I
could get left holding the bag. Jerry's court stunt terrified
the hell out of upper management. Sasha fled to Greece, a

bad omen for their exemplary economy. Even though he was too related to qualify as a scapegoat here, he couldn't resist witnessing his own country's flogging firsthand. With Jerry gone, there's only me and Mort left, and one of these days, Mort will disappear. He has enough money to become someone else. He can change his fingerprints and his face if he wants to. That leaves me.

I have more than selfish regrets about Jerry though. As a Gemini, I kicked myself when the final truth dawned on me, that Jerry was Saphora. She was smart enough all right. She was my most profitable trader, made eight million in dollar-yuan, of all things. Looking back on it all from a management standpoint, I can't believe I gave a woman such a big trading limit. She was part of our family. I would have talked Sasha into saving her from the axe if I weren't so damn insulted that she had chosen that spoiled nephew of the president of the board over me. All I could see was red, so I left her there with Mort, and when I got back from Vegas, he had already puppeted her away.

I never noticed Jerry's restaurant on Wall Street. It's not the kind of joint I typically frequent, and frankly, I'm repelled by the clientele. In my day you had loads of people at demonstrations. Now, you walk through Zuccotti Park, and everybody's dragged all their junk out there. It's like a garage sale with only a few people milling around. I got up the nerve to go into Jerry's restaurant last week. I had to wait in line outside for ten minutes. There were two hipsters behind the counter and another one waiting on tables. 'Fuzzy' was a euphemism. He was tall, hairy, and hardcore. I asked about Jerry.

"She's at the other damn vegan restaurant."

She was opening a second restaurant!

I'm gonna have lunch at Vegan Cure again today. I hope she's there this time. I haven't seen her since the day Mort fired her, except on the news.

She was holding a vigil outside a foreclosed home in Queens. The homeowner, her three kids, and two dozen neighbors were occupying a home to stave off eviction. You could see it made her feel sad. Hell, it made me sad to see the housewife and two kids wrapped in blankets in front of that 'Foreclosed' sign put up by banks that had just received $7.77 trillion from the Federal Reserve to rescue the financial system — more than fifty percent of the goddamn GDP. The housewife was beside herself. "At least the kleptocracy turned the heat back on before the pipes froze."

From a purely financial standpoint, letting human beings maintain bank-owned housing adds more value than leaving vacant houses to rot, even if banks theoretically benefit from a depreciating asset at some unknown date in the future. So why do they do it? There's a mystery for you. You have to watch where the money goes. *Who* profited? Yeah, Lehman blew up. The reality is the six largest U.S. banks' total assets increased thirty-nine percent, to $9.5 trillion between 2006 and 2011, according to Fed data.

They only aired the police raid on the late night news. Jerry was 'liberating' an abandoned home that had been foreclosed since 2009 so a homeless family could live there. Police arrested the activists who were defending it as well as a handyman team that was working to make the house habitable. The police used beanbag guns and pepper spray

370

to disperse the rest of the protestors.

They slapped handcuffs on Jerry. I stared at the TV. She'd painted her fingernails green. Her fingers tore at the handcuffs. As the police led her away, she yelled, "The courts are throwing out invalid foreclosures!"

An announcer asked her how it felt to be right.

She done me proud the way she dodged the oncoming kick in the butt.

She said, "It has its downsides."

Acknowledgements

Thanks to Georgina Tate for her encouragement and light touch and to all the wonderful editors in the Harvard Fiction Workshop without whose help I might never have finished this novel. I'm grateful to Florence Cunningham for holding it down when I most needed to hammer out this tale. Most of all, a *grand merci* to my confidants, Maureen Sheehan and Gina Ramoz for their astute advice, patience and on-target criticism.

J.L. Morin grew up in inner-city Detroit. Morin was nominated for the Pushcart prize, was Gold medalist in the eLit eBook awards in 2011, and has also won a Living Now book award for the Japan novel, *Sazzae* written as a creative thesis toward an AB at Harvard. Other novels include *Travelling Light* and *Trading Dreams.*

J.L. Morin traded derivatives for six years while studying nights toward an MBA at New York University's Stern School of Business and has worked for the Federal Reserve Bank posted to the 103rd floor of the World Trade Center, Agence France-Presse in the wire service's Middle East headquarters, and as a TV newscaster. She writes for Huffington Post and is adjunct faculty at Boston University.

Other novels published by

Harvard Square Editions

The Conjurer's Boy, Michael Raleigh

Gates of Eden, Charles Degelman

Patchwork, Dan Loughry

All at Once, Alisa Clements

A Weapon to End War, Jonathan Ross

Spiders and Flies, Scott Adlerberg

Sazzae, J. L. Morin

303842LV00002B/1/P
LVOW080549221012
Printed in the USA
CPSIA information can be obtained at www.ICGtesting.com